The GREEK PRINCE of AfGHANISTAN

DAVID AUSTIN BECK

First paperback edition December 2020

Book design by Rafael Andres

ISBN 978-1-7361840-0-4 (paperback)
ISBN 978-1-7361840-1-1 (ebook)

Published by Endless Horizon Publishing LLC

Acknowledgments

Many people supported me on the journey that became this book: thank you, Eric, Dushyant, and Gemma, for your perspective and advice; thank you, Jasmine and Constance, for your wonderful editing; thank you, Rafael, for the beautiful book design; and thank you, Mom, Dad, Aunt Nancy, Katie, Andrew, and Vandana, for your endless support.

208BC

SCYTHIA

BLACK SEA

MACEDONIA

PAPHLAGONIA

BITHYNIA

PONTUS

CAPPADOCIA

ARMENIA

MEDIA ATROPATENE

ATHENS

SELEUCID

MEDITERRANEAN SEA

CYPRUS

ANTIOCH

PALMYRA

TYRE

BABYLON

COELE-SYRIA

ALEXANDRIA

MEMPHIS

PETRA

PTOLEMAIC EGYPT

NABATEAN KINGDOM

RED SEA

ARABIA

A UNIQUE TIME AND PLACE

Afghanistan has been a crossroads of peoples and ideas for as long as history has been recorded. Among the ancient peoples to move through its passes were the Aryans, Persians, Indians, Macedonians, Greeks, Scythians, Kushans, and Parthians. They brought, or in some cases developed, the tenets of Buddhism, Hinduism, and Zoroastrianism, and they pushed new boundaries in art and architecture.

In the fourth century BC, much of Afghanistan was called Bactria, and it was the jewel of the Persian Empire. In 330 BC, during his decade-long conquest of that empire, Alexander the Great attacked Bactria with a brutality only hinted at during his earlier campaigns. Cities were destroyed, villages burned, populations massacred. In response, Bactrian fighters adopted guerrilla tactics and a similar ferocity. It took Alexander years to conquer the region, and even then, he deemed it necessary to garrison thousands of Greek mercenaries across the land.

Alexander died in Babylon in 323 BC. Before his last breath, however, he promised his empire to the "strongest" of his generals. Perhaps unsurprisingly, given the enormity of the prize, those generals fought each other to claim that title. During the ensuing years of chaos—which saw thousands of people slaughtered across the Eastern Mediterranean and the Middle East—the Greeks in Bactria forged an existence among wary locals. Over the years, lines between local and invader appeared to blur, but tensions remained.

In the mid-third century BC, a man called Diodotus declared Bactria's independence from the Seleucid Empire, the largest polity to have risen from the blood-soaked ruins of Alexander's conquered domains. Our story starts in 208 BC, roughly thirty years after Diodotus's declaration. It centers on Demetrius, the Greek prince of the nascent Greco-Bactrian kingdom. Demetrius is a curious young man and, while he worships as a Greek, he sees himself as native to the fields, mountains, and rivers of Central Asia. But his home is under threat. Antiochus III, the Seleucid emperor, wants to reconquer Bactria. With the invasion approaching, Demetrius's mind, like his region, will become a battlefield.

CHAPTER ONE

Demetrius, 208 BC. North of Bactria

Demetrius straightened his back and shifted in the saddle. Sunlight caressed his face and sweat pooled beneath his woolen tunic. The seemingly endless Eurasian Steppe extended before him, its tall grass swaying rhythmically in the wind.

"Grass and sky," said Demetrius, running his fingers through his tangled hair. "Nothing but grass and sky."

"Not necessarily a bad thing," said Roshan, riding beside him, his beard covered in dust.

Demetrius nodded. In many ways, Roshan was right. The barren landscape was a good thing: Maybe the rumor of a large and approaching Scythian horde was unfounded.

"Either way," said Demetrius, "we need to secure a peace treaty with the Scythians before Antiochus's invasion. We can't fight on two fronts."

"Yes, your majesty," said Roshan.

Demetrius squinted at the empty steppe. "They can't be that far away. Have the men wear armor, just in case."

Roshan relayed the order to the eleven other soldiers, who all began to dress.

Demetrius dismounted and pulled plates of armor from the sack behind his saddle. After hours in the sun, the metal was scalding hot, and wherever possible, Demetrius used his loose tunic to maneuver it.

"It's strange to think that just weeks ago, we were celebrating the annual games in Zariaspa," said Demetrius, as he secured his chest plate.

"Feels like a different life," said Roshan, strapping bronze greaves to his shins. "We weren't at war then."

"But we knew it was coming."

"Yes, I suppose we did."

Once his armor was in place, Demetrius remounted his horse and surveyed his men, each covered in plates of metal. In the places where the plates failed to protect—such as the neck, armpits, and groin—they had wrapped thick pieces of leather. If it came to a fight, each man would prove a worthy adversary. If they stayed in a group, they could hold off a force twice their number. But they had to stick together.

"Let's get moving," said Demetrius, nudging his horse forward. "The Scythians must be close."

As Demetrius rode, he reminisced on a childhood filled with tales of the nomadic people of the north. Tales of how they fed their sick to the dogs. How they lived and fought on horseback. How they moved like the wind, in one place one day and miles away the next. Demetrius grasped the hilt of his sword and counted the arrows in his quiver.

Over the following hours, the caravan moved deeper into the grassy abyss. When the sun approached its zenith, they entered an ocean of pink poppies. As the flowers passed below his feet, Demetrius spotted a group of riders. And they were only shouting distance away.

The roughly twenty figures approached from across the field, sunlight glinting from the bronze, gold, and iron armor worn by riders and horses alike. Half of the warriors carried a small shield and a sturdy, thrusting spear; the other half were armed with bows. Demetrius knew immediately that he had found the Scythians.

He called for his companions to halt.

"Look," said Roshan, "women ride among them."

"I'd heard as much." Demetrius eyed the long-haired woman who rode at the front of the group, an ax held in her hand.

"Well," said Demetrius, looking back to his company. "We found them."

"Your highness, let me speak with the Scythians," said Roshan. "You stay among the men. You didn't bring me here for company. I promised Menon I'd keep you safe."

"He's right, your majesty," said Phlotas, one of Demetrius's long-time bodyguards.

Demetrius nodded.

"Phlotas," said Roshan, "you and Feroze come with me. And keep your weapons down. If you flinch, they may attack."

Phlotas and Feroze brought their horses alongside Roshan's.

"Be ready if things go badly, your majesty," said Roshan, catching Demetrius's gaze.

As Roshan led his companions into the pink field, Demetrius watched the Scythians. Some pointed and spoke, while others nocked arrows to their bows or pulled axes from their belts.

Roshan, Phlotas, and Feroze stopped at the midway point between the forces. The flanks of the Scythian line fanned out. More and more of the warriors pulled arrows from quivers and fitted them against bowstrings. Demetrius itched to recall his men, but he knew that doing so could trigger an attack if misunderstood by the Scythians. Still, with each passing second, an attack seemed increasingly likely anyway.

Roshan and the others waited, motionless. Demetrius held his breath. The Scythians watched.

After a short time, Roshan turned his horse and led Phlotas and Feroze away from the Scythians and back toward Demetrius.

Demetrius let out a sigh of relief, but it was cut short as an arrow pierced Feroze's neck. A moment later, Feroze dropped from his horse and crumpled in the grass, a motionless heap.

Perhaps the fight had been inevitable, thought Demetrius, as he pulled his sword from its sheath. He ordered his comrades to do the same and called his horse to action.

As the animal pulled him toward the enemy, Demetrius's mind traveled to the city games just weeks before—to the excitement, the competition, and the revelry. As he tightened his grip on his sword, he pushed the memory from his mind. That had been a different life, indeed.

CHAPTER TWO

Demetrius, One month earlier. Zariaspa

"Chapatis! Fresh from the oven!" a woman yelled in Bactrian from a stall on Demetrius's left. As his mind translated her words into Greek, Demetrius watched dough sizzle on an iron plate over a crackling fire.

"Taking bets on today's horse race!" called the man beside her.

Demetrius breathed in the smells of cooking, sweat, and perfume—the latter offering notes of oil, sandalwood, and flowers. Across the capital's bustling market square, a man struggled to control his horse.

"Join us outside the city walls for the annual games!" the horseman shouted to the crowd as his horse scratched the ground with its front hooves. "This year's sports are unlike any we've had before."

The crowd's cheers mingled with the din of the market.

"Your majesty," said Menon, drawing Demetrius's gaze to his father's advisor, "you were right about including games from the east." Menon wiped the sweat from his forehead with the edge of a gold-laced tunic. "The people seem to appreciate it."

"Greeks have lived here for a century. It's about time we embrace local customs. But who knows? We'll see if the nobles agree."

"I wouldn't be too optimistic. You know how conservative they are."

"Well," said Demetrius, observing the diversity of the clothes, smells, and sounds that surrounded him, "that's their loss."

"Javelin throwing! Discus throwing!" the horseman yelled to the ecstatic crowd. "Wrestling, both Greek and Indian rules! Foot and horse racing!"

"Speaking of customs," said Menon, "I noticed your absence at the bull sacrifice."

"Did you?" said Demetrius, his attention drawn to the large Greek temple where the sacrifice had been carried out.

"The king noticed, too."

Demetrius sighed and kicked the dirt. "My father knows my reasons for skipping."

"Your majesty," said Menon, "I understand the sacrifice angers your friends—"

"Not *just* my friends," said Demetrius, cutting him off. "It angers half the kingdom. Only a minority of us are Greek. Most subjects are Buddhist, Hindu, or Zoroastrian."

"Your father just wants you to observe tradition."

"Whose tradition? Greek tradition? Bactrian tradition? Both? You and I have discussed this plenty. You know my feelings on the matter."

"And I respect them." Menon ran his hands across his bald head.

"I know. I know. I'm just tired of my father's complaints."

There was a brief pause. "I'll come up with an excuse for your absence," said Menon.

Demetrius smiled and placed his hand on Menon's shoulder. "Thank you, my friend."

"At your service, my prince." Menon bowed.

"Now," said Demetrius, "shall we head to the gaming fields?"

"You should," said Menon. "But I must meet your father. Antiochus sent another message. I fear a Seleucid invasion might be only weeks away."

"I see." Demetrius did not want to think of the threatening Hellenistic empire to their west. At least not today. "Perhaps you'll join later, then?"

"Of course, my prince."

"Very well," said Demetrius. "I'll be off then."

With his bodyguards around him, Demetrius followed the crowd to the city's main gate. The jostle of people filled the thin street with dust, its billows mingling with the smoke of food stalls.

"Your majesty!"

Demetrius turned to see a man and woman approaching. His bodyguards looked to him for direction, and he indicated they should let the couple through.

"Ashok, Priya," said Demetrius, making room for them to walk beside him. "I was hoping I'd see you."

"How could we miss it?" said Ashok, through his thick black mustache.

"Although," said his wife, "it did take forever to get through the city."

Priya wore a green-and-purple saree, and her long, braided hair lay on her shoulder, interwoven with flowers.

"The crowds seem to get bigger and bigger each year," said Ashok.

"Sure," said Priya. "But tell me. Why can't women compete? We make up half the city, after all."

"Because you'd beat all the men!" Ashok laughed. "And men can be so sensitive."

"If you say so." Priya tossed the braid over her shoulder. The flowers crunched against her back. "I guess I'll find something to sell outside the walls. Maybe I'll make enough to get you a new outfit. Wedding season is coming up—and your birthday."

"Don't remind me." Ashok rolled his eyes.

Demetrius had known Ashok for most of his life. Ashok's mother had served as his wet nurse and aide, and she had often brought Ashok with her to the palace. Demetrius grinned as he watched the couple joke. It was nice to see them happy—especially during a time when the army, in which Ashok served as a bowman, was preparing for war.

"We've reached the gate," said Ashok.

Demetrius looked past his bodyguards and at the large stone structure. Soldiers waved them and the masses through the archway. Shade blanketed Demetrius as he passed below the rock. To either side sat thick wooden doors. Metal spikes, each capped with a coconut, protruded from their red-painted surfaces.

Once outside, light streamed into Demetrius's eyes. A trench extended along the fortress wall and beneath the bridge. Wooden stakes projected from its waterless trough, which had cracked in the dry heat.

Demetrius had seen the city's defenses upgraded many times. Scythian raids from the north were not uncommon, and there was always the possibility of rebellion—the same path his father had followed to the throne. But more recently, the threats came from the west, from other Greeks.

Once across the bridge, the crowd dispersed along the flat clearing that surrounded the city. Tan dirt crackled under Demetrius's feet and dust rose into the air. Usually, the army kept the clearing free of structures to ensure there was no place for an enemy to hide, but during the games, vendors set up tents to cater to the needs of the crowd. Even the threat of invasion by Antiochus and the Seleucid Empire couldn't stop them.

Past the clearing, in green fields, men and women bent over and pulled crops from the dirt. Sunlight glistened on their sweaty bodies. Beyond them, the leaves of orange trees swayed in the wind.

"A beautiful day," said Priya.

"Perfect," added Demetrius.

A horn blared in the crowd to Demetrius's right, where a diverse array of people stood together, some wearing colorful sarees, others adorned with shining armor or linen tunics.

"What's going on?" said Ashok.

"Must be the start of the footrace," said Priya. "That's always first."

Priya led Demetrius and Ashok into the throng, and Demetrius's bodyguards created an opening that brought them to the edge of the track. The track was fifty meters long, its end marked by a wooden stake. The runners were to follow a chalk-lined path, pass around the stake, and return to the starting point. It was nothing like the tracks in Greece, but it had become Zariaspa's custom.

Six runners gathered behind the starting line, which was little more than crushed limestone sprinkled across the compacted dirt. A few athletes stood still, while others stretched, jumped, and practiced their starting sprint. They wore nothing but delicate white loincloths. In Greece, participants competed naked, but here in Bactria, customs had changed to respect local sensibilities. At least, *some* of them had.

"Your majesty!" someone called.

Demetrius scanned the starting line and spotted his childhood friend, Eucratides. The man had always been an excellent athlete, and as the dust grazed his muscular body, it was clear to Demetrius that he was among the city's fittest. Eucratides kept his face clean-shaven—a style popularized by Alexander—and his black hair was cut in the latest Greek fashion. He came from a traditional family, and his father served as the city governor of Maracanda in the north. As was tradition among nobles, Eucratides had grown up with Demetrius in the royal palace.

"My friend." Demetrius grabbed the man's extended hand. "How are you?"

"Annoyed to be running beside Bactrians." Eucratides jerked his head toward the other athletes, whose skin tones varied.

"We're Bactrians, too, you know," said Demetrius.

"You know what I mean." Eucratides eyed the runners.

"These are the city games," said Demetrius. "Greek-only events are a thing of the past."

"So it seems," said Eucratides, running his fingers through his hair.

Of the six runners at the starting line, four could trace their heritage back to Greece or Macedonia, the land of Alexander. The other two were native Bactrians, men whose families had lived in Bactria long before Alexander's invasion. As Demetrius looked at the runners, he thought of the years of conflict and fusion that had brought them together.

Demetrius stepped back from Eucratides. "I'll leave you with my well-wishes."

"Thank you, my friend." Eucratides returned to the starting line.

"How was he?" said Ashok, when Demetrius rejoined him.

"As arrogant as ever."

Ashok smiled. "At least he's consistent."

When the referee told the runners to prepare, the crowd fell silent. The runners leaned down and their fingers pierced the dirt. A man stepped forward with a glistening bronze horn, which he pressed to his lips, releasing a low hum. The runners dashed forward in a cloud of dust and cheers.

Eucratides ran beside a tall, well-built man: Roshan, one of the best soldiers in the kingdom's unit of native Bactrian infantry—a group still segregated from the ethnic Greeks. Roshan's muscles flexed and twisted as he pumped his arms and drove his knees toward his chest.

"Look at them go!" yelled Ashok, jumping.

Eucratides and Roshan reached the wooden stake and, after elbowing one another to maneuver around it, they sprinted back toward the chalk line. They panted, the tendons in their necks taut. The crowd roared.

"Here they come!" cried Priya.

A gust of wind swept dust into Demetrius's eyes. Blinking, he made out Eucratides's arms tangling with Roshan's. He wiped his eyes, and saw Roshan rolling on the ground. A moment later, Eucratides crossed the finish line, exultant, his sweaty body glistening like metal. The crowd cheered, but whimpers of concern punctuated the jubilee. Demetrius watched Roshan push himself from the dirt and wipe grit and pebbles from his body. Lines of red appeared across his left arm and shoulder; blood dripped from the outer corner of his right eye.

Eucratides paced the finish line, while the crowd draped flowers around his neck. Demetrius thought back to the race, unable to decide if Eucratides had pushed Roshan.

Wincing, Roshan wiped the blood with a rag. A man approached and poured water on his wounds.

With the crowd massing around the finish line, Demetrius could no longer see Ashok or Priya, but his bodyguards cleared a path through the crowd. Demetrius tried to look back to Roshan, but even he had been lost among the throng.

Demetrius found his friends beside a fruit stand. "When is the buzkashi match?" he asked. Greeks and native Bactrians had learned buzkashi from the people of the steppe. It was a dangerous and exhilarating game designed for the grassy, endless plains to the north. Two teams of horsemen used hooked sticks to transport a goat carcass into one of two circles on the ground.

"This afternoon," said Ashok, returning a mango to the table. "We're going early to find good seats. Are you in?"

Priya laughed. "He's the prince. He can have whatever seat he wants."

"Unfortunately, I can't join you," said Demetrius. "I should visit my father after his meeting. There's news of Antiochus."

"Do you really think there will be a war?" Priya looked from Demetrius to Ashok.

"Of course not," said Ashok. "Antiochus has enough to worry about in the west. He has no reason to come here."

Ashok wasn't wrong. Over the past few weeks, the palace had heard reports of Antiochus's troubles in Parthia, a region just to the west of Bactria. Apparently, the Parthians had fought the Seleucids into a stalemate.

"Demetrius, what do you think?" said Priya.

"I'm not sure yet," said Demetrius. "My father doesn't seem worried, but Menon has his concerns."

"Well," said Priya, "if you and Ashok deploy, I'll come with you. There's always room in the caravan, and I won't have someone else looking after my husband."

"Enough war talk." Ashok swatted the air. "What about food? Have you got time for that, at least?"

"I always have time for food," said Demetrius.

"Predictable as ever," said Priya, as they followed Ashok to a large food tent.

"Rice cakes! Rice cakes!" yelled a man beside a small cart.

"I'll take three," said Ashok, nodding toward the dull-white snacks.

After handing over his coins, Ashok handed rice cakes to Demetrius and Priya. Demetrius bit into the savory snack.

"Amazing," he said.

"You should try Priya's!"

Priya blushed and shrugged.

As he ate, Demetrius scanned the gaming fields, where people laughed, sang, and relaxed. Nothing about the scene suggested a region on the precipice of war.

But a commotion at the clearing's far end caught his attention. He squinted against the sun and made out a group of soldiers in the midst of two crowds of men. They seemed to be holding the two groups apart with drawn swords. The men paced and yelled at one another across the soldiers, their fists clenched. One group appeared to be native Bactrians, many of them wearing colorful cloaks. The others were dressed in traditional Greek tunics.

"They're probably arguing about the outcome of the race," said Ashok at Demetrius's side.

"Perhaps." Demetrius wanted to get involved, but Menon always said that a prince must be seen as above such disagreements. He relaxed his fists and turned from the fight. "I must excuse myself and return to the palace."

"Alright," said Ashok. "But come back when you can."

"Of course." Demetrius forced a smile, but as he headed to the palace, his mind remained on the fight. Tension between native and Greek Bactrians was nothing new. In fact, it had existed since the time of Alexander. But since that time, it had rarely manifested in violence. This was a bad omen. A bad omen on the eve of war.

CHAPTER THREE

⧗

Menon

Far above the gaming fields, Menon walked through the palace halls. Light cascaded between columns and pooled on the tiled floor. With each gust of wind, leaves scattered before his feet.

People scampered from Menon's path in tightly packed groups, some of them whispering. Menon knew they discussed the king and the threat of war; it was all anyone in the palace was talking about. But he also knew that some of Zariaspa's Greek elite favored Antiochus over the king. Ever since King Euthydemus had begun lowering the political barriers between Greeks and native Bactrians, the neighboring Seleucid Empire's ethnic segregation was gaining admiration. If Euthydemus didn't assert his authority soon, such talk could become a problem.

Menon reached the king's audience chamber and, nodding to the guards, entered. Royal attendants and petitioners filled the spacious hall, and the king sat before them on a wooden, gem-studded throne. On the red wall behind him, painted figures played musical instruments. Colorful murals of Greek gods covered the walls on either side.

"Menon," the king said. "I've been waiting for you. What did you wish to tell me?"

"We received another letter, your majesty," said Menon, stepping toward the center of the room. "From the Seleucid emperor."

"Ah, Antiochus." Euthydemus rose from his throne. "What does the old warmonger want now?"

"Just that, your majesty," said Menon, wishing the crowd would disperse. "He threatens war."

"And what's new? Have his demands changed?" The king resumed his seat. An attendant offered him a fur for the cold, but was waved away.

"No, your majesty," said Menon. "His request remains the same. He demands the restoration of imperial sovereignty over Bactria, Margiana, and Sogdiana."

"Ha! Margiana. Does he really think we still hold sway over that land? He must know the Parthians run wild among those hills. He's been fighting them, after all."

"Perhaps he is suggesting the empire will ensure our control over Margiana if we pledge our fealty," said Menon.

Euthydemus stared at a groveling petitioner, who bowed.

"What response should we send, your majesty?" said Menon, again wishing the petitioners would depart.

"Oh, please," said Euthydemus, turning to Menon. "A response is unneeded. Antiochus only just finished fighting the Parthians. He's licking his wounds. He is bluffing."

"I don't think so, your majesty."

"Let's discuss this later," said the king. "What else do you have for me?"

Pushing back his frustration, Menon looked to the next item on his list. "Our garrison at Merv. I feel that it is too small to hold back an attack from the west."

"I thought I was clear, Menon," said Euthydemus. "I don't want to discuss Antiochus right now. Talk to me about something else or nothing at all."

Menon moved down the list. "The Scythians, your majesty. They have sent another request to trade within the walls of Maracanda."

"And what does the governor of Maracanda say about this?" said Euthydemus.

"I've received a letter asking that we deny the request."

"Then that's that. I defer to him. He's north of us and in much better contact with the Scythians."

"I fear the governor fails to give the request its due. Yes, the Scythians attacked in the past. I of all people understand that." Menon's chest pounded. "But they have a new chief now, and he has shown a genuine interest in trade, not war."

"I won't ignore the advice of our northern kin," said Euthydemus. "The Scythian request is denied."

Menon sighed. Time was running out. "Perhaps we can turn again to the issue of Antiochus."

He watched Euthydemus scan the room. All eyes were on the king. Any response would be analyzed for cracks that suggested weakness. Judged for signs of impending war. The king was in a delicate position. The nobles didn't want war, but Euthydemus could not look weak before them.

"What response should I send, my king?" Menon repeated, louder.

Euthydemus scanned the room. He stood and the crowd stepped aside to let him walk to the door.

"Your majesty," said Menon, "a response for the emperor?"

Euthydemus whipped around.

"Emperor?" His gaze darted from one person to the next. "That man is no emperor to me. He is a king, as I am a king. And the last time I checked, kings don't bow to other kings."

He turned and strode from the room.

Still lacking answers, Menon pushed through the mumbling crowd and made his way to his private chambers. The potent smell of incense welcomed him, but otherwise, he despaired of his quarters. A small table stood to his right, stacked high with parchment and unfinished glasses of wine. An unmade bed sat to his left, the sheets rumpled against the cracked walls.

Pushing the disheveled state from his mind, Menon moved into the principal room, where he found his wife sitting on the edge of a waterless marble pool.

"Cleo," he said.

She looked at him, wiped her eyes, and smiled. She wore a light-green chiton and had her hair wrapped close to her head in a strip of red wool.

"My love, you're back."

She stood and embraced him. Over her shoulder and next to the window, incense burned on a small table. Several objects were arranged on either side of the scented stick. A painted plate bore the image of Erastus, their brave young son, his eyes depicted in striking blue, his hair wavy and blond. There was a bronze helmet beside the plate. It was a near-flawless example of Greek metal-smithing, and a gift from Menon's relatives in Greece. He remembered how proud he had been the day he gave it to Erastus. It had been sunny, exactly one year ago, and Menon had shielded his eyes to look up at his son.

"Thank you, Father," Erastus said, sitting atop his horse, the sun beaming behind him.

"It will keep you safe," Menon replied, swallowing through the discomfort in his throat.

"Don't worry, Father. We'll be back in days."

The king had ordered a scouting mission north to investigate Scythian movements. Such incursions had been increasing, and for months the king had ignored Menon's advice to send a permanent force to Maracanda to solidify the northern border.

"We'll be thinking of you every day," Cleo said, as Erastus touched her long and wavy blond hair, so like his own.

"And I, you."

Memories were a painful gift from the gods, Menon now thought, turning from the memorial.

He moved to the window, where Cleo joined him, and they looked at the buzzing market below. Sheets of colorful linen shaded the stalls, and traders from Syria, Persia, and India mingled with the crowd.

"What did the king say?" said Cleo.

"About what?"

"About the emperor's demands."

"Nothing." The tendons in Menon's neck tightened. "He said nothing, which means he's doing nothing."

"His usual strategy," Cleo said, bitterly. "At least until it's too late."

Menon thought of his son, knowing his wife was doing the same. If only Euthydemus had addressed the Scythian incursions before the situation had grown so dire.

"He needs to make a decision," said Menon. "Either he needs to prepare the kingdom for war, or he needs to negotiate. He can't continue to do nothing."

"But preparing for war will only aggravate the nobles who don't wish to fight fellow Greeks."

"Exactly." Menon began to pace. "But this kingdom is more than a few Greek nobles. He has to think about everyone, which has left him paralyzed. The nobles are unhappy that he's spending money on the Zoroastrians, Hindus, and Buddhists, and the rest are unhappy when he doesn't. He needs to be stronger. He needs to share his vision for what this kingdom is—or else, why should anyone fight for it?" Menon stopped and forced himself to breathe. "At the very least, the king needs to make a decision."

"Maybe Demetrius can help," said Cleo. "Can you ask him to speak with the king? I know you two are close. All those years of tutoring must count for something."

"Perhaps," said Menon, musing. Demetrius had been an eager student, reading whatever Menon provided. Science, philosophy, theater—he loved it all. He even read texts from his friend, Ashok, or those he found in the royal library. He studied Hinduism, the religion described in the *Mahābhārata*; Buddhism, the faith of the Mauryans; and detachment from the world, a theme common to both. While the king disliked Demetrius's self-directed learning, Menon encouraged it. A future king should accept all knowledge, no matter its source. And the kingdom needed such open-mindedness to pull together its many parts.

"You're right," said Menon, facing his wife. "Demetrius may be young, but he has the makings of a great king. It's time he played a more active role."

Menon wrapped his arm around Cleo and returned his attention to the market below. He closed his eyes and listened to the laughter and bartering, breathing in the spices of the street food as the cool mountain breeze brushed against his face. It all meant so little without his son.

He opened his eyes and looked at Cleo. "I love you."

"I love you, too."

He kissed her and left the room.

CHAPTER FOUR

Demetrius

Demetrius entered the palace to find Menon pacing the hallway.

"Your majesty," said Menon, lifting his head. "You're just the person I was looking for."

Demetrius stopped in front of Menon and noticed that his eyelids were puffy. "Is everything alright?"

"Yes. Everything is fine. For now."

"What is it?"

"I have a favor to ask. The king has not been listening to me recently, but I think he'll listen to you."

Demetrius nodded, familiar with his father's stubbornness.

"It's about Antiochus," said Menon. "I think he'll invade. He has just signed a treaty with the Parthians and, to my mind, that means he's coming here next."

"You really think so?" Demetrius asked. Perhaps he'd been keeping thoughts of war at too far a distance.

"I do," said Menon, his expression betraying concern. "It has long been his interest to unite the lands that Alexander conquered."

"What can I do to help?" Demetrius was eager to serve his mentor.

"It's imperative that we reinforce the garrison at Merv."

"In the desert?" said Demetrius. "Near Parthia?"

"Yes," said Menon. "If Antiochus captures Merv, it will not take him long to reach Bactria, and we need more time to prepare. However, your father worries that mobilizing the army will anger the nobles, many of whom are not yet resigned to war. They are not interested in fighting fellow Greeks or Macedonians. Moreover, they fear that mobilization will push Antiochus into attacking."

His mentor's words pushed Demetrius's mind toward familiar thoughts. He had spent many nights lying awake and wondering what made one Greek. Especially when so far from Greece.

"So you're saying that if we don't mobilize now," said Demetrius, slowly, "we won't be ready if the invasion comes?"

"That's what I fear."

"I'll speak with him." Demetrius placed his hand on Menon's shoulder.

"Thank you, your majesty. And please also remind him of my earlier request for more mercenaries from India."

Demetrius studied Menon's face. "You're sure everything is alright?" he said. "I mean with you. You don't look well."

Something was clearly on Menon's mind—something other than Antiochus. Demetrius had known the man for years. It was Menon, not his father, who had played games with him. It was Menon who had explained the gods and told stories of Achilles and Troy, Leonidas and Thermopylae, Alexander and Persia. It was Menon who'd been preparing Demetrius to be king.

"Today is . . ." Menon stepped back, and Demetrius's arm fell. "Today is the anniversary of Erastus's death."

Demetrius's stomach clenched. How had he forgotten?

"I'm so sorry, Menon," said Demetrius. "I've just been so busy with the games."

"It's alright, your majesty. We all need to move on. The Scythians have a new chief now, and he sent a message of apology for the attacks of his predecessor. It's time I move on, too."

"Really, Menon, I'm sorry. Please let me know if you need anything."

"Thank you, your majesty." Menon bowed.

Leaving Menon, Demetrius made his way to the royal chambers. Statues watched his passage like crowds at a parade, and attendants lowered their heads. Demetrius found his mother, Helen, in the room she had dedicated to artistic endeavors. She was sitting on a stool and adding the finishing touches to a vase she had been painting for days.

"That's coming along nicely, Mother," Demetrius said of the narrow piece of amber-colored pottery.

Helen swiveled on her stool and smiled up at him. Sunlight from the window painted shadows across her face.

"I've spent days on this man's face and hair, and I'm still not satisfied," she said, pointing at the figure on the clay. "But it will have to do."

"It looks perfect, Mother," he said.

"I just hope it gets all the way to Greece," she said. "The trade routes have been unpredictable ever since Antiochus started his eastward march."

"I actually wanted to speak with Father about Antiochus," said Demetrius. "Is he here?"

"In the flesh."

Demetrius turned as Euthydemus entered. The king dragged the extra fabric of his cloak behind him, and a servant dashed to lift it from the floor.

"My love," said Euthydemus. "The vase is beautiful."

"You said that three days ago," said Helen.

"And it was beautiful then, too."

Euthydemus stopped beside Demetrius and placed his hand on Helen's shoulder.

"How were the games, son?" he asked. "I was sorry to miss the beginning."

"They're going well," said Demetrius. "And people have noticed the extra expense on decoration."

"Excellent," said Euthydemus. "Excellent. Any winners I should know about?"

"Eucratides won the footrace," said Demetrius, his mind filling with the image of Roshan rolling on the ground.

"Always a great sportsman," said Euthydemus, smiling. "Now tell me. What is on your mind?"

"I was just speaking with Menon," said Demetrius, "about the need to increase Merv's garrison—"

His father cut him off. "Menon is always worrying."

"I think he *should* be worried. Antiochus is in Parthia. That is just west of here, and if he releases his soldiers into Bactria, we may not be able to hold him back."

"Ah, my son." Euthydemus patted Demetrius's shoulder. "Already speaking as a king." Euthydemus breathed deeply, his chest rising in satisfaction, before continuing, "But Menon must understand that I'm still working to build support among the nobles. Mobilizing right now won't help."

"But if we don't mobilize now, it may become too late," said Demetrius, starting to share Menon's frustration. "Menon also mentioned a request for more soldiers from our ally in India."

"While I would like more mercenaries from Taxila," said Euthydemus, "the nobles are complaining about their presence. They don't like that non-Greeks make up more and more of our army. They think it makes our position here weak. Native Bactrians already form the majority of our forces. Adding more Indians will only infuriate the nobles."

"That is the reasoning of a conqueror, not of a ruler," said Demetrius, channeling his many philosophical discussions with Menon. "Why should the native Bactrians accept us as their own if we're unwilling to act the part?"

"There's the king in you again," said Euthydemus.

"So you don't think Antiochus will come?" said Helen, pulling Demetrius's attention from his father.

"Don't worry about the Seleucids," said Euthydemus. "They'll never come. Not in our lifetime. They've had enough with the Parthians. They have no energy for us."

Demetrius strode to the wide balcony that overlooked Zariaspa. Most of the square buildings that made up the city had bumpy walls of dried clay, while others featured columns and statues of Greek influence. Small alleys snaked between the structures, and temples rose among them like shrubs in the desert. Smoke flowed from their sacred fires into the dry, dusty air.

As Demetrius looked past the city walls to the hazy horizon, he thought of Antiochus. If the monarch was in Parthia, he was only weeks away.

CHAPTER FIVE

Antiochus

"Mark my words," said Antiochus III, sixth emperor of the Seleucid Empire. "I'm not done with these Parthians. They may have forced us into a truce, but I'm not done with them."

He looked to his general, Dropidas, who rode beside him through the army's tent-filled camp. Dropidas nodded his strong, clean-cut jaw. His light-brown hair fell across his face.

"Yes, your highness," he said, struggling to calm his horse, "but we signed the peace treaty. We are allies now. What choice do we have but to return west?"

"I didn't come all this way to go home with my tail between my legs," said Antiochus. "I will not shame this dynasty like those before me, no matter how dire my situation."

Though Antiochus's reign had so far been brief, it had already been eventful. He had become emperor in Syria, the political heart of the Seleucid Empire, at the age of eighteen. The day before he learned of his destiny, his biggest responsibility had been picking which animal to hunt. The day after, his duties were overwhelming. There were the simmering threats of Ptolemaic Egypt to the south, Pergamum and Lydia to the west, Armenia and Atropatene to the north, and the Parthians, Bactrians, and Indians to the east. And then there was the steppe. There was always a threat from the steppe.

Antiochus, Antiochus. . . . Even his own name reminded him of his shaky inheritance. The last emperor to hold that name, Antiochus Theus, had fought the Ptolemaic Greeks of Egypt to no avail—and worse, when that peace was finally made, Antiochus Theus was poisoned by his own wife! It was also his distinction to have lost Bactria and Parthia to revolt.

Nudging his horse into action, Antiochus considered the other name popular among emperors: Seleucus. Unfortunately, it offered no better record. Antiochus's father, Seleucus Callinicus, had failed to take back Parthia and died shortly into his reign after falling off his horse, while Antiochus's brother, Seleucus Ceraunus, lasted only three years on the throne.

"No," said Antiochus, "I will not fall from my horse. If Alexander could take these mountains, I can, too."

Dropidas opened his mouth and then closed it.

"I have no intention of going west," Antiochus continued. "We're going east. To Bactria."

"Are you sure that is wise, your highness," said Dropidas, "considering how our campaign ended here?"

"This is simply a setback, Dropidas. And regardless, an attack on Bactria could bring immeasurable wealth. Wealth we greatly need to recuperate our losses. And remember, I have not been without my fair share of victories."

Since taking the throne, one after another, Antiochus had destroyed the enemies that weaker leaders before him had allowed to rise. He had attacked Atropatene and Armenia and won, and he had spread his power across the rebel kingdoms of Asia Minor. He had even destroyed his rebellious cousin. Yes, defeat in Parthia was only a setback. So what if problems festered at home? His empire's future was not in the west. It was in the east.

"Tonight," said Antiochus, tightening his hold on his horse's reins, "I dine with Arsak, the self-declared king of the Parthians. He says he is now my ally. Let's put that to the test."

Hours later, Antiochus, Dropidas, and their entourage left camp under an orange sky. The breeze was calming, and the surrounding mountains—bare of vegetation—glowed at the edges.

After a brief journey, the Parthian camp came into view: A wall of wooden spikes surrounded hundreds of tents that extended across the valley and up its slopes, with no uniform size or color. Soldiers sat in groups beside fires. The camp must have contained at least fifteen thousand men.

Two Parthian riders approached, the sunset light bouncing from the small, interlaced squares of metal that flowed down their bodies and across their horses. Only the riders' eyes were visible through small holes in the armor. Antiochus had learned from Dropidas that this form of cavalry was called cataphract—and they were formidable, indeed.

"Welcome," said one rider, coming to a stop. "Arsak II, king of Parthia, permits you free passage through his camp and his land, and welcomes you to dine."

Free to pass? His land? The insinuation infuriated Antiochus. The terms of the treaty were clear: Arsak would retain control of Parthia, but he would recognize the ultimate authority of the Seleucids. But Antiochus decided he would not mention it now. Perhaps later, with Arsak. And alone.

The riders led Antiochus and his entourage through the gates of the camp where Parthian soldiers—who only days before had been his enemy—stared at him. Their faces were scarred and bloody, their armor dented and dirty.

On the path ahead, long strips of linen—green, gold, red, and purple—hung from wooden frames at least twice the height of a man, forming a wall. A tent projected from the installation. At the entrance of the vibrant structure, Antiochus stopped.

"The king has set up a dining pavilion specifically for this occasion," said a Parthian. "Please leave your horses here and join his royal majesty inside."

The man raised his arm toward the flaps of fur that covered the tent's doorway.

"If this is a trap . . ." said Dropidas, leaning toward the Parthian, "our army will burn this camp to the ground."

The Parthian dismounted and looked at Dropidas. "I will disregard your words, soldier," he said, "but I sincerely advise that you never again insinuate dishonor from the royal majesty."

"He meant nothing by it," said Antiochus, dismounting as well. "He was only joking. It's our way."

He turned to Dropidas and gave him a sharp look. There would be words later.

Dropidas smirked and placed his hand on the hilt of his sword.

"Your entourage may not follow you past this point, your highness," said the messenger, as Antiochus moved toward the tent door. The man pointed at the thirty-odd men that Antiochus had brought with him. "Only one companion."

"Very well," said Antiochus, over Dropidas's exaggerated sigh.

Followed by Dropidas, Antiochus stepped under the lifted fur and into the tent, where a cloud of incense engulfed him. He suppressed a cough.

Arsak's tent was long, divided into sections by hanging linens and furs. Colorful and intricately embroidered carpets covered the floor. Antiochus decided he would never invite Arsak to his own tent. It was tiny compared to this and might give an impression of weakness.

A Parthian soldier lifted a sheet in the middle of the room and beckoned them in. Here, Arsak sat atop an imposing, gold-speckled chair. The Parthian chief was large and wore a gold diadem from which his black curls burst across his strong shoulders. A purple tunic flowed to his feet, its gold and jewels sparkling in the firelight. Two attendants stood on either side of him, and a muscular soldier stood quietly in the corner, bow in hand.

"Welcome, your majesty," said Arsak.

"Thank you, your highness," said Antiochus, bowing his head no less than he would for a friend, but no more than he would for an equal. "Are we to dine here?" he asked, studying the luxurious surroundings.

"Why, no." Arsak offered a gentle laugh. "This is a welcoming tent. Come, I'll take you to the pavilion."

He disappeared through a door at the back of the tent, and Antiochus and Dropidas followed.

Once again under the sunset sky, Antiochus looked up in wonder at the shifting colors, then drew his gaze to the pavilion. Fabric walls enclosed a vast space, in the middle of which a long rectangular table sat waiting. Pillows lined either side of the table, and a small, though considerably taller, table capped the long one.

Antiochus turned to Arsak for direction, despite sensing how the Parthian leader intended everyone to sit.

"Your majesty," said Arsak, pointing to the foot of the table. "If you would."

Of course, Antiochus thought, but I'll entertain this act. He sat on a large blue pillow and looked down the length of the table at the small, but taller, platform directly opposite him. A moment later, Arsak took his place behind it.

As Dropidas settled onto a pillow at Antiochus's left, two men entered through the fabric door.

"Your majesty," said Arsak to Antiochus, "let me present two of my best generals."

Antiochus nodded.

"Directly to your right," said Arsak, "is Heron."

Heron collapsed onto a pillow beside Antiochus. The man's curly black hair curved around a gold band on his head, and he wore an open purple robe, revealing a gold chest plate decorated with red and blue gems.

"Heron leads my cavalry," said Arsak, "both the archers and cataphract."

Antiochus thought back to the campaign and to fighting Heron's mounted archers. The riders had hovered on the flanks of his army like vultures, shooting arrows and then pulling back when Antiochus sent his own cavalry in pursuit. And then there were the cataphract, heavy cavalry unlike any he had seen before.

"And beside me, here," said Arsak, smiling widely, "is my son, Phriapa. Or Phriapatius, as some Greeks call him."

Antiochus looked at Phriapa, trying to remember if he had heard the name during the campaign. The man was tall and thin, but his shoulders were broad and his arms thick. Wavy black hair fell just below his shoulders, and a short black beard and mustache covered his angular face. His piercing green eyes were impossible to read.

"Have we faced one another in battle?" said Antiochus, staring at the young man.

"Unfortunately, no," said Phriapa. "Although many of my friends fell by the spears of your phalanx. As did my brother."

"I will drink tonight in their honor," said Antiochus, lowering his head.

"Phriapa has been in the north," said Arsak. "The Scythians encroached on our land, and a response was required. He pushed them back. It has become a yearly affair."

"I understand," said Antiochus. "The steppe warriors harass my borders, as well."

Antiochus took a sip of wine.

"Tell me, Arsak," he said, setting the cup delicately against the table. "Am I right that your father came from the steppe like the Scythians?"

Arsak stared silently for a moment, then smiled. "You are correct that my father brought our people from the steppe. But no, I would not say we're like the Scythians."

Antiochus held the Parthian's gaze as he drank his wine.

"Now," said Arsak, finally looking away and lifting his arms. "Let us eat."

Attendants covered the table from end to end in delicate gold plates and elaborately arranged food.

While Antiochus and Dropidas had to eat on faith, a taster hovered beside Arsak, ready to test each course. It was a scene to which Antiochus was well accustomed, as he followed the same procedure in his Syrian palace. Still, as a guest, it was hardly something he could demand, especially when he sought to build trust and a fruitful alliance.

"I hope one day we can celebrate a victory together with such a meal," said Antiochus, grabbing a pheasant leg.

"Most certainly, your highness. But first, let's agree to the foe. The Scythians, perhaps?"

"Bactria," said Antiochus, not wishing to waste any more time.

"Ah, yes, Bactria," said the Parthian king, his mouth twisting into a smile that seemed less than genuine. "The biggest prize of them all. The gateway to India. Do you have an interest in extending your control to that far land, as well?"

Antiochus set down the pheasant bone. "I have an interest in reasserting control over the lands of my illustrious predecessor." He tried not to blink, but to no avail.

"Yes," said Arsak. "Alexander. It's always Alexander. But surely you think our lands are included in that dream?"

"Perhaps," said Antiochus. "But rarely do dreams manifest after waking. You have taught me this most violently." He thought back to the war. The Parthians had hidden in the mountains, never meeting him in open battle. They chose instead to raid his supply lines, ambush his scouts, and fill the wells along his route. His campaign was never lost, but it was also never won. It dragged into a stalemate, then this uneasy peace. He pushed the humiliation from his mind. "Your people are no friend to the Bactrians. They were on our side during your war of independence."

Arsak took a long drink. "You know," he said, setting down the cup, "you Greeks are a peculiar people. One day, you control all of the known world, and the next, you kill each other to have slivers of it."

"This is the fate of power, is it not?"

"Perhaps. But your collective weakness opens the way for a new power in the west. Rome, I believe it's called. I hear they are eager to invade your Macedonian neighbor."

"That may be," said Antiochus. "But the Romans are too busy with the Carthaginian general, Hannibal, to invade. Either way, you need not worry about them, your highness. Your people will never face Rome as long as the Seleucid dynasty reigns in Asia."

Arsak did not respond. Antiochus gnawed his pheasant bone.

"Yes," said Arsak, after a lengthy pause. "We will help you conquer Bactria."

Phriapa leaned forward, glaring at Antiochus. "But, Father—"

Arsak silenced him with a wave of his hand. "If you give us full control of Margiana and Sogdiana when this is over," he said to Antiochus, "then yes, we will join you."

"Deal," said Antiochus. He could return for those regions later. "They shall be yours."

"But may I ask," said Arsak, "that we solidify this understanding in marriage?"

Antiochus let out an involuntary laugh. The man must be joking! Alexander may have allowed marriages between his men and the people of the east, but those days were long gone. Still, he played along. "What do you have in mind?"

"I have been told of your youngest daughter's beauty. And I have a son." He nodded at Phriapa, who sat stone-faced.

"I mean no offense," said Antiochus, "but such an arrangement is out of the question. Her hand is destined for the needs of the west. She will marry some Ptolemaic prince after I avenge a recent setback."

"We shall see," said Arsak. "We shall see."

"Will you still join us?" said Antiochus, flustered by these cryptic words. "Or should I consider our friendship as faint as a dream?"

Arsak smiled.

CHAPTER SIX

>>>———→

Phriapa

After the Seleucids left, Phriapa and his father settled on bulbous pillows beside the pavilion's small fire. The flame had burned to embers, causing the carpet's gold embroidery to flicker.

"We shouldn't have agreed to fight beside them," said Phriapa, sinking deeper into his blue-and-gold cushion.

"You shouldn't challenge my judgment."

"Yes, Father." Phriapa paused for a moment, but couldn't help himself. "We would have beaten them," he blurted. "Why did we agree to a truce, let alone this Bactrian campaign?"

"Yes, we could have beaten them." Arsak leaned forward and lowered his voice. "But at too great a cost. We need our strength for the fights to come. I am thinking in years. And in due time, not only will Bactria, Margiana, and Sogdiana be ours, but all of Asia, the Seleucid lands included."

"How can this be?" said Phriapa. "The Seleucids will rule Bactria—and with our help, I'll remind you. And with them in Bactria, enemies will surround us."

"Because times are changing, son, and the Seleucids are weak. Their hold on power is shaky at best, even when all they face are the Ptolemaic Greeks of Egypt and the Antigonids of Macedonia. But soon, they will face Rome as well, and from all I've heard, that enemy is unlike any other." Arsak sipped his wine. "Antiochus will leave soon enough. And once his wars have softened him up, we will take his place."

Draining his wine, Phriapa considered his father's words. "And you suppose that we can oppose these Romans any better than the rest?"

"I do, son. I do."

"Your ambition is admirable, Father," said Phriapa. He'd heard a great deal of the Romans' martial abilities. "But we have yet to beat even the Bactrians."

"Don't worry about that. We'll let the Greeks do most of the work against their own. But rest assured, we'll be there to pick up the pieces."

Leaving his father, Phriapa stepped into the breezy evening. The sky was a light pink, and the horizon red. He looked out at the army's tents and the fires around which the soldiers sang, joked, and commiserated. He thought of the many friends lost in the previous months' fighting—his brother included. Yes, they had stopped the Seleucid advance, but at considerable cost. And now his father agreed to help remove the thorn in Antiochus's side. Better to leave the thorn alone.

With his mind clouded, Phriapa found Heron sitting alone beside a fire.

"Can I join you?"

"Of course, your majesty," said Heron. "There is no need to ask."

Phriapa sat on the cold ground and stretched his feet toward the flames.

"What did you think of Antiochus?" said Heron.

"He's ambitious," said Phriapa. "I'll give him that. But he's also naïve. These lands differ from the west. The mountains, the roads. He'll find things take longer here."

Nodding, Heron threw a stick onto the fire. Its bark twisted in the flames.

"What do you think of the alliance?" Phriapa asked.

"It is the king's will, so it is the right decision," said Heron.

"Heron," said Phriapa, "you don't need to speak like that with me. Tell me what you really think."

"Well," Heron hesitated. "I guess I'm frustrated. We fought them for months, and they were slowly grinding away. We ought to have finished them."

Phriapa nodded.

"You agree, your majesty?" said Heron, clearly looking for Phriapa to back him up.

"I agree," said Phriapa, "but as you've said, the king has spoken, so I will follow him to Bactria." He clenched his jaw.

"As will I," said Heron. "As will I."

Phriapa focused on the crackling fire.

"How did my brother die?" he asked. The question had been on his mind for weeks.

He caught Heron's glance, eyelids glistening.

"He died a hero," said Heron, looking away.

"I know, I know," said Phriapa, wanting to get past the veil of hero talk. "But were you there? What happened?"

"Why do you want to know, your majesty?" said Heron.

"I just do," said Phriapa. "Please tell me."

"He died during a cavalry charge," said Heron. "We had been softening up the enemy with arrows, and when the time seemed right, your brother led the heavy cavalry. The phalanx was disordered, and it looked like we could break through. Maybe it was the dust, or just the chaos of battle, but we misjudged. By the time your brother and the cataphract were upon the enemy, the phalanx was in order, their long spears pointed out like a porcupine."

Phriapa's breathing sped up, and his fingers tightened.

"Most of the horses slowed," continued Heron, "unwilling to gallop into the blades, but your brother's horse didn't flinch. It took him right into them."

"That horse was crazy." Phriapa let out a pathetic laugh. "I always told him to find another."

"The horse fell," continued Heron, "your brother with it. But then we saw him stand, sword in hand. He fought ferociously, but eventually, he was cut down. Like I said, he died a hero."

Phriapa thought of the times he and his brother had pretended to be soldiers as children. They had faked their deaths many times. But now it was real, and his brother was gone. Phriapa breathed deeply and closed his eyes, vengeance on his mind.

CHAPTER SEVEN

Demetrius

On the second day of the games, Demetrius decided to watch the chariot race from atop the city walls. The welcome breeze caressed his hair, and he wiped the sweat from his forehead. Directly below and just beyond the spiked moat, vendors sold food from across the region. Parathas gurgled on iron pans, transforming from a doughy paste into flaky discs, and chunks of skewered meat roasted over a fire. Elsewhere, there were baskets of fruit, vegetables, and nuts. Vendors announced fresh batches of different fares, while a young boy with a large barrel strapped to his back pushed through the crowds offering wine. When a woman stopped him, he lifted a metal cup that dangled from a string and filled it with dark liquid from a nozzle on the barrel's side. Once the woman finished drinking, she dropped the cup, leaving it to swing as the boy walked on.

Demetrius struggled to imagine what the same area might look like if the Seleucids did invade. If there was a siege, the Bactrian army would carve the gaming fields into successive ditches, and burn their own agricultural fields so the attackers could gain neither food nor shelter. Demetrius looked past the farmland to the wavy horizon. What had been their haven could become their tomb.

"Not looking to mingle with the crowd?" said a voice to his right. Demetrius turned to see Menon.

"I was down there before," said Demetrius. "It takes a certain energy to stay within it for too long."

"You don't need to tell me," said Menon, his large stomach pressing against the wall. "It's hard to be there. Erastus loved the games. I only watch now to keep track of the general fitness of our men."

"I remember Erastus competing in the footrace," said Demetrius. "It's one of my earliest memories."

"That was a long time ago," said Menon. "We live in different times now."

"So, are you here to watch the chariot race?" Demetrius asked, believing Menon wanted a subject change.

"That, yes." Menon wiped sweat from his forehead. "But I'm more interested in the hoplite race afterward."

"As a child, I would always laugh at that race," said Demetrius. "They look so ridiculous running in their armor."

"Today, it's more important than just a race. It's a test of our hoplites' stamina. They will form the center of our battle line soon enough, and they will stand face to face with the emperor's best soldiers—men who have fought for years."

"Do you think we're ready?"

"Unfortunately, no," said Menon. "Not right now. But I think we can be."

"What do you mean?" Demetrius asked.

"If I may say, your majesty," said Menon, "the city is divided. Much work is needed to bring everyone together. But you, Demetrius, may be the one to do this."

Menon's words disturbed Demetrius. As his tutor, Menon often spoke frankly with him, but this felt like something else.

"I've seen your instincts for getting to know people across the city, no matter their rank or heritage," said Menon. "It is that attitude that we need right now. How else can we expect the non-Greeks to fight for this government, or the Greeks to fight against people they consider kin?"

The deep hum signaled the start of the chariot race, which would take the participants in a wide loop around the walls. A dust cloud billowed out beside the green fields as the four chariots pulled away. Each chariot was drawn by two horses, and their frames were devoid of any extra weight—no umbrellas, no arrow quivers, and no soldiers. Just wood, leather, and a driver.

The crowd below erupted in cheers as the chariots approached, one far in the lead. Pebbles and dust flew from the wheels, and the horses bobbed their heads violently as they pushed against fatigue and the whip. As the chariots passed beyond his view, Demetrius's heartbeat slowed.

"In the coming months," said Menon, drawing Demetrius back to the conversation, "if this kingdom is to have any chance of survival, you will need to step into a leadership position. Your father needs help. He believes that this kingdom is on the edge of collapse, and that the Greeks here favor Antiochus if it means an end to including all of our citizens in the polity. He doesn't understand that only a few feel that way—albeit a loud few. I think that's why he is being indecisive at the exact moment when we need strong leadership."

Demetrius had never heard Menon speak this way.

"I want you to follow your instincts," continued Menon. "If you think something, then say it. If you disagree with your father or the nobles, voice your concern. If you don't, I'm afraid the kingdom will be rudderless, and that is no way to approach a storm."

"I don't know if I'm ready to be that man," said Demetrius. "I don't know if I'm ready for war."

"You're more ready than most of your subjects, your highness. You have trained for this moment your entire life. In due time, you will achieve the greatness that we expect of you." Menon paused. "You must."

The conversation was far from comforting, but Demetrius knew he would appear weak if he pushed the matter further. Menon may have mentored him since childhood, but Demetrius was still the prince.

"I understand," said Demetrius, hoping his voice hid his doubts.

Below, the city's best soldiers stepped through the gate, covered in bronze armor. The spectators greeted them with cheers. Once the chariot race was over, the hoplites would take their turn at the starting line, and at the sound of the horn, they would sprint the length of a stade. The race tested their readiness for a battlefield charge, and Demetrius knew that many of the onlookers would be eager to see something to instill confidence.

As the hoplites tightened their armor and shined their shields, the chariots circled back into view. The crowd yelled encouragements to the drivers, the two in the lead racing side by side. The drivers looked at one another as they approached the finish line, and when they crossed, it was too close for Demetrius to tell which of them had won. He would find out soon enough, though, as the games' various winners were to feast with the king and queen that night.

"Here we go," said Menon, pointing at the small army of hoplites lumbering toward the starting line. From above, the men—standing shoulder to shoulder—looked like a giant bronze sword left in the dust.

The game administrator stepped before the infantrymen and pointed at a distant line. When he stepped aside, the horn hummed, and the race began. What had once been a straight line disintegrated as soldiers ran at different paces, few of which could be considered fast. By the time the first soldier crossed the finish line and collapsed, others had only covered half the distance.

Menon sighed and turned away. "I'll be speaking with Lander about this," he said, referring to the kingdom's most experienced general. "Drilling will double moving forward."

He bowed to Demetrius and descended the stairs.

CHAPTER EIGHT

Roshan

In the gaming fields, Roshan ran to the chariot from which his friend, Feroze, was stepping down. Feroze wore nothing but a leather loincloth, and sweat and dirt stuck to his body. His horses sneezed amid a cloud of dust.

"You did it!" yelled Roshan as he embraced Feroze. "You won!"

"Did I?" said Feroze, clearly exhausted. His eyes were bloodshot.

"Yes!" Roshan patted him hard on the back. "The judge just announced it. The race was close, but you won."

Feroze forced a smile between two heavy breaths and looked over Roshan's shoulder. Roshan turned to see another chariot amid a crowd of Greeks. He couldn't see the driver, but two people were arguing with the judge. One of them threw his hands in the air and yelled. Roshan squinted against the sunlight. It was Eucratides, the Greek he'd competed against in the footrace.

Roshan's face prickled, and he ran his fingers through his long beard. He remembered running ahead of Eucratides; he remembered rolling in the dirt and watching the Greek cross the finish line.

As the judge walked away, Roshan's gaze moved to Eucratides, who stared back at him and spat in the dirt. Roshan spat back and turned to Feroze, who was speaking with an older Bactrian couple. They wore matching green tunics, but the woman had covered her hair with a transparent red shawl. She pulled it to her mouth and coughed. As the couple walked away, Roshan said to Feroze, "This win is a great way to end the day."

"Better than the hoplite race," said Feroze. "That couple was telling me that some men couldn't even finish."

Roshan looked to where a group of men in bronze armor ambled toward the gate. One man dragged his shield beside him.

"Yes," said Roshan. "But I mean it's wonderful that *you* won. It shows those Greeks that we can beat them. That they're not better than us."

Feroze frowned and threw his arms up.

"What?" said Roshan.

"Why is everything like that for you?"

"Like what?"

"Like us and them," said Feroze. "We this. Greeks that. I raced to win. I didn't care against who."

Roshan resented the scolding. "Whatever. I'm just glad you won."

"So am I," said Feroze. "Now, let's wash up for the victors' dinner. Your buzkashi team earned it."

They entered the city and peeled away from the main street, coming to Roshan's neighborhood. It was inhabited by Zoroastrian Bactrians who could trace their roots in Zariaspa to before the Greco-Macedonian invasion.

Parting ways with Feroze, Roshan walked through a small market where people sold homemade handicrafts and food from their family gardens. A few of the stalls sold linens and furs, gold and precious stones, decorated knives and composite bows. The products were imported from near and far, many of them across the northern steppe. A young boy ran through the crowd selling oranges, while another brought people to a stall where he grilled dough into roti and chapati.

A nearly completed Zoroastrian temple sat at the far end of the market. For a time, the palace had funded the temple's construction, but recently, the money had stopped coming. Supposedly, some nobles had complained because they wanted the funds for their own temples. Roshan grew angry every time he thought about it.

Roshan's family home was in a thin alley that ran between the incomplete temple and the wall of the upper city. The wall imposed itself on their neighborhood, and little natural light landed directly on the road. In front of his house, a woman set a pile of trash alight; the government sweepers avoided this neighborhood.

Crammed between two shops, Roshan's house was small, and its wooden door rested unevenly. Upon entering, Roshan found his mother sitting beside the small window that provided the room's only light.

"My son," she said, standing. She was short and thin. Gray striped her black hair, and wrinkles cut across her face. "I heard your team won at buzkashi. That is wonderful news. The neighbors will be thrilled."

"I don't care about that win," said Roshan. "I wanted to win the footrace. And I would have if that Greek hadn't pushed me."

"Now," said his mother as she opened the window shutter wider, "that's no attitude to bring into this house."

Roshan could hear the pain in her voice.

"You're right, Mother," he said. "I'm sorry."

He looked to a shelf on his right, which contained keepsakes from his late father. Roshan had been an infant when he died.

"You know, Roshan," said his mother. "People have been asking about your marriage interests."

Roshan sighed. "Not now, Mother. Anytime but now."

"You've said that for years," she said. "All the women will be taken by the time you want to talk."

"I'm to go to the palace tonight," said Roshan, trying to change the subject.

"What an honor." She joined him at the center of the room.

"If you say so."

"Do you know how many people would love to take your place?"

"Yes, I know."

"So show a little gratitude," she said. "At least around the others."

Roshan nodded as he gazed at their home. When he was small, he'd spent much of his time playing with clay toys in the dark corners of the house, but as he grew older, he would leave the claustrophobic structure to steal oranges from the royal gardens. Caning scars told the stories of his missteps. Eventually, he went to work with his uncle in a carpentry shop, where they made whatever the palace needed. The work helped keep the family fed, but Roshan never excelled at it. Given the opportunity, he joined the native infantry within the kingdom's army, where he quickly distinguished himself as a good fighter. Though he resided in the barracks, he returned home as much as he could. Especially after his father died.

"Perhaps you can help me decide what to wear." Roshan smiled sheepishly.

"Now that's more like it." His mother ruffled his hair, rattling the bangles on her wrist. "I won't have my son looking dirty in front of the king and queen. Or the prince for that matter." She sighed. "You know, I still hope you'll meet the prince one day. I hear he's a good man."

"If you say so." Roshan was tired of his mother's constant deference toward the nobles.

After dressing, Roshan made his way to the upper city. Passing through the imposing gate that separated the haves from the have-nots, he studied the large, clean buildings before him. Here, the walls were painted red and were largely devoid of the cracks that plagued the lower city. Smooth pillars supported roofs, the edges of which were decorated with murals and statues.

At the foot of the palace staircase, Roshan gave his name to the guards, and after consulting their list, they let him pass. When he reached the top step, he turned to look out at the city. The view was beautiful. From this high perch, it was impossible to see the rot and ruin that had spread further with each year.

Roshan ran his hand through his beard and entered the palace.

CHAPTER NINE

Demetrius

The feasting had already begun by the time Demetrius arrived in the banquet hall. Perhaps one hundred winners—most from the kabaddi and buzkashi teams—sat on colorful pillows behind the small tables arranged on the floor. Musicians played harps, double-fluted aulos, and water organs, and in the center of the room, a boar rotated on a metal pole above a massive fire. Demetrius's parents reclined on a large red pillow, feeding each other from a golden plate of fruit. Beside them, Menon drank wine and spoke with the enormous general, Lander, who towered over the table. Demetrius assumed they were discussing the hoplite race and the army's preparedness for war.

Demetrius couldn't help but note the way the guests were organized. His father and mother sat at the front of the room and conversed with other Greeks, while Indians and other foreign mercenaries perched throughout the room. Meanwhile, the native Bactrians sat at the far side of the room, near a lively fire. The scene felt like a metaphor for Bactria: Its people lived beside one another, but they were not yet one.

The fires' waving flames and the terracotta lamps did little to fend off the moonlight, which pressed into the room from the courtyard, where bushes and leaves swayed and shook as peacocks roamed. In the middle of the yard, a large cauldron, painted with ships cutting across the Mediterranean, collected water during the rainy season. When he was a child, Demetrius had called the cauldron "the little sea" and swam in it, until a winter swim nearly killed him—as his mother liked to remind him.

"Demetrius, come join me!" Eucratides called, leaning back against a purple pillow. He waved to a nearby attendant and pointed at his cup. The attendant refilled it, pouring first from a bronze vase of wine and then from a pot of water to dilute the alcohol.

"Congratulations again on your victory yesterday," said Demetrius. "It was a close one."

"It was," said Eucratides. "And you know what? Some of them—" he pointed to the native Bactrians, "—claim I cheated. That I tripped Roshan, their champion."

"*Our* champion."

"What?" said Eucratides, his face contorting.

"Roshan," said Demetrius. "He is one of the city's champions. As are all of you here tonight."

"Stop the nonsense." Eucratides pushed Demetrius's shoulder. "You know what I mean. Save that talk of us and we and whatever for when you're king."

Demetrius decided against pressing the matter. Whenever Eucratides drank, he liked to argue. Instead, Demetrius told Eucratides that he needed to make the rounds. It was his duty as prince.

"Very well," said Eucratides, waving Demetrius away with his now empty cup. "Off you go." He turned to the large man who had won the hoplite race. Eucratides's tone was unacceptable, but Demetrius chose not to mind.

For much of the evening, Demetrius moved from group to group, congratulating people on their victories and discussing strategies for their respective sports. Most attendees were polite. His friends, on the other hand, made fun of him for being at the dinner when he wasn't a champion. He agreed with them.

He spotted Roshan, the man who had fallen during the footrace, and though he didn't know why, Demetrius sensed that he and Roshan should meet.

"Congratulations on your buzkashi victory," he said, stopping in front of the Bactrian. "Your name is Roshan, right?"

Roshan swallowed his food and nodded. "Yes, your majesty."

Roshan was strong, with broad shoulders and thick arms. His brown hair sat in a knot behind his head, and his long beard swayed along his chest.

"I also saw your footrace," said Demetrius. "It was close."

"Very close," said Roshan, looking past Demetrius to glare at Eucratides. "But there is always next year."

"An admirable attitude." Demetrius tapped his wine cup against Roshan's goblet. "Again, congratulations."

Later that night, when the queen had retired to the women's chambers and the men were drunk, Euthydemus stood from his chair to give a speech. He wore a fresh white tunic, its edges embroidered with red thread and gold foil. The guests were slow to quiet, but that was expected on a drinking night.

"Countrymen," he declared, "it is a great honor to drink with you tonight. You are the champions of our great city. You have brought honor to yourselves, your families, and our country."

Applause cascaded across the room.

"The first city games," continued Euthydemus, "were held by Alexander in celebration of taking the city. Since then, they have become a symbol of continuity and growth. Continuity with our ancestors, and growth through the expansion of our polity. It was with great pleasure that I watched not only the sports of Greece but also the sports of the east, the south, and the north."

Cheers erupted again, although unevenly.

Euthydemus, who had only watched a few of the games, spent most of his speech mentioning those highlights from the two-day festivities that the palace attendants had relayed to him. But eventually, the speech turned to the subject that everyone, Demetrius supposed, had on their minds: Antiochus.

Euthydemus set his cup down. "If only Antiochus had seen your performances, he would take his army and run back to Syria. But he was not here, so he might foolishly try to impose his will upon us. But I'm fully confident that you, the champions of our city, will stand by me and grind his army into dust."

The room erupted into the loudest cheers yet, and Demetrius noticed that his father seemed almost surprised by it.

Soon after, Euthydemus took his leave and the party slowed. A few people, Eucratides included, would drink till morning, but most of the guests cleared out. Demetrius wasn't tired, but he had no interest in staying, and he wondered if Ashok would be awake at this hour. The lower city was always full of parties during the games. Even a walk would be nice, and so he donned a dull gray cloak and left.

With the moon high in the sky, the whole city was visible. Its straight edges and stark shadows combined beautifully with the dark, rolling horizon. Terracotta roof tiles reflected moonlight like ripples in a pond. Demetrius passed through the upper city gate, and could hear the clattering and cheering from parties down the hill.

As the hill leveled, the crowds grew dense and Demetrius found the market alive as ever. Vendors called to potential customers, who pushed and shoved in the chaos.

Demetrius kept the hood of his cloak pulled over his face and wove through the crowds, ducking under clotheslines and twisting past stalls. Finally, after much effort, he reached Ashok's house, a small mud hut in the city's Indian quarter. The door was blue, and below it, a chalk drawing of a flower graced the ground. A coconut swung from a string beside the door. Demetrius knocked, and after a pause, the door opened.

"I know it's late," said Demetrius in greeting. "But I thought you might be up."

"We're up alright," said Ashok, smiling. "The whole city is up. Come in."

Demetrius stepped across the mud-brick threshold and felt the weight of the previous hours lift from his shoulders. The feast had felt more like a burden than a party. It was becoming more and more difficult for him to look past the tension and the divides of the city. But Ashok's house had always felt like a home away from home. When he had grown old enough to leave the palace alone, Demetrius had often returned to the lower city with Ashok and his mother when she was done working. He would listen to Ashok's stories of Ram and Sita, Hanuman and Krishna, and imagine life in India.

For the rest of the night, Demetrius and Ashok shared stories from childhood and discussed the games. The horizon glowed with the rising sun before Demetrius fell asleep, and he woke with a headache. After eating a simple breakfast with Ashok and Priya, he left for the palace. As he walked, he rubbed his temples and tried to clear his mind. With the games over, the palace would turn entirely to the threat of invasion, which was appropriate, because somewhere to the west, their enemy was on the move.

CHAPTER TEN

>>⟶

Phriapa

Atop a bluff, Phriapa and his father watched the Seleucid and Parthian armies marching in a long, twisting column. The soldiers had broken camp the day before, and now, with the sun rising on their second day of marching, they approached the Parthian homeland. Birds of prey flew in the sky, dust hugged the moving armies, and yellow flowers blanketed the hills around them.

"It's nice to be in the open again, isn't it?" said Arsak.

Phriapa turned in his saddle to face his father, who sat on a large white horse ornamented with strings of gold.

"I'm glad to be heading to Saddarvazeh," said Phriapa. "Although it's strange to be taking the Seleucids with us."

Antiochus came riding up the bluff on a light-brown horse armored in bronze plates. Phriapa clenched his fists as Antiochus stopped beside them.

"It's a beautiful sight, isn't it?" said Antiochus.

"Yes," said Arsak. "We love this land very much."

"I meant my army."

Phriapa twisted his horse's reins.

"See there, just below the bluff?" Antiochus pointed. "Those are the Katoikoi. They form the bulk of my army. Most of them are Greeks who I encouraged to move to Asia. In return for settlement in towns across the land, they render military service when called upon. Packed into a phalanx hundreds of men wide and a dozen deep, they are as strong as a fortress wall."

The Seleucid infantry lumbered before the forest-covered mountains. Their pikes—known as sarissas—waved back and forth in the air, catching the light and making the sky sparkle. Thinking of his brother, Phriapa wanted to break them in two.

"Just behind the Katoikoi," continued Antiochus, "are the Argyraspides, or Silver Shields. They, too, carry the sarissa for when a fight of phalanx proves most appropriate. But their skills extend far past that, and they have quite the reputation. Under Alexander, the Silver Shields were always the first over the wall during any siege. They fought in dire circumstances and never retreated. Then again, they rarely lost. It was this group that hacked a path through the Hindu Kush to India."

Phriapa had seen enough. He turned to Antiochus and quoted a play he had read as a child: "'Zeus hates with a vengeance all bravado, the mighty boasts of men.'"

"I see you know *Antigone*." Antiochus grinned.

"One must study their enemies," said Phriapa, glad that Antiochus understood the reference, though annoyed that the emperor smiled.

"They absolutely should," said Antiochus.

"Fighting on a horse," said Arsak, moving his own steed between them, "is surely the noblest of skills."

"On this, you and I agree," said Antiochus, leading his horse closer to the bluff's edge. "And I have been most interested in your armored cavalry. It's a wonder they can move under all that metal."

"The cataphracts," said Arsak, joining him. "It takes months to prepare the armor for each man and horse. And patience. Each piece must be bent and twisted and sewn together. And at the end of it all, it must fit the rider. No tailor in the world can rival the artists who dress our cavalry."

"I'm sure the skill can be learned," said Antiochus.

"Perhaps," said Arsak, "but mastery takes years."

They sat in silence for a moment, and Phriapa watched the birds hovering above the moving armies.

"Ah, the Companion Cavalry," said Antiochus, pointing at a group of riders at the base of the hill. "They are the empire's pride."

"Do I recall correctly," said Phriapa, "that the friends within this group killed each other after the death of Alexander?"

Antiochus glanced at him. "You know your history."

"As any leader should," said Phriapa.

Antiochus sat straight. "Times have changed since then. Rest assured, young prince. My Companions are most loyal."

"If you say so." Phriapa was pleased to see Antiochus's face twist with irritation.

"I've decided to send my son to look at the defenses of Merv," Arsak announced, in a clear attempt to break the tension. This was the first Phriapa had heard of the plan. "We need to know if the Bactrian stronghold is heavily guarded. With the Scythians always harassing the Greeks in the north, it is possible there's only a small garrison at Merv. If it is any larger, it will be too difficult for us to take the city, surrounded by desert as it is."

"Very well," said Antiochus, "but I insist that some of my riders join him. It is important that they, too, see what lies ahead."

"That is fine," said Phriapa, eyeing the monarch. "But I won't slow for them."

"Nor will you have to," said Antiochus, holding Phriapa's gaze for a moment longer than needed.

"Well," said Arsak, "while we wait for Phriapa's return, we can practice."

"Practice?" said Antiochus.

Arsak smiled. "You shall join us in Saddarvazeh. Perhaps I can teach you a thing or two."

Disgusted with this conversation's increasing geniality, Phriapa led his horse down the hill.

"I can't stand that man," he said, pulling beside Heron.

"Don't worry, your highness," said Heron. "We'll be rid of him soon enough."

Phriapa smiled as he thought of Antiochus running back to Syria, bloody and humbled.

But when the army reached the irrigated fields that surrounded Saddarvazeh, Phriapa pushed back tears. He had grown up on this land. He and his brother would go hunting among the hills, often staying away for days. It was overwhelming to ride across it now. Alone.

"I can see the walls," said Heron.

Phriapa raised his arm to block the sun. The walls were so tan and dusty that it looked as if the ground simply became the sky. Purple-and-green flags fluttered on tall poles that rose from the fortifications. As the army approached, people on the walls called down to the Parthians galloping below.

Reaching the city, Phriapa left the crowd that welcomed the returning warriors and made his way to the palace where he assumed his mother was waiting. He found her in the small garden that she managed. Seeing him, she placed a spade on the ground and stood. Her long black hair lay straight against her back, but as she stepped forward, it swayed behind her waist.

"The warrior returns," she said, her smile revealing cracks in her bright lipstick. "I wanted to greet you in the square, but you know how uncomfortable I get among crowds."

Phriapa pulled her into a hug. "How else would I know to find you here?"

"I'm glad you're back," she said, clinging to him. Her voice was scratchy. He tightened his grip when she started crying. "I only wish that both of you had returned," she sobbed.

"I know, Mother." He felt his throat tighten. "I know."

In this very courtyard and much to their mother's chagrin, he and his brother had often uprooted the sturdy plants and used them as swords. Fighting was their obsession. They were so naïve.

Phriapa stepped back and looked at his mother. Tears wove down her cheeks, pulling her makeup with them.

"And now your father makes allies of his killers," she said, wiping her face.

"You heard." Phriapa sighed. "I wanted to be the one to tell you."

"A messenger came this morning," she said.

"This alliance will help our people in the long run," said Phriapa, repeating an argument he hardly agreed with, but hoping it would help his mother deal with the news. "And my brother played his part in getting us here. Parthia's successes will honor him."

His mother nodded and cried again. He pulled her close, and the tears he had thus far held back streamed down his face.

"Come," his mother said, stepping back. "I've prepared a feast."

"I look forward to it," said Phriapa, wiping his face. "But you should know that I depart tonight."

"So soon?"

"Unfortunately, yes." He was fully composed now. "I must scout Merv. If it's heavily defended, Father wants to head south."

"So war with Bactria is inevitable," said his mother, looking to the sky.

"So it seems." Phriapa placed his arm around her. "So it seems."

CHAPTER ELEVEN

Demetrius

"Antiochus is coming," said Menon, as he stepped into Demetrius's room.

Demetrius set aside a parchment and stood. "You received word?"

"Your father did. Now come with me. He called a meeting."

Demetrius rolled the parchment and placed it on a shelf before following Menon from the room.

"What were you reading?" Menon asked, as they moved through a wide corridor. "You've already read much of the library."

"There's always something new," said Demetrius. "And in this case, it was a report on mathematical theories developed at the Library of Alexandria. I can't say that I understand it, but I'm trying. And I wanted to get my mind off the coming war."

"I understand," said Menon. "The war is all I think about lately. This way."

Menon led Demetrius through a doorway into the meeting room. At a long table, Euthydemus sat beside Lander and Arjun, the kingdom's most trusted generals. On the bare walls behind them, a window opened to a small courtyard.

"Menon, you were right," said Euthydemus, as Demetrius and Menon took seats across from him. "Antiochus is coming."

Menon bowed his head in silence.

"But it's no matter," continued Euthydemus. "We will beat him just as the Parthians did."

"The Parthians didn't exactly beat him," said Menon. "They achieved a truce, which is hardly a victory."

"No," said Lander, leaning against the table. "They've done more than that. My spies say the Parthians have joined Antiochus in his march here. They've probably already reached Saddarvazeh."

Demetrius watched his father close his eyes and exhale slowly.

"We should have destroyed the Parthians years ago," he said, looking to Menon.

"There's no way we could have anticipated this," said Menon.

"Well." The king settled further into his chair. "The past is past. Now we must face its consequences. I guess the question we must ask is how easily they can get here."

"I've put some thought into this, your majesty," said Menon, standing.

"Of course you have." Euthydemus leaned forward.

Menon beckoned to an attendant, who placed a map on the table. As Demetrius helped to spread it flat, he studied the ink marks that indicated mountains, rivers, and roads.

"So now we know that he will attack." Menon's rings tapped loudly against the table as his large hands came to rest on the parchment. "And we know the Parthians will help him. But there is much we *don't* know, such as the route they will take, and when. Now, the quickest route would be to move east from Saddarvazeh toward our stronghold at Merv. From Merv, it would be a rapid march to Bactria."

"They won't take that route," said Lander. "They would be without water along an unprotected stretch of desert. Their survival would entirely depend on their ability to take the fortress. And quickly."

"Unfortunately," said Menon, "the garrison at Merv is too small to survive an attack. It desperately needs reinforcements."

Menon's gaze turned to Euthydemus, who looked away, and Demetrius considered his father's flushed face.

"If we can reinforce it in time," said Euthydemus, finally looking up, "can we hold it?"

"I believe so, your highness," said Menon. "But we must send an army quickly."

"Then let's hope they take the route to Merv," said the king.

"If we reinforce it in time, then yes," said Menon. "But I agree with Lander. It is unlikely that Antiochus will go that way."

"You see, alternatively," said Lander, standing and motioning Menon out of the way and back to his seat, "Antiochus could take his army north and around the desert. He would then make a wide arc through Scythia and descend on Bactria from our stronghold at Maracanda."

"And how likely do you find this route?" said Euthydemus, eyeing the general.

"It's possible," said Lander.

"Antiochus's main force contains much heavy infantry," said Menon, moving to the edge of his chair. "Taking them through the steppe would be a slow and arduous process. And most importantly, very dangerous. The Scythians would attack them the entire time. It's a huge gamble, even with the Parthian cavalry by their side. If beaten on the steppe, by the Scythians or by us, they would have nowhere to run. I can say with near certainty that they will avoid this route."

"So how *will* they come, Menon?" Euthydemus threw up his arms. "Give us your assessment."

"The third way to approach," said Menon, "and this is the one I believe they will take if we reinforce Merv, is to follow Alexander's route through the southern mountains. Then, after reaching the Kabul Valley, they will swing north and break into the heart of Bactria."

"Seems too dangerous," said Lander, stroking his beard as he stared at the map. "Why would they risk it?"

"Because there are advantages to this route, despite the dangers," said Menon. "To start, we may lose track of them and only learn of their location when they descend from the mountains and arrive at our doorstep. Further, Antiochus may want to ally himself with Sophagasenus, the king of Kabul. At one point, the kingdom of Kabul was vassal to the Seleucids."

"I met Sophagasenus once," said Euthydemus. "Many years ago. A very strategic man, I recall. Able to be reasoned with."

"I've heard he has hundreds of war elephants and plenty of warriors," said Arjun, speaking up for the first time.

Demetrius had only conversed with Arjun a few times, but the man's reputation was considerable. He hailed from India, but since joining the kingdom's Indian mercenary unit, he had quickly risen to the highest rank.

"Yes," said Menon, "Antiochus has many reasons to take this route. But there are advantages for us, too. This route takes time— time that we could use to better prepare Zariaspa's defenses. Ideally, Antiochus will go south but fail to secure an alliance with Sophagasenus. Even better, *we* should secure such an alliance with Sophagasenus and attack Antiochus from both sides while he's stuck in the mountains."

"I think it's unlikely that we can form an alliance with Kabul," said Arjun. "Sophagasenus resents our alliance with the Indian kingdom of Taxila to his east."

"Nonetheless, it's worth a try," Menon said.

Euthydemus reached for his cup and took a long drink of wine. Impatience flared in Menon's eyes.

"Alright," said Euthydemus, setting down the cup. "I will go west with most of our army and reinforce Merv as Menon suggests. If Antiochus attacks, we will destroy him. If we force him south, so much the better. We will use the time to prepare. Lander, you will remain here and make provisions for a siege. I hope it doesn't come to this, but we must be ready."

"Yes, your majesty," said Lander.

"Now, Menon," continued the king. "Have the soldiers from Maracanda arrived yet? I recall you asking for them weeks ago."

"No, your majesty," said Menon. "They haven't come. And judging by a letter I just received, I doubt they will."

"What does that mean?" said Euthydemus, his voice giving away his exhaustion.

"Laodice, the governor's wife and the one who actually holds power in Maracanda, has written that attacks along their Scythian frontier prevent her from sending soldiers."

Laodice was Eucratides's mother, and Demetrius remembered her fondly from childhood. A cold woman to some, she had always been kind to him.

"She can't be serious," said Euthydemus, leaning forward. "You're telling me that she's refusing us soldiers? All because of a few raids on the Scythian frontier?"

"More or less," said Menon. "She writes that Scythians attacked traders just a few days ago. Although, knowing how she conducts policy toward the Scythians, I can't be certain the attack didn't happen the other way around. The new Scythian chief, Kulka, is known to possess far less war-lust than his predecessor."

Euthydemus ran his fingers through his thinning hair and nodded.

"We need their soldiers," said Menon. "That's a full third of our army."

Euthydemus nodded again and, this time, rubbed his temples.

"My king," said Menon, "now is no time to buckle to the nobles."

"Excuse me?" Euthydemus barked, slamming his palms on the table.

"My apologies, your majesty." Menon bowed his head. "I spoke too freely."

Euthydemus breathed heavily and dragged his hands across the map. He looked to Demetrius. "My son. Menon, your admittedly outspoken tutor, tells me that you are ready for more responsibility. Is this true?"

Demetrius swallowed and looked to Menon, who nodded. "Yes, Father."

"Good," said Euthydemus. "You will go to Maracanda and demand that Laodice's soldiers deploy. She can leave a suitable garrison in place to maintain security within the city, but no more. You will bring her army to me at Merv. Is that clear?"

"Yes, Father." Demetrius looked from his father to Menon, who nodded again.

"Menon," continued Euthydemus, "you and Arjun will leave immediately for Kabul to see if Sophagasenus is open to an alliance. Then go to India and ask the raja of Taxila the same. He has offered us soldiers in the past. Ask him to do so again."

"Yes, your majesty," said Menon. He nodded to Arjun.

"Good," said Euthydemus. "Now get to it."

The room cleared, leaving Demetrius and Menon alone.

"Do you really think I'm ready?" Demetrius glanced at Menon.

"I do," said Menon, placing his papers in two neat piles on the map. "This kingdom needs strong leadership if we are to survive this trial. It is time for you to step up."

"Menon," said Demetrius, slowly. "I've been thinking a lot about what you said. About a leader understanding their people."

"Have you?" Menon pushed the papers aside.

"Yes," said Demetrius, "and toward that end, I'd like the soldier called Roshan to join me on the journey north. I want to get to know him."

"That's an excellent idea, your majesty," said Menon. "The non-Greek soldiers respect him greatly. I'll have a messenger sent to the barracks."

"Thank you, Menon." Demetrius stood and moved toward the door.

"Your majesty," said Menon, drawing him back. "I think you may find that Laodice is different from what you remember."

"What do you mean?"

"I mean that she has grown stern and more conservative since you were young. At least, so I've been told. You may find it difficult to secure the soldiers your father requested."

"Thank you for your concern, Menon. But I've known her for a long time. She is Eucratides's mother, after all."

"Times change," said Menon. "And it's not just her. Greeks here face an identity crisis. And it has made some people more fanatical and close-minded. We've become a bitter version of our former selves, with people framing themselves by who they aren't, rather than by who they are. And with the Seleucid Empire maintaining a clear division between Greek or Macedonian rulers and non-Greek or Macedonian subjects, I'm afraid some of our conservative colleagues will be attracted to Antiochus."

"It can't be that bad," said Demetrius, hoping for some reassurance. Cultural tension was nothing new to Bactria: After he had taken over the region, Alexander had tried to integrate his customs with those of the locals, to mixed results.

"It's not good," said Menon. "But not everyone is like that. Yes, some people are conservative, but others are open to integrating with our neighbors—as you have done. And that is important. Because that is our future."

"I think Laodice will agree when I speak with her." Demetrius wasn't sure what else to say.

"I hope so," said Menon. "Now, if you'll excuse me, I'll see to having Roshan join you."

"Thank you," said Demetrius.

"Of course, your majesty."

As Demetrius entered the corridor, he struggled to breathe.

CHAPTER TWELVE

Roshan

In the city's largest barracks, Roshan polished his shield.

"My mother wants me to marry," he said, glancing up from the metal and at Feroze.

Feroze laughed and ran a rag across his sword. "My parents have been telling me to marry for ages."

"I hate to disappoint her," said Roshan, "but it's not going to happen. I've met all the women in our community, and I'm just not interested."

"There's no way you've met them *all*," said Feroze.

"You know what I mean."

"Your problem is that you want adventure. You want something different." Feroze grinned. "Like a Greek."

"Ha," said Roshan.

As he spat on his shield and wiped it with the rag, Roshan heard the grinding of dirt behind him. He turned to see a captain of the Bactrian guard, tall with wide shoulders. His tan face was covered in a white beard, and his bald head was blistered by the sun.

"The prince asked for you," said the captain.

"The prince what?" Roshan pushed aside his shield.

"He's going north to Maracanda," said the captain, "and he asked that you accompany him."

"Why?"

"Maybe he enjoyed your foot race." The captain smirked. "I don't know."

"When are we leaving?"

"Tomorrow."

"What about me?" said Feroze. "Did the prince ask for me?"

"Probably doesn't even know you exist," said the captain. "But if you'd like to join, the position's yours."

"Looks like we're going north!" said Feroze, slapping Roshan on the back. He looked to the captain. "And who else is going?"

"I understand that you'll be joining the royal bodyguard and some Indian mercenaries. Apparently the prince chooses his own companions."

Roshan nodded.

"And another thing," said the captain. "Be careful. The Scythians have been especially active lately, and I don't need to tell you the consequences of running into them."

"Of course not," said Roshan, his mind at once escaping to the past.

"Good. Now, get packing."

"Are you excited?" asked Feroze, as the captain strode away. "I've never been north."

"Not particularly," said Roshan.

"You're scared of the Scythians?"

Roshan glared at his friend. "Not at all. I've just had enough of this work."

"But this is what we do," said Feroze.

"It's what we've *done*," said Roshan, tugging at his beard.

"What do you mean?"

"I don't know." Roshan looked to the sky and then back to Feroze. "Do you remember the fistfight with the Greeks after my footrace?"

"My face still hurts," said Feroze, patting his swollen right cheek.

"Do you remember when the soldiers came to break it up? Did you notice where they pointed their blades? They shouldn't have been pointing them anywhere, but do you remember where they did point them? At us. And only us. And you say we belong? I used to think we had a future in the military. You know, opportunities to gain rank and influence. But we've never escaped the bottom, despite the many times we've bled for the kingdom."

Feroze looked to the dirt.

"And then there's the freeze on temple funds," continued Roshan. "Our community worked for years to get approval for that temple, and now there's nothing to show for it. I thought things were changing, but apparently not."

"The prince is different," said Feroze. "At least, that's what I've heard."

"Everyone keeps telling me that," said Roshan. "But he didn't seem that different at the dinner. He just walked around smiling like any other noble."

"You never know," said Feroze. "And regardless, I've met lots of Greeks, and plenty of them are friendly. And even if they're not right now, people can change. I've always believed that."

"I guess we'll see soon enough. But I'm not holding my breath," said Roshan. "Now, let's get packing."

The next morning, Roshan and Feroze made their way to the stables near the city gate and signed out two city-owned horses and a pack mule.

They passed through the gate, where workers were hacking at the ground with pikes and shovels. The defensive trench-digging had begun.

"That must be them," said Roshan, pointing past the workers to a group of men and horses.

Roshan scanned the soldiers. Seven were royal bodyguards, made clear by the red-and-black crests that ran atop their helmets. Two were Indian mercenaries, who carried long bows and had secured their quivers to their horses. Demetrius, the prince, sat straight on his white horse. He wore a blue tunic and a simple bronze chest plate shaped to resemble a muscular torso.

One of the royal bodyguards approached Roshan and Feroze.

"You must be the Bactrians assigned to us," he said, coming to a halt in front of them. "I am Phlotas, a friend of his majesty and one of his bodyguards."

"I am Roshan, and this is Feroze. I understand we are to join you."

"You are," said the soldier. "But be sure to keep your distance from the prince. He's our responsibility."

Roshan knew what the Greek meant by "our."

"We'll do our best," said Roshan, sarcastically.

"Good." Phlotas led his horse away.

Roshan glanced at Feroze. "Not a great start."

Feroze shrugged.

There was a clattering behind them, and a large column of armored men stepped through the gate and into the sun. Their armor glittered, and their feet kicked up dust. The leaders' bronze helmets bore colorful plumes, which whipped in the wind like flags.

"It's the army," said Feroze. "I heard the king is taking much of it to Merv."

"The war's begun, then," said Roshan, squinting at the men before turning back to Demetrius.

An Indian man on a tan horse broke off from the group surrounding the prince and approached Roshan and Feroze.

"Hello," said the man. "I'm Ashok."

"I'm Roshan. And this is Feroze."

"I'm happy to meet you," said Ashok. "The more soldiers, the better. Especially when going north. Don't you agree?"

"I'd say so," said Feroze.

As Ashok and Feroze chatted, Roshan's returned his attention to the prince. He watched him conversing with the other Greeks.

"Phlotas be damned," he said, nudging his horse into action. He rode forward and drew up alongside Demetrius. Phlotas scowled.

"Your majesty," said Roshan in a clear, calm voice.

Demetrius looked at him. "Ah, Roshan," he said. "I'm glad you were able to join us."

"If I may ask," said Roshan, "why did you request my presence? You already have plenty of companions." He glared at Phlotas.

"Well," said Demetrius, "I've heard much about you. You saved my father during a Scythian attack some years back."

"Yes, your majesty."

"And you survived the massacre one year ago," said Demetrius. "So you have experience with Scythians."

"I just barely survived," said Roshan. "Many didn't come home."

"I'm sure you did your duty," said Demetrius. "And I look forward to speaking with you further during our journey."

"Yes, your majesty," said Roshan, sensing that the conversation had come to a close.

Without looking back at Phlotas, Roshan rejoined Feroze and Ashok.

"How was the prince?" said Feroze.

"He seemed fine," said Roshan. "Although I'm still not sure why we're here. He has enough guards already."

"Was that your first time meeting Demetrius?" said Ashok.

"Second time," said Roshan. "But both were brief."

"I've known Demetrius for many years," said Ashok, clearly proud. "You could even say we grew up together."

Roshan had a hard time believing the man, but didn't voice his doubts.

"Then I suppose you know Phlotas? I can't imagine him being anyone's friend."

"Oh, don't worry about Phlotas," said Ashok. "He may talk a lot, but he's harmless."

"I guess we'll have to take your word for it," Roshan scoffed.

After Demetrius met with men in the infantry column, he addressed the group he was to travel with, detailing his expectations for the journey north. It seemed simple enough to Roshan: Demetrius wanted to visit the governor of Maracanda and return with soldiers.

"And make sure you're always aware of your surroundings," said Demetrius. "The Scythians have been particularly active lately. While I don't think we'll see them, we must be prepared."

Roshan thought of the Scythians. They were fierce fighters, but only time would tell if they would come between the caravan and its mission.

CHAPTER THIRTEEN

Beleen

Beleen stood on the flat expanse of the Eurasian Steppe below a purple sky. Grassy hills and a wagon-filled camp surrounded her. It was simple, but typical of Scythian organization.

"Alright, let's get the pole in," she said, looking at the wooden cart beside Tul, one of her closest friends. While usually pulled by oxen, the cart was now motionless and serving as one wall of a domicile. A piece of fabric lay beside it.

Beleen picked up the pole, and with Tul's help, guided it into the fabric ceiling. Securing it in place took longer than expected, as the pole was taller than needed. After rearranging the fabric, they finally got it to work.

"You know," said Beleen. "It's strange to be putting this together. The last time I set up a home was with my brother."

Tul paused. "We can stop if it's too difficult for you."

"No, no," said Beleen. "It's good to move on."

"Well, I don't know about you," said Tul, "but I need a break from this work. I'm going outside to practice a bit."

"I'll join you." Beleen appreciated Tul's initiative.

They emerged from the newly formed tent, and Beleen walked past the three huts they had built that morning and over to her horse, Kasen. She pulled her bow from its place beside the saddle and a handful of arrows from the gold-plated case that hung from Kasen's left side.

"I know you're restless," she said to the horse, before walking into the open steppe. The grass swayed gently in the wind as far as the eye could see. A line of orange hugged the horizon, dividing the hills from the increasingly star-speckled sky.

Tul stood ahead of Beleen. Tattoos passed beyond the sleeves of his sheep's-wool tunic and covered his hands in swirling blue designs. He had a short brown beard and mustache, and he kept his long hair tied in a tight knot at the top of his head.

Beleen placed an arrow on the bow, aimed at the sky, and released. It flew in a steep arc, and she followed it with her eyes as it slowed, turned, and plummeted to the ground.

"Far, don't you think?" said Tul, who had come to stand at her side.

Beleen looked at the arrow sticking from the grass. The black-painted shaft pointed to the sky, and the white feathers at its tail jutted out like blades.

"You think I can't hit it?" said Beleen.

She and Tul had competed since childhood. For many years, Tul had bested her in many things. But times had changed, and now Beleen's bow skills were the talk of the community.

"I have my doubts," said Tul, grinning.

"Care to try first?" said Beleen, handing him the bow. He looked at the arrow sticking from the ground and then back to Beleen.

"You know," he said, as he pulled an arrow against the string and aimed at his target, "it's getting dark."

Beleen didn't respond. He was just making excuses.

Tul let the arrow fly. It glided an inch or two away from the target and slid into the grass.

"I've always been better on a horse," said Tul.

"Aren't we all?" said Beleen, reaching for the bow, which Tul handed her with a sigh.

Beleen grabbed an arrow that bore a crisp white tail and pulled it against the bowstring. Looking past the arrowhead, she let her gaze focus on the target's plume. She exhaled and released the arrow. It tapped the side of the target, flew past, and hit the ground. It hadn't been a direct hit, but it counted.

"See?" said Tul. "You also missed. It's just too dark out here."

Beleen was about to argue her case, but a yell from behind pulled her from the task.

Back at the camp, someone was pointing at the horizon. Beleen looked back to the target arrow and then beyond, at the orange point where sky met steppe. There was the flicker of sunlight reflecting against metal. With her hand to her forehead, she studied the figures that crested the nearest hill.

"They're Royal Scyths," said Tul. "Can you believe it?"

As the riders neared, Beleen noticed their clothes were made of a colorful and gold-laced combination of fur, wool, linen, and leather.

The riders stopped in front of one of the makeshift tents. A woman stepped down from her horse and approached Beleen. She had bright green eyes that shone above sharp cheekbones. Her blond hair fell down her face, and across her fur-covered chest, and the hat she wore was impressive. While Beleen wore common leather headgear, which lifted to a point a few inches above her head, this woman's hat was at least three times taller and made of gold-studded wood. The whole thing rose from her head like the neck of a goose rose from its body.

"Greetings," said the woman. "I am Alora, and I wish by the gods I find you well."

"Thank you," said Beleen, stepping forward. "And I wish the divine deities have protected your journey."

"They have," said Alora. She looked past Beleen to the tents. "What is going on here? A new settlement?"

"Yes," said Beleen. "But not for our tribe. It's for our northern kin. Conflict in the north has been pushing more and more people south each year. Kulka asked me to organize the building effort."

Beleen had known her chief for many years. He had mentored her following her parents' deaths.

"The camp looks orderly enough," said Alora. "If you could point me to Kulka's settlement, I would be grateful."

Beleen pointed at the horizon to her right, where the grass picked up the orange of the falling sun.

"It will be dark by the time you reach it," said Beleen, "but you will find him beyond those hills."

"Thank you." Alora led her horse past Beleen and toward the darkening horizon, her retinue following.

"What do you think they want?" asked Tul.

"I'm not sure." Beleen watched the riders disappear beyond a hill.

"I hope it's not war in the west," said Tul. "We have our hands full here."

"We certainly do," said Beleen, thinking of the population pressures from the north.

When they completed the last tent, Beleen opted to return to her chief's camp instead of remaining in the new settlement. She wanted to know why the Royal Scyths had visited. After bidding Tul goodbye, she mounted her horse and rode into the darkness.

By the time Beleen approached the camp, the moon and stars afforded the only light. Three hundred wagons, organized in an expansive circle, formed the settlement's border. Wooden towers rose from the wall of wagons, and spikes projected forward.

Along the edge of the wall, hundreds of oxen grazed within a fenced pen. In another enclosure beyond them, hundreds of horses did the same. Armed soldiers sat on horses and patrolled the animals.

Beleen led her steed through the gate, the top of which was adorned with gold statues of men fighting against winged horses. Colorful tents covered most of the settlement's open space.

Beleen dismounted in front of the largest tent—Kulka's tent. Linens and furs covered the wagons that formed its foundation, and it featured a quilted leather awning.

"I'll be back, Kasen," she said, patting her horse on the neck.

Kulka's tent was dimly lit by a central fire. Carpets covered the ground, and the gold-and-silver-embroidered fabrics draped along the walls sparkled against the firelight.

Beleen looked at her chief, perched atop his throne. He was a tall man, even when seated, and his black beard, like his body, was thick. He wore a blue robe covered almost entirely in ovals of gold, and a ceremonial cap like that of the Royal Scyths. It rose from his head like a flagpole and featured animals carved in wood, stacked one on top of the other. Alora sat beside him and silently watched a ceremony being performed before the chief.

Beleen caught Kulka's gaze through the crowd. He smiled and indicated she should wait at the edge of the tent. Standing with a red-and-purple carpet at her back, Beleen watched women present their children at the foot of Kulka's throne. The attendees had dressed up for the occasion, in outfits of intertwined leather, wool, linen, gold, silver, and fur. Many had also braided their hair, plaiting it with colorful linens and horsehair to add volume.

It took over an hour for the ceremony to end, and by then, Beleen was doing all she could to contain her boredom. When the women and children finally left, Kulka stepped down from his throne and sat cross-legged on the ground in front of it. Beleen considered the intricately designed soles of his shoes. A hunting scene in miniature had been sewn into the leather.

Kulka turned to Alora, who sat at his right. "I'm sorry I had to cut short our conversation earlier," he said. "I had forgotten about the mothers' ceremony. Now, you were saying something about your master's concern?"

"I was saying," said Alora, "that our master is displeased by the interruptions to trade. He has noted a steep decline in products from the far east, and many of the items we now get, we have to buy from foreign peoples at extortionate prices."

"I understand," said Kulka. "But your master must understand what is going on here."

"Our master," snapped Alora.

"*Our* master," Kulka agreed. When Alora nodded, he continued. "There are wars north of here."

"And what concern is that to you?"

"It has created chaos among the tribes there. Their patronage systems have fallen apart. They are now one against another, which hinders trade. And worst of all, the wars are sending refugees south into our land. We're trying to avoid war, but it is becoming increasingly difficult."

"We also deal with war on our borders," said Alora. "You think the wars along the Black Sea have not affected us? They have. But we find a way."

"As will we," said Kulka. "But it takes time. And we need new land and new places to trade. The pressure from the north is too great for us to stay, but the Greeks attack us whenever we move south."

"I have not come with solutions," said Alora. "Only advice. You need to take control of your domains, or our master will send someone to take control for you."

"I don't take well to threats," said Kulka, his expression turning stern.

"And our master doesn't take well to disappointment," said Alora.

There was a long pause, during which Kulka and Alora stared at one another. Beleen held her breath.

"Shall we drink to a better future then?" said Alora, finally breaking the silence. Her mouth curved into a discomfiting smile.

Kulka looked away. "Certainly." He then signaled to an attendant. "Bring the koumiss," he said, sending the man scurrying for the fermented milk.

"Not koumiss," said Alora. "I hope you don't think I came all this way without gifts. I brought wine."

A servant handed Kulka an ox-horn cup of unfiltered wine.

"We must negotiate with the Greeks of Bactria," Kulka said, sounding defeated. "It may be our only way. We need access to the land they control, and our traders need access to their markets. And the gods know we've tried to establish relations with those in Maracanda. But they turn us away and attack our trading posts."

"Perhaps you're being too timid with the Greeks," said Alora. "Maybe they need a reminder of our power."

"Yes," said Kulka. "Perhaps they do." He took a sip of wine and continued, "A few days ago, we sent a trading caravan south. Let's wait and see what becomes of them."

CHAPTER FOURTEEN

Roshan

Roshan was exhausted. The sun had fallen by the time they entered the narrow gatehouse of the famous fortress known as the Sogdian Rock. For two days, he and the others had traversed thin passes of the Pamir Mountains to the north of Bactria. The journey had been difficult, with Roshan balancing both the demands of the march and disparaging comments from Phlotas and his fellow bodyguards.

Beyond the gatehouse, a thin street ran ahead, from which small alleys extended like streams from a river. Apart from the fires of the nearby soldiers' barracks, the town was barely lit, making the alleyways dark and uninviting.

After depositing his belongings in the barracks, Roshan joined the others atop the gatehouse, where a small fire crackled and the men shared a jug of wine and tales from home. Some discussed concerns about the harvest, while others stuck to more jovial subjects, like meeting women in the market. As conversation slowed, Roshan poured water into a flat bowl and placed half of a nutshell on the surface. It floated like a small boat. The others used their fingers to flick drops of wine at the nut to make it sink. It was a common and simple game, but it passed the time.

"So, Alexander really came here?" said Ashok, when the boat was sunk.

"That he did," said Demetrius. "In fact, he met his wife, Roxana, here. Menon told me the story when I was a child."

"Then it's your turn to tell us," said Ashok.

"Well," said Demetrius, catching Roshan's gaze across the fire, "it was during a time of great turmoil in Bactria and Sogdiana. Alexander had captured the region, but just barely, and the locals continued to fight. One such rebel was Oxyartes. His soldiers controlled this fortress, and his family, including his daughter, Roxana, took refuge here."

Roshan had heard the story many times before. Oxyartes was a controversial figure among the native Bactrians.

"When Alexander arrived, he saw the difficulty of the situation: This fortress is built halfway up a steep mountain. So, hoping to avoid a bloody siege, he sought to negotiate with the defenders. They rebuffed him, telling him that only men with wings could take the fortress. Undeterred, Alexander offered money to those of his soldiers who would scale the cliffs and attack the fortress from above."

Roshan looked at the cliff that rose behind the town. Its steep surface appeared to offer few foot- and handholds for intrepid climbers.

"So," continued Demetrius, "the selected men attached tent pegs to their feet to best grab the rock, and in the darkness, they climbed. The next morning, when the defenders saw soldiers on the mountain above them, they surrendered without a fight."

"Incredible," said Ashok.

"Yes," said Demetrius. "And importantly, Oxyartes went on to be one of Alexander's most valuable allies. Alexander's wedding to Roxana solidified the agreement and demonstrated Alexander's ambition to have his people integrate with the locals."

Phlotas clucked his tongue and whispered to one of the other bodyguards.

"Such epic times," said Ashok.

"Don't worry," said Feroze, playing with the wing-shaped cheek protectors on his helmet. "We'll have stories like that soon enough. We're getting closer and closer to Scythia, after all."

"Don't be too eager," said Roshan, standing.

He walked away from the fire and to the gatehouse wall, beyond which a few stars broke through the blackness.

As he breathed the chill air, Roshan imagined fighting at Sogdian Rock against the invading forces of Macedonia and Greece. He wondered if he would have surrendered and collaborated like Oxyartes, or if he would have died fighting like the most famous rebel of the time, Spitamenes.

"Care for some company?"

Demetrius had come to stand beside him.

"Your company is always welcome, your majesty," said Roshan. He clenched his fists in frustration—not at Demetrius, but at himself.

"I'm not sure I believe you," said Demetrius. "But I'm grateful for the opportunity to speak with you."

Roshan looked back into the darkness.

"Tell me about the lower city," said Demetrius, placing his hands on the wall. "How do people feel about the possibility of war?"

"Things feel tense," said Roshan, watching an owl dive into a clump of grass.

"That's understandable. People are scared."

Roshan paused as he considered his next words. He watched the owl fly into the sky with a squirming animal in its claws. "It's not exactly that, your majesty. The city was tense before we heard of the invasion."

Roshan looked from the owl to Demetrius, who furrowed his brow and seemed to await Roshan's elaboration.

"It's the temple building, I think," said Roshan, his body prickling with sweat. "Sure, diverting funds from the new temple of Zeus to new temples for Zoroastrians and Buddhists angered many of the Greeks. But after so many years of Greek temple building, the move sent a strong and welcomed message to others in the city. When that funding was recalled halfway through construction—" Roshan stopped, feeling he had spoken too brashly.

"Please continue," said Demetrius.

"When the funding was stopped," said Roshan, still uncertain, "it sent the completely opposite message. On the eve of war, people are unsure what they are fighting for. People may have a hard time dying for a kingdom that doesn't value them."

His heart pounded, and he worried how Demetrius would respond. But the prince surprised him.

"You're absolutely right," said Demetrius, nodding. "I can see how that would lower morale. All I can say is that the king is in a difficult position. Many of the nobles want funds for their interests. It is the nature of nobles, I guess. With that said, I will see what I can do. The king values all of his subjects, and when we're shoulder to shoulder in the phalanx, the enemy doesn't care who is behind the armor."

Roshan gazed out across the darkness and contemplated Demetrius's words.

"Moving forward," said Demetrius, "I'd like you to join me in meetings. Your perspective will be valued, and you can help me see things that I may have missed."

"As you wish, your majesty," said Roshan, though he was skeptical that Demetrius truly meant it.

"Well," said Demetrius, moving away from the wall, "I think we should get some sleep."

Roshan followed the prince back to the fire.

"Get some sleep, men," said Demetrius. "We're leaving soon."

Roshan walked with the others to the barracks. Without torches, they felt around for their places on the ground. As he settled against the cold floor, Roshan thought of Oxyartes's relationship with Alexander and of his own with Demetrius. His mind moved to the fall of

Sogdian Rock. He wondered how different Bactria would have been had the Greeks never come.

Roshan fell asleep cold and awoke the same. It was easy to pull himself from the ground—even the breezy air was warmer than the rock surface. As he was packing his things, Demetrius stepped into the room.

"Good," he said, "you're already packing. We'll leave as soon as you are ready."

"We're not staying for breakfast?" said Ashok.

"We'll eat breakfast after we get some land behind us," said Demetrius. "There's no time to waste. Antiochus is on the move."

CHAPTER FIFTEEN

Antiochus

"We ought to be moving," said Antiochus as he walked to the gate of Saddarvazeh. He swatted at a fly that zipped before his face. "This delay is giving our enemy time to prepare. Why hasn't Phriapa returned with news of Merv?"

"I'm not sure, your majesty," said Dropidas, who walked beside him.

The air was chilly, and Antiochus rubbed his arms as he walked through the twisting street. Pots and pans tapped beyond the shutters of mud-brick homes.

Ahead of him, a man and a young boy stood beside a rickety wooden cart. A small fire crackled beside it, on top of which sat a black pot.

"At least we can use this time to study Parthian archery," said Antiochus.

It had been days since Arsak invited Antiochus to watch an archery practice, and today, Antiochus was finally taking him up on it.

"And don't forget," said Dropidas, "more of our soldiers arrive every day."

"We already have enough soldiers to destroy every city between here and India," said Antiochus. "What we don't have is time. The longer we stay here, the more likely it becomes that our enemies in the west will take advantage of our absence."

"Yes, your majesty," said Dropidas.

Antiochus turned a corner and faced the gatehouse. Without the crowds that had flocked to it when the armies first arrived, the gate now looked like the entrance to a countryside villa back home. Plants grew in the cracks along the walls, sprouting white flowers.

Passing through the gate, Antiochus found a group of men tending to their colorfully adorned horses. Arsak was among them, a hand on his horse's reins.

Beyond the riders, in the clearing surrounding the fortress, lay Antiochus's camp. Its thousands of tents filled the horizon. A handful of men at the edge of camp pointed toward him. Antiochus turned from his army and approached the horsemen.

"Your majesty," Arsak hailed him. "I was afraid you wouldn't join."

"I wouldn't miss an opportunity to study the famed Parthian horse archers," said Antiochus.

"I only hope that you will train with us," said Arsak. "Your renown as a horseman precedes you."

"Perhaps." Antiochus watched the surrounding men string their bows and pack leather quivers with arrows. "But first, I will observe."

"Very well." Arsak turned to Heron, one of the men Antiochus had met in the mountains. "How about you show Antiochus today's challenge?"

"Yes, your majesty," said Heron, bowing. He led his horse away from the group and mounted it. The sun reflected against the gold laced across his tunic and the silver foil on the horse's green saddle-cloth.

As Heron prepared, Antiochus said to Arsak, "I understand that Phriapa and my men should return from Merv soon."

"If they didn't kill each other on the journey." Arsak laughed and slapped Antiochus on the shoulder.

"Your majesty, do you see those wooden stakes?" said Heron, pointing into the rocky plain at four large stakes sticking from the ground. Each was as wide as a tree trunk and the height of a man.

"Yes, I see them," said Antiochus.

A moment later, Heron galloped toward the stakes, his horse's hooves kicking dust into the air. Through the haze, Heron bounced up and down on the horse, one hand on the animal's reins and the other on his bow. The horse took him toward the first pole, then past it.

"That was as close as he was going to get to that target," said Antiochus, not talking to anyone in particular. "Now he must come back around."

But then, as if on a pottery swivel, Heron twisted at the waist so that he faced backward, pulled an arrow against the bowstring, and released it. The arrow stabbed the pole.

Coming upon the next poles, Heron did the same. He passed each, twisted backward on the horse, released an arrow, and hit the target. When he reached the far end of the course, Heron galloped back to the main party and stopped only feet from Antiochus. The following wave of dust enveloped them.

"Your turn," said Heron, smirking at Antiochus. "Unless you're unable to do it."

"Only one way to tell," said Antiochus, lifting his arms with open palms. "May I?"

Heron dropped to the dirt and placed the horse's reins in Antiochus's right hand, the bow in his left. The quiver remained latched to his horse's saddle.

"No need to be ashamed if you can't do it," said Heron, his voice infused with sarcasm.

"Of course I can," said Antiochus, frustrated by his limp response.

Antiochus's gaze moved to his army's tents. While only a handful of soldiers had watched his arrival, a crowd now lined the edge of the camp.

Antiochus mounted the horse. After adjusting his position in the saddle, he reached for the quiver to get a feel for the distance. He then studied the bow. The weapon was unlike any he had ever held before.

"It's a composite bow," said Heron, at his horse's side. "It's made of wood and sinew. With it, a talented soldier can shoot faster and farther than any you'll find in your own country."

Antiochus wrapped his fingers around the string. It was remarkably difficult to pull back.

"Alright," he said, letting go of the string and sitting straight in the saddle. He looked at the four poles.

"Alright," Heron repeated.

With nothing more to say, Antiochus nudged the horse's abdomen with his ankles and was off. The horse quickly achieved a gallop, its body swaying forcefully beneath him. Antiochus felt a rush of adrenaline. Once he found his equilibrium, he looked at the four poles.

Antiochus pulled an arrow from the quiver and struggled to latch it to the taut bowstring. When he did, he realized he would pass the pole in seconds. He was distracted by guiding the horse, looking past its moving head, and aiming at the fast-approaching target. He pulled the bowstring back, and as the pole whipped past him on his right, he let the arrow fly. It missed the mark and stabbed the rocky ground beyond.

Antiochus slowed the horse. He looked back at the pole where Heron's arrow remained embedded, and then at his arrow in the ground. Parthian laughter traveled with the wind. Antiochus looked at his men to make sure they were not laughing with them.

"Try it as we do," yelled Arsak. "Trust that the horse can guide itself. Turn back and shoot, so you concentrate on the target and only the target."

Very well, thought Antiochus.

He guided the horse back into a gallop and approached the second pole. He placed an arrow into position, but this time, as he approached the target, he didn't aim. Instead, he and the horse passed the pole. As it disappeared to his right, Antiochus twisted his body at the waist.

With the horse's head out of the way, he had a clear view of his target. While it was getting smaller and smaller, it remained clear in his view, not zipping past him as it had before. He pulled the arrow against the string and released.

The arrow hit the ground and slid to a stop next to the pole.

Antiochus twisted forward and slowed the horse. He turned to the Parthians, far in the distance and dwarfed by the tall walls behind them. He rode back.

"Better," said Arsak, as Antiochus reached him.

"It takes practice, indeed," said Antiochus, sliding from the horse. He handed the reins to Heron, who remained stone-faced.

Antiochus glanced at his army's camp, where hundreds of soldiers now stood watching.

"Dropidas!" Antiochus yelled.

"Yes, your majesty?" said Dropidas, running to him.

Antiochus leaned in to make sure the Parthians weren't listening. "Why are our men standing around?" he said. "Get them working. They look weak."

"Yes, your majesty," said Dropidas, lowering his head. "I'll have them busy in no time."

"Good." Antiochus turned back to Arsak.

"Now, come," said Arsak, meeting his gaze. "Let's eat."

"I won't say no to that," said Antiochus, finally feeling a bond with the Parthian monarch.

Perhaps Arsak would remain a loyal vassal. Phriapa, however, was a different matter.

CHAPTER SIXTEEN

»———→

Phriapa

Phriapa looked at the Tapourian Mountains. They had been his constant companions during his reconnaissance trip to and from the Bactrian stronghold at Merv. The low sun cast one side of the range in bright gold and left the other in darkness. It looked as if an ax-wielding god had hacked the land to pieces. To his right, the foothills flattened into the Karakum Desert, where sand dunes extended as far as Phriapa could see. A white haze obscured the horizon, beyond which the steppe lay open and waiting. Not far behind Phriapa and his companions, Bactrian scouts followed. They had been on his tail ever since he pulled away from Merv.

"How far until Saddarvazeh?" said one of the Seleucid soldiers who rode beside him, looking back at the enemy scouts.

"Not far," said Phriapa, having grown tired of his assigned comrades.

"You always carry that bow?" The soldier pointed at the weapon on Phriapa's lap. Perhaps he was bored.

"Yes," said Phriapa. "What of it?"

"It's just a weapon of distance," said the man. "It doesn't allow you to get in close and prove your valor."

"I'm perfectly capable with a sword," said Phriapa, placing his hand on his sword hilt. "I can show you here and now if you'd like."

"That's not necessary," said the man.

"Then what are you trying to say?"

The man studied the sky and smiled. "I just find it unfortunate," he said, "that you and the others never faced us man to man. You know, in a phalanx."

Phriapa's fingers tightened around the handle of his sword. "I guess we value strategy over basic shows of force."

"There's a strategy in what we do," the other snapped.

"Just not enough to win," said Phriapa, staring him in the eyes.

"Last time I checked, you were Antiochus's vassal."

"You can call me whatever you want," said Phriapa. "It won't stop me from killing you and your countrymen someday."

The man's face grew stern, and he drew his sword from its sheath.

"Enough," said the second man, pushing the sword's blade toward the ground. He turned to Phriapa. "Just get us to Saddarvazeh."

"I'm not your guide," said Phriapa. "And I didn't ask you to join."

"Just take us there."

Phriapa turned away, and the group rode in silence. Later, as they approached Saddarvazeh, the ground grew lush. Fog hovered above knee-high shrubs, and birds darted from one refuge to the next. Eventually, they came across small farming communities, their mud shacks arranged beside streams.

Soon after, the stark outlines of the city appeared on the rolling horizon. The walls were impressive, framed by the pink sky beyond. Flags of purple and green fluttered in the wind and horns blared as Phriapa and his party drew near. He breathed deeply and let his mind fill with memories of racing across the hills with his brother.

But the sight of the Seleucid camp poisoned these joyful thoughts. There were more tents now than when he had left Saddarvazeh. The

Seleucids had received reinforcements. Phriapa nudged his horse into a gallop, leaving his "allies" behind.

After making his way through the crowded city, Phriapa entered the largest of the many palace courtyards. His father sat beside Antiochus and Dropidas on colorful pillows, but stood to pull Phriapa into an embrace.

"Son, welcome," Arask said. "We've just been exchanging war stories."

"Not from our recent war, I hope," said Phriapa, his gaze darting to Antiochus.

"No, no." Arsak laughed. "Of course not. How was your journey?"

"Quiet," said Phriapa, as his riding companions joined them in the courtyard.

Antiochus rose. "I'm eager to hear of Merv. Is the city lightly defended?"

"Unfortunately, no," said Phriapa. Clearly, they had moved on from pleasantries. "By the time we arrived, the Bactrians were reinforcing the city with a large army. I stayed for a few days to better understand their numbers."

Antiochus looked at one of the Seleucid soldiers who had traveled with Phriapa. "Is this true?" he asked.

Phriapa stepped between Antiochus and the soldier. "You don't trust my report?"

"I do. I do," said Antiochus, placing a hand on Phriapa's shoulder. "But you know as well as I do that it's wise to hear from multiple sources."

Phriapa pulled Antiochus's hand from his shoulder.

"Yes, your highness," the soldier said from behind Phriapa. "The Parthian speaks the truth. Merv is heavily defended. We also scouted the water sources. Many are dry, and the few available are near the city. We would fight skirmishers daily just to get the water we need."

Antiochus nodded, and Phriapa was furious that the voice of a Seleucid was needed before Antiochus would give his words credence.

"That decides it then," said Antiochus. "We'll go south and follow the route of Alexander."

"Are you sure that is a wise decision?" said Dropidas, standing.

Phriapa had been wondering the same thing. Moving through the mountains would put both the Parthian and Seleucid cavalry at a significant disadvantage.

"It's the best option we have," said Antiochus. "And regardless, there is a wayward vassal in the Kabul Valley that I would like to visit. Like the Greeks of Bactria, he has slipped from the fold. My visit will allow him the opportunity to gain my trust and form an alliance. Further, he has war elephants, and I have lost many."

"But, your majesty," started Dropidas, "what about the mountain people? We will waste too much time fighting them."

Again, Phriapa agreed.

"Dropidas," said Antiochus, "am I emperor of those mountains or not?"

Dropidas looked to the ground and then back to Antiochus. "Yes, you are, your majesty."

"Then I never want to hear again where I can or cannot lead my soldiers. Is that clear?"

"Yes, your majesty." Dropidas stepped back.

Phriapa smiled. He enjoyed watching the westerners bicker.

"The tribes ahead, the Arians," said Antiochus, turning to Arsak. "What are they like?"

"It seems you're more scared than you let on," said Phriapa.

Antiochus and his father both glared at him.

"The tribes are each fairly small," said Arsak, pulling Antiochus closer and away from Phriapa. "But they will defend their land. They know it well and command the heights. We have been told that Alexander suffered greatly while fighting them and we, too, have bled at their hands."

"We'll be careful then," said Antiochus, glancing at Phriapa. "But it's settled. We will visit Sophagasenus. And with his elephant core, we will crush Euthydemus."

After leaving the meeting, Phriapa roamed the palace halls aimlessly and recalled moments from his childhood. In a small courtyard near the main audience chamber, Phriapa approached a statue of his father, dried leaves crunching beneath his feet. The statue was a few heads taller than Phriapa and flattered the subject. His father's face was chiseled, his arms strong, and his stomach lean. Phriapa had stopped liking the statue when he'd learned how heavily it was influenced by the art of the west. Parthia had its own art to be proud of.

Now, looking at the statue's stone face, Phriapa reflected on the year his father carved Parthia from the former Seleucid domains. "Rule, or be ruled," his father had told him. Perhaps his father wasn't so different from Antiochus after all.

Phriapa's mother entered the courtyard, wearing a delicate green dress and a gold belt that added a note of royal flair.

"I've never cared for that statue," she said, coming up beside him. "It looks nothing like him."

"Not even close. But that was never really the point."

"No. I suppose not."

"We're to leave soon," said Phriapa, his mind returning to the campaign ahead.

"This is becoming a pattern."

"I know. But now we are to move south."

"Toward the kingdom of Kabul?"

"Yes," said Phriapa. "To meet King Sophagasenus and form an alliance."

"I met him once," said his mother. "He is part Greek. Did you know that?"

"I didn't." Phriapa sat on a stone bench and watched the leaves dance in the breeze.

"Well," said his mother, "Antiochus can certainly try to form an alliance with Sophagasenus. But I wouldn't be surprised if the Bactrians got there first."

CHAPTER SEVENTEEN

☥

Menon

Menon stood at a large window and watched hawks circle above the Kabul Valley. Jagged mountains pierced the horizon behind the birds of prey, their sharp peaks cutting slices from the sky. Mud-brick huts rose and fell across the valley's hilly terrain, but there were a few significant buildings among them, such as the fire temples of the Zoroastrian faith.

Beyond the palace's stone walls a market bustled. A large pillar rose among the shops. The Indian emperor, Ashoka the Great, had planted it there when the Mauryan Empire held sway from the coastline of eastern India to the Hindu Kush. It was covered in Sanskrit, Greek, and Aramaic scripts, as Ashoka had intended his edicts to reach a wide and distant audience. And this they had indeed reached. Buddhism was now just as prevalent in Kabul as Zoroastrianism.

Menon breathed deeply and turned to his host, the king of Kabul.

Sophagasenus lounged on a pillow, leaning on his left elbow, with his right arm draped across his bent leg. The rings on his fingers sparkled in the light of the terracotta lamps, as did the gold foil adorning his red robe. He looked at Menon with hazel eyes, and his black mustache twitched.

"Thank you for seeing us, your majesty," said Menon, nodding toward Arjun, who sat in a wicker chair.

"So," said Sophagasenus, "you bring a message from Euthydemus, your king in Bactria?"

"That is correct." Menon left the window and took a seat across from Sophagasenus.

"Alright," said Sophagasenus, "let's hear this message."

He leaned forward and assumed a cross-legged position.

"I'm sure your spies and diplomats have told you that the Seleucids recently formed an alliance with the Parthians," said Menon.

"Perhaps they have," said Sophagasenus.

"Then they've also told you that the Seleucids plan to attack Bactria."

The king nodded and his earrings swayed forward and back.

"Now, I'd venture to guess," said Menon, "that you're not too pleased that the Seleucid emperor is getting involved in affairs so far east. Especially considering the freedom you've enjoyed while he and his predecessors have been busy killing their enemies in the west. Your kingdom was in vassalage to them once, after all."

The king turned toward the window and said, "It is true that the Seleucid preoccupation with their Greek cousins in Egypt has given us space to develop our land without their interference. And this is important. My kingdom needs constant attention: Our position on the road to India has us stuck between your Bactria and the Taxila of Raja Manish. I know your alliance with the raja is peaceful, but from my perspective, I am surrounded by potential adversaries." Sophagasenus drank from a bronze cup and then looked back to Menon. "Now, what does your king want?"

"King Euthydemus requests an alliance," said Menon. "He asks that you combine your army with that of Bactria and stand against the forces of Antiochus."

"I assumed as much," said Sophagasenus.

"And what do you think?" asked Menon.

"That Antiochus is a fool if he thinks a western emperor can rule these lands again."

"So you will stand with us?" said Menon.

"No."

Menon massaged his temples. He looked to the ceiling and closed his eyes. "What would it take for you to join us?" He returned his gaze to the king.

"There is one condition," said Sophagasenus.

"Name it," said Menon, sitting up straight.

"That you stand with me against the forces of Taxila."

Menon exhaled and slumped back into his pillow. He thought of the Indian kingdom to the east. "I'm not in a position to promise that," he said at last. "And regardless, you know that Taxila is Bactria's ally. I am going there next, actually."

"Then you must take your chances with Antiochus," said Sophagasenus, sinking deeper into his pillow.

"As will you," said Menon. "Because, believe me: He is coming."

"Empires come and go," said Sophagasenus. "It is dangerous to bet on the long-term success of any one of them. And more to the point, Antiochus must get through the tribes north of here before he reaches us. I've spent years trying to control them, and to no avail. I have no reason to think that Antiochus will fare better."

"Very well." Menon stood.

Sophagasenus took a sip of wine. "You're welcome to stay here as long as you like. Could I offer you some wine?"

"No," said Menon, looking to Arjun. "We will continue east."

"Well, in that case," said Sophagasenus, "please send my regards to Taxila."

As he and Arjun left the room, Menon whispered, "We needed this alliance. If Taxila also says no, we'll be in a very difficult spot."

"Want to stay longer?" said Arjun. "Maybe Sophagasenus will change his mind."

"No." Menon picked up his pace. "Let's leave as soon as possible. I'm not sure how pleased he is that we're headed to his enemy's domain."

"He wouldn't be foolish enough to do anything to us," said Arjun, as they entered a wide corridor.

"Times are changing," said Menon. "And I feel that our luck is running thin."

"Perhaps you're right. Let's just hope Demetrius is having better luck than us."

CHAPTER EIGHTEEN

Demetrius

Demetrius leaned forward and ran his fingers through his horse's mane.

"I know you're tired," he said. "I am too."

He watched Ashok gallop toward the top of the next ridge before closing his eyes against the wind. How many more ridges would they crest before they reached their journey's end?

"We're here," Ashok yelled from the other ridge, bringing Demetrius's internal conflict to a close. "We've reached Maracanda!"

When he, too, reached the top of the ridge, Demetrius studied the city with heavy eyes. It sat on the southern edge of a slow-moving river and had high walls. It looked like a smaller but more fortified version of Zariaspa. Beyond the irrigated farms that surrounded the city, the land was rocky desert, scattered with small shrubs.

At the market just outside the main gate, riders came out to hail them.

"Welcome to Maracanda, your majesty," one rider said to Demetrius.

"Thank you," said Demetrius. "We look forward to meeting with Heliokles and his wife, Laodice."

"Yes, your majesty," said the man. "Although Heliokles cannot visit for long, if at all. He has been unwell for some time and spends much of his day in bed. Laodice, however, will return from surveying the land later tonight. The servants will prepare a feast for you upon her arrival."

Demetrius nodded and led the caravan toward the large, imposing city gates. Moments later, his stomach tightened. Along the stone defenses, at least ten bodies hung from nooses.

"You think they're criminals?" Ashok drew up beside him.

"No," said Demetrius, looking at the trousers the bodies wore. "I think they're Scythians." He looked away in disgust. None of the dead looked to be of fighting age or build.

As they continued on toward the upper city, Demetrius took note of the large number of armed and armored soldiers standing around on the city streets, and he wondered just who they were meant to protect and why. He would ask Laodice about it at their evening meal.

Later that night, Demetrius sat in his chamber, dressed and alone, waiting to be summoned for dinner. He didn't wait long.

There was a knock on the door, and Demetrius opened it to a servant, who said, "Are you ready, your majesty?" He was short and wore a simple tunic held by a knot below the shoulder.

"I would like one of my men to join me," said Demetrius.

"Certainly, your majesty."

"Good," said Demetrius. "Please have Roshan meet me at dinner."

"Yes, your majesty."

Demetrius followed the servant down a long corridor and into a wide courtyard lined with columns and trees. A statue of Dionysus guarded the center of the square.

The servant led him a short distance further, into a dining hall where three fires blazed and torches flickered along intricately painted walls. The black-and-white tile floor was dotted with pillows and tables.

A woman stood at the room's far end, rising above two men seated on pillows beside her.

"Demetrius, is that you?" she said, walking toward him.

Demetrius smiled as he recognized Laodice, and his mind surged with memories of childhood games he had played with her and Eucratides. Gold jewelry secured her gray hair behind her head, and she wore a bright-red dress that felt coarse as they embraced.

"It's been years," said Laodice, releasing Demetrius and stepping back. "You have grown so much."

"And you haven't aged at all," said Demetrius. He looked past her at the two men who still sat on pillows. They were young and strong. "I'm sorry to hear that Heliokles is unwell."

"Thank you," said Laodice. "The gods can be mysterious in their ways."

She looked down and played with her gold bracelets.

"So, Demetrius," she said, affecting a smile, "why isn't Eucratides with you?"

"He is visiting the cities of eastern Bactria, where he is quite popular among the nobles," said Demetrius. "We are consolidating supplies in case of a siege."

"I see," said Laodice, her face turning stern. "And how is he otherwise?"

"Good," said Demetrius. "He won the footrace in the city games. I saw it myself."

"He's a true sportsman," said Laodice, shooing away the servant who filled her cup and taking a drink.

As Demetrius watched the servant hurry away, Roshan entered, and Laodice stared at him as if he had broken a priceless heirloom. Seeing her face, Demetrius explained that he wanted Roshan there as an advisor—that he valued his counsel.

"Let's sit," said Laodice. She didn't acknowledge Roshan, but instead said, "Excuse us," to the two men at the end of the room. They nodded, rose, and left.

Demetrius followed Laodice's lead and settled onto the pillows. A servant placed a cup of wine on the small table beside him, and Demetrius let the servant dilute the red liquid considerably.

"How long will you stay?" said Laodice. "Tomorrow, the theater performs some of the newest plays from the west. You must join."

"Perhaps," said Demetrius. "But first, I have something to discuss."

Laodice took a long sip of wine and took her time setting the cup on the table.

"Demetrius, I know why you're here," she said, her tone notably colder than before. "You're here to lay claim to my soldiers. You want them to defend Zariaspa against our Greek cousins from the west."

"That is the short of it, your highness," said Demetrius, suddenly feeling a need for formality.

"Well," said Laodice, "the king, your father, must understand that I need my soldiers here. The border with Scythia is wide and dangerous. The king knows he cannot leave us unprotected against those barbarians."

"We do not require all of your men," said Demetrius, taken aback by the bluntness with which she spoke. "But we need many of them to defend against the Seleucids."

"Well," said Laodice, "I would remind you that the Seleucid threat is more of a threat to the royal family than to the people of Bactria. Some Bactrians may even ask if it matters which Greek rules. What *does* matter to them is whether or not their lands are overrun by large groups of people interested in staying."

"We require only the standard amount expected from your city," said Demetrius, choosing to ignore her inflammatory statements. "This obligation, after all, is one reason your husband holds power here." He knew the last part would drive home his seriousness. She may have been his friend's mother, but he was at her court on behalf of his people.

"I hold power—" Laodice began, before stopping abruptly. "*My husband* holds power because of the efforts of our ancestors. And I will again remind you that we need our soldiers to defend against the Scythians. I don't mean to speak frankly with you, Demetrius, but you're not a child anymore. Your father's policies concerning the Scythians have been unsatisfactory at best, negligent at worst. He has done very little over the past few years to stop Scythian encroachments onto our land. I suppose it's been easy for him because he lives in Zariaspa and not in the north. But they *are* coming."

"Perhaps he wants to avoid war with the Scythians and believes there is room for negotiation," said Demetrius. But these were his own ideas—not those of his father. "Even Alexander formed a treaty with them."

"Only after killing them by the thousands on the battlefield," said Laodice. "And he still saw the logic of creating a fortress north of here. Not that the men who garrisoned it lived long, I should remind you. No, you don't know the Scythians. I do, and they cannot be trusted."

"Why not?" asked Demetrius. "I understand that *you've* been attacking them, and not the other way around. I saw the bodies hanging from your walls. Those people were not soldiers."

"We attacked them because they moved too close. They move closer and closer each year, and I'm tired of waiting for your father to do something about it. Their movement is not just an inconvenience. It is a matter of survival. You know what the Scythians did to our men last year." Laodice drank her wine. "Diodotus shed Seleucid control because he felt that only local rule could ensure the right resources went to securing our borders. I only wish your father had understood that before taking over. Instead, he spends money on non-Greeks." She looked sharply at Roshan. "Oh, I've heard about the temples he's building for the Zoroastrians, and the Buddhists, and the Hindus."

Disgust distorted her face.

"Now you want us to mix with the barbarians?" She turned to Demetrius. "Such policies have already gone far enough, and they weaken our hold on power."

"You think that embracing other cultures makes us weak?" Demetrius could feel Roshan watching him. "My father sees it as our strength. And are those of us who come from Greece really so different than those who don't? As Isocrates once said, 'The name Greek is no longer a mark of race but of outlook and is accorded to those who share our culture as well as those who share our blood.'"

Laodice scoffed.

"We only have a future in these lands," continued Demetrius, "if we integrate with the people who live here, and have them integrate with us. I believe that the Scythians will continue to come, whether we fight them or not. In fact, if we continue to push them back or bar them from trade, they will fight us even more. But if we incorporate them into our trading networks—which could help us, too—they may become our allies. Alexander saw this. That is why he married Roxana in this very palace."

"Alexander, Alexander," said Laodice, wiping wine from her lips. "Everyone hangs their arguments on the legacy of Alexander." She set her wine on the floor and stood. "Come," she said, waving for Demetrius to get up, too, "follow me, and I'll show you the legacy of Alexander."

Demetrius and Roshan followed Laodice into the airy courtyard.

"Do you know where you stand?" she said, twisting in place and leaving no time for an answer. "It was here, in this very courtyard, that Alexander killed Kleitus for speaking his mind."

Demetrius looked around. A peacock pecked at the ground in the corner.

"You probably know the story," said Laodice. "But I enjoy telling it, and now it seems particularly relevant."

She paced between the columns as she spoke, dragging her gold-covered fingers against the red-painted rock.

"There was a great feast the night of the killing. Everyone was drinking, but none more than Alexander," she said. "They were celebrating their victories against the barbarians of this area. And of course Alexander was joyous. He had led those battles. But it wasn't just that. He had adopted the ways of the east. He made his comrades bow to him and attend to his every whim. Who wouldn't be happy? And he called himself the leader of Greece! But not everyone was pleased with such displays—Kleitus among them. He hated the bowing, and he despised Alexander's ridiculous attempts to make them fuse their lives with this region's culture. The dress, the food, the marriages to locals. And he said as much. He challenged Alexander in front of the others."

Laodice breathed deeply and continued. "Perhaps it was stupid to challenge a drunk man, especially one drunk on power, but Kleitus did it. And his words so infuriated Alexander that Alexander grabbed a sarissa—the spear wielded by all those loyal to home—and stabbed him through the heart."

Laodice strode to the middle of the courtyard and stopped beside the statue of Dionysus. "It is said that Kleitus died here," she said, pointing to the ground, "on this very spot. He died because he stood up for his heritage, and Alexander killed him because he'd abandoned his."

"The story was more complicated than that," Demetrius protested. "Kleitus spoke of more than just Alexander's adopted customs. He also insulted his honor."

"Perhaps. But one must not forget Kleitus's honor." Laodice placed her hand on her chest. "Our honor."

"I sense we now speak of something different," said Demetrius.

"Different, yes, but also the same."

Laodice stepped toward Demetrius. "You want us to leave our border unprotected against the barbarians so that Euthydemus can wage war against our kin? No! My obligations are to the safety of my people in Maracanda. You can tell the king that as long as my men must guard against Scythia, he will get no more than a handful of my soldiers."

She sneered.

"Very well," said Demetrius. "I shall secure your border with Scythia."

"Excuse me?" said Laodice.

"You heard me," said Demetrius, closing the gap between them. "You need your soldiers to protect your lands from the Scythians. If we enter an alliance with the Scythians, most of your soldiers will be free to join us in the defense of Bactria. I will thus go into Scythia and form such an alliance."

"Your majesty," said Laodice, her breathing erratic. Foolishly, she looked to Roshan for support.

Demetrius lifted his hand to silence her.

"This is my final decision," he said. "I am a prince of Bactria, son of the king, and we have debated this long enough."

Laodice blinked rapidly, and she opened and closed her mouth like a fish.

"We will leave in the coming days," said Demetrius, glancing at Roshan. "But for now, we will call it a night."

Without waiting for a response, Demetrius turned and left. Roshan walked beside him, shoulder to shoulder.

"Are you sure you're up for this?" said Roshan, as they approached their rooms. "The journey will be exceedingly dangerous, and there's no telling if the Scythians will form an alliance even if we do reach them."

"I've made up my mind," said Demetrius. "I've been hearing about our conflict with Scythia for long enough. It's time someone did something about it. And if we can have them at our side, we may just balance out our enemy's forces, Parthians included."

"Your majesty." Roshan stopped at Demetrius's door, and Demetrius turned and faced him. "Thank you for including me in that meeting. I appreciate knowing what's going on."

"I know you didn't speak much," said Demetrius, "but in time, I hope that will change."

"Yes, your majesty." Roshan bowed.

As Demetrius entered his chamber, he let out a long sigh. His conversation with Laodice had disappointed and exhausted him. Menon was right. She had changed.

The window shades creaked as Demetrius pulled them open, revealing the city below and the steppe beyond. He breathed slowly from the cool air and thought of the next leg of their journey. It would be a gamble, and a dangerous one. But how else could they stop Antiochus?

CHAPTER NINETEEN

Antiochus

Amid the mountains of Ariana, Antiochus led his forces along a thin and winding road. His army looked tired and dejected; the mountains were taking their toll. There'd been attacks without warning and ravines that swallowed men whole and screaming.

Behind the column of men, a pillar of smoke billowed in the distance, and watching it, Antiochus felt a pinch of guilt. Dropidas approached on a light-brown horse.

"What is it?" said Antiochus, studying the dust-covered man. "Are the men dragging their feet?"

"No, it's not that . . ."

"Then speak," said Antiochus, eager to be left alone.

"It's about the village." Dropidas looked past Antiochus, presumably at the smoke.

"What of it?" Antiochus's heart beat faster.

"Was is really necessary to burn it? It will not endear us to the locals. I'm afraid it will invite retaliation—and when we control these lands, such treatment may breed rebellion."

"Rebellion?" scoffed Antiochus. "You know better than most that I have faced my share of rebellion. And let me tell you, Dropidas. Did my cousin rebel because I was too hard on him? No. He rebelled because he perceived me as weak."

The smoke from the village twisted.

"I shouldn't have to explain that what we do here is studied by our adversaries in the west," Antiochus said, "both without and within our borders."

"But your majesty," said Dropidas, "that village didn't house the people that attacked us this morning."

"People lie," said Antiochus.

"But burning the village will only build hatred among the tribes we must still pass."

"Hatred, yes," said Antiochus, recalling the moment he'd ordered his cousin's crucifixion. "But also fear."

Antiochus nudged his horse and rode off. The crackling of the burning village and the cries of protest rung in his ears. He hadn't always been cruel. But that was before those closest to him rebelled. There was no more room for mercy, no matter how much Dropidas protested. Dropidas was only a general. He didn't understand the weight of being king, let alone emperor. Antiochus straightened his back and lifted his chin. The world was anarchy. A leader must rule or be ruled.

Antiochus breathed deeply from the mountain air and tried to think of brighter things. Though his journey east had been beset with difficulties—the war in Parthia being the largest—he couldn't help but feel like a reborn Alexander. His army was carving paths that no western army had done for over a hundred years.

Antiochus called to Phriapa, who was riding ahead of him.

"You're riding on the path of Alexander," said Antiochus. "Can you feel it?"

"He must have been tired," said Phriapa, his voice flat.

"Perhaps," said Antiochus. "But don't you feel the energy?"

"No." Phriapa did not look back. "I don't share your obsession with the man. He conquered the world. So what?"

"If he hadn't died so young," said Antiochus, "the world would be a very different place."

"A better one?" said Phriapa. "Or one of dead villagers and burning homes?"

"Of course a better one."

"And I suppose you think you can achieve his dream?"

"I'm here, aren't I?" said Antiochus, annoyed by Phriapa's condescending tone. "I'm only sorry that your father couldn't join us. But it's good that he is consolidating forces in Saddarvazeh. I plan to use them."

Phriapa didn't respond, instead leading his horse further up the column.

An hour or so later, Antiochus approached the middle of the column as it entered a narrow gorge framed on both sides by cliffs and steep hills. He craned his neck as he studied the jagged rock formations, and he squinted at the top of the cliffs high above.

"Keep moving," he said to the man beside him.

Though only a few men could hear Antiochus's command, just saying it assuaged his anxiety. Marching through a ravine was always a dangerous gamble.

"How much further to Kabul?" Antiochus called to the guide, who passed beside him.

The guide pointed at a wall of mountains in the distance. Their dark foundations gave way to snow-capped peaks. "It's past that range," he said.

Antiochus studied the many hills between him and that distant point. He pulled at the collar of his breastplate and closed his eyes. They were almost to Kabul, he told himself. Alexandrian glory was only days away.

A sharp pain in his left thigh ruined his tranquility. Antiochus opened his eyes and discovered a wooden shaft sticking from his leg.

At first, he was baffled. He knew he was looking at an arrow, but the gravity of the situation entered his mind only slowly.

The clanking of metal and the screams of men further ahead pulled Antiochus's attention from his wound. He pushed himself higher on his horse and looked over the men of the column and through the swaying forest of sarissas. His heart pounded as he realized the front of the column was under attack.

"Shields up!" Antiochus yelled, as he pulled his sword from its sheath.

Antiochus heard shouting behind him. He twisted and saw figures armed with clubs and swords descending the steep hills and crashing into the middle of the column. A large boulder fell beside him, crushing a man beneath it. More dark shapes hulked on the cliff edges above, then plummeted to the ground. Men around him screamed and pushed as the boulders landed among them—on top of them. Shrieking filled the moments between thuds.

Antiochus pulled the arrow from his thigh and nudged his horse into action. He rode to the front of the column, where soldiers formed a rough line. With the enemy so close, the sarissas were useless, and the Seleucid soldiers fought with swords and stones. Antiochus jumped from his horse and joined the front line. Leg throbbing, he swung his sword frantically at the mass of assailants, who clamored down the steep hill.

A man fell beside him, so Antiochus picked up his blood-covered shield. Sweat made the handle slippery, and it took Antiochus a moment to find a secure hold. Pulling it up, he pushed his left shoulder against the metal and aligned the shield with those on either side of him.

"Push!" he yelled, stepping forward and grinding his shield into the enemy. "Push!"

The shield wall moved forward and soldiers stabbed with swords and broken sarissa staffs. Antiochus jabbed his sword over the top of his shield and pierced a man's throat. Another enemy tripped over the falling body.

"Push!" Antiochus shouted again.

With the shield wall moving another foot, the enemy broke and men stumbled over one another as they ran. Antiochus stabbed at their backs, catching those unable to retreat. He pushed up the hill, stepping over the dead and dying.

CHAPTER TWENTY

Phriapa

Further down the line, Phriapa watched Antiochus and a large contingent of soldiers work their way up a steep hill. The monarch's red cloak stuck out among the soldiers.

"Let's go!" Phriapa called to Heron. "We'll get up top and draw the attack away from the column."

"There's a path to the left," yelled Heron as they moved forward.

As they rode, Phriapa studied the infantry column. Three bodies lay on the ground, blood spreading beneath them. Without warning, a large boulder smashed into the line, crushing another man. Arrows followed, felling more.

Phriapa's horse was unsure of its footing as he led it across the boulder-strewn path Heron had identified. There was a deep ravine on Phriapa's left, and a cliff face on his right.

"We'll have to leave the horses behind," said Phriapa, realizing his animal would go no further.

He dismounted, waited for his companions to do the same, and ran up the mountain path. By the time he reached a small, flat ledge,

Phriapa was winded. The ledge overlooked a wide valley dotted with low shrubs.

"We must be behind them by now," said Phriapa. "Do you see anyone?"

His comrades said no.

"Then we'll keep climbing," he said, running to an incline. He was exhausted after only a few feet of climbing. Each inch of progress required careful planning, as sharp stones protruded all around him. Yelling and the ringing of metal ricocheted across the rocks.

When Phriapa turned back to check on the others, he spied movement below. The ledge had filled with figures, many of them with bows in hand.

"They're attacking from behind!" yelled Phriapa. "Take cover!"

His warning came too late. Arrows zipped through the air, piercing his comrades or slamming against rocks. The man beside him screamed and fell backward, his body tumbling down the hill.

Realizing they had no cover and that upward progress was dangerously slow, Phriapa decided to charge the enemy. With arrows landing around him, he ran back down the hill. There was no time to use his bow, so he pulled the knife from his belt. He, Heron, and another man ran into the enemy fighters. Phriapa ducked below a swinging sword and jabbed his knife into the wielder's abdomen. A club crashed against his arm. His elbow burned, and he dropped the knife and stumbled back. A man lunged at him, swinging the club at his skull. Phriapa darted left and grabbed the club still in his opponent's grip. He and his enemy fell to the ground. Phriapa punched at whatever he could reach. He swung his elbow back and his assailant went limp.

Phriapa looked up. A soldier in bronze armor stood above him, bloodied sword in hand. As the man helped him stand, Phriapa recognized him as Dropidas, the Seleucid general.

"They nearly got you," said Dropidas. Blood was splattered across his dirty, sweaty face.

"If you say so," said Phriapa, patting the dust from his clothes and looking at the dead body.

He pushed past Dropidas, making sure his shoulder slammed into the Seleucid's.

"Hey," Dropidas called to him.

Phriapa turned and faced the Seleucid.

"You and your monarch caused this by burning that village," said Phriapa.

"We don't all agree with what happened there," said Dropidas.

Phriapa turned away and approached Heron, who was tending to a wounded soldier.

"How many did we lose?" said Phriapa.

"Twelve," said Heron.

Phriapa ran his fingers through his sweaty hair.

"What a waste," he said, walking away.

CHAPTER TWENTY-ONE

Demetrius

It took Demetrius and his companions a couple of days to prepare for their journey into Scythia. During that time, Demetrius let the men roam the city and allowed them to take their horses to the river just beyond the walls.

On the day of their departure, they gathered before the main city gate. Laodice approached with her retinue of advisors, servants, and soldiers.

"Your majesty," she said. "I can't believe you're off so soon." Her tone betrayed the sarcastic nature Demetrius had only recently come to know.

"These times demand swiftness," said Demetrius.

"Of course," she said, pulling her crimson gown from the dirt. "Your aim for the north is ambitious. And dangerous, I should add."

"Which is why we have employed a guide."

"Don't tell me you found the man called Peers," said Laodice, rolling her eyes.

"I understand he is a student of their ways and customs," said Demetrius. "And he offered his services at a reasonable price."

Demetrius looked past Laodice at an approaching man. He was slender and of average height. His light-brown hair fell across his face and partially covered his dark eyes.

"You're a welcome companion," said Demetrius, as Peers stopped beside them. Demetrius turned to Roshan. "Ensure that Peers has a good horse."

"Yes, your majesty," said Roshan.

"I don't understand his fascination with the Scythians," said Laodice, as Peers walked away, "but perhaps he'll convince you of your mission's futility before it's too late."

"I assure you," said Demetrius, "we will only return when our mission is complete."

"Very well," said Laodice. "If I hear of your success, I will head to Zariaspa with my army."

"Good," said Demetrius. "And I'm sure Eucratides will be delighted to see you."

"I certainly hope so," said Laodice, faking a laugh.

"And one more thing," said Demetrius, stepping forward and straightening his back. "Remove the bodies hanging from your walls. They've been there long enough."

"I'll consider it," said Laodice.

"No," said Demetrius. "You'll do it."

"Acting the king already."

Demetrius stared into Laodice's twitching eyes until she looked away.

"Take the bodies down," she called to a soldier.

She glared at Demetrius and, with her retinue close behind, left the clearing.

Not eager to stay longer than was needed, Demetrius mounted his horse and led his companions from the city and toward the hilly steppe.

"Are you sure about this?" said Roshan, riding to Demetrius's side. "We can still turn back."

"That time has passed," said Demetrius. "And regardless, we must take risks to beat Antiochus."

Roshan sighed.

"More importantly," said Demetrius, "we can't give Laodice any excuse for withholding soldiers."

"I don't know," said Roshan. "Perhaps it's safer to wait and see what Menon and Arjun accomplish."

"Perhaps," said Demetrius. "But we don't have time."

"Yes, your majesty."

Demetrius turned back to look at the walls of Maracanda. A soldier cut one of the ropes, and a body fell to the ground. Demetrius closed his eyes and breathed slowly. He was glad the bodies were being removed, but the damage, unfortunately, had already been done.

Demetrius nudged his horse to go faster. It carried him toward a horizon obscured by fog. Appropriate, Demetrius thought. He had no knowledge of what, or who, awaited them.

CHAPTER TWENTY-TWO

~

Beleen

Beleen sat beside Alora, sharpening her ax. Children chased one another between the tents.

"It's nice to see the children having a good time, isn't it?" said Alora. Many of them had arrived with a caravan of northern refugees. "They're still at the age when they know nothing of the outside world."

"Is the world really so bad where you come from?" said Beleen, still fearing civil war in the west.

"I wasn't talking about my home," said Alora. "I was talking about yours. War between you and the Bactrians seems inevitable. It's only a matter of time."

"Perhaps our people can integrate with theirs," said Beleen. "I've heard that in the west, the Bosporan Kingdom is ruled by Thracians and is populated by a mix of Greeks and Scythians."

"That's true," said Alora. "It's a remarkable place. But there's a conservatism among the Greeks here that I don't see back west. Perhaps the distance from home makes people more rigid in their ways and more closed to outsiders."

"It just takes time for people to understand one another."

"No doubt," said Alora. "But much death generally precedes such a transition." Alora shifted to face Beleen and said, "Let me tell you a story."

Beleen nodded.

"Years back," Alora began, "There was a man called Scyles. He was the son of a Scythian king. But his mother was a Greek from Istria, and she raised him to speak and read the Greek language. It wasn't long before Scyles secretly preferred Greek culture to his own." Alora took a breath, extended her legs in front of her, and continued, "Eventually, the king died and Scyles became king of the Scythians. But his secret urge to be Greek hadn't gone away. So, for an entire month, he left his community and lived in a Greek city on the border of his land. When among the foreigners, he dressed, spoke, and worshiped like them. He even married a Greek woman."

"What happened?" said Beleen. "Did his people find out?"

"Of course they did," said Alora. "And things ended the way you'd expect. The people revolted and Scyles was beheaded by his own brother."

Beleen tried to imagine what she and her comrades would do if Kulka became a Greek. The notion seemed preposterous.

"You know," said Alora. "The Greeks are not the only ones who are conservative. And I doubt we'd act any differently in Bactria if the roles were reversed. But, alas, we are here and they are there."

As Beleen reflected on Alora's story, a horseman entered the clearing. He dismounted and ran up to Beleen.

"Where is Kulka?" he said.

"Inside." Beleen tilted her head toward the tent, and the man ran in. Beleen followed, Alora close behind.

Kulka sat on the floor in front of his throne reading from a parchment, but as the man approached, he looked up and set the paper aside.

"My chief," said the man, bowing.

"What is it?" said Kulka.

"The traders that we sent to Maracanda. They were executed. Their bodies hang from the city walls."

Beleen tightened her fists and clenched her jaw.

Kulka let out a long sigh and stroked his beard. "Now we know the kind of people we're dealing with." He looked to Beleen.

"Only one response is appropriate," said Alora.

"And what is that?" Kulka asked.

"In the west," she said, "when the southern people close their borders to trade, some of the tribes attack them. And with time, the southerners realize that trading is more acceptable than death."

"But that could start a war," said Kulka.

"The Greeks need to know that we're serious," said Alora. "That there are costs to their actions. Only then will they negotiate and open to our traders."

Kulka nodded. "You're right." He sighed.

Beleen lowered her gaze. Her mind filled with the image of her brother dead in the grass, vultures tearing at his face.

"Beleen," said Kulka, startling her. "In the days ahead, raid their outposts and attack their soldiers."

Beleen ran her fingers through her hair. "Yes, my chief," she finally said, her voice wavering with fear for what the future held.

Stepping from the tent, Beleen looked up at the gray sky. She pulled her ax from her belt, sat down, and began to sharpen it.

CHAPTER TWENTY-THREE

Demetrius

"Peers, how close are we?" Demetrius asked the guide.

A day and night had passed since they had left Maracanda, and the air had grown cold.

"There's a settlement beyond those hills," said Peers, pointing ahead. The sun, which had just risen above the horizon, shone red. There were gentle hills of swaying grass as far as Demetrius could see, punctuated in some places by tall rocks.

"Alright," Demetrius said, turning to his companions. "It's not much further. This should be the final day."

"If only I had known about all of this riding before we left home," Ashok groaned. "I'd have brought a pillow."

Demetrius laughed, and others added to the joke.

As Demetrius resettled on his horse, he thought of their journey from Zariaspa. Yes, it had been physically demanding, as Ashok had suggested. But it had also been mentally taxing. The days were long and monotonous, and the men spoke to one another only briefly and often with an underlying tension. Offensive comments from Phlotas never helped, nor did Roshan's stonewalling of conversation with him.

"What do you think is beyond the steppe?" Roshan asked, bringing his horse beside Demetrius's. A layer of dirt covered his mustache and beard, and his eyes were bloodshot.

"I don't know," said Demetrius. "More of this, I guess."

"The Scythians say the northern lands are covered in feathers," said Peers.

"Feathers?" said Roshan. "Like bird feathers?"

"That's what Herodotus wrote," said Peers.

Roshan laughed. "You need to read something else."

Demetrius thought of Herodotus, the famous Greek historian. He had only read some of his accounts of the world and of the wars between Greece and Persia. But he had read enough to know that Herodotus traced the conflict between east and west to the time of Achilles and Hector. He wondered if those men were all that different from him—if they struggled to understand their place in the world and their relationship to those they called enemy.

Soon after, the group fell back into silence and the journey resumed its monotony. Despite the periodic excitement of birds diving for their prey, little seemed to happen.

"Alright, I'll admit it," said Demetrius, an hour or so later. "This is getting tedious. Who's up for a race?"

"I'll race," said Roshan, still beside him.

"Very well," said Demetrius. "Do you see those rocks ahead? The ones sticking from the grass?"

"Yes, your highness," said Roshan.

"I'll race you there. You ready?"

"I'll go when you do," said Roshan.

Demetrius grinned, faced forward, and nudged his horse. The animal jolted ahead, and he guided it toward the rocks. The wind whisked through his hair as he rode. The breeze had grown throughout the early morning, and it was a welcome companion.

A moment later, Roshan pulled past Demetrius, his horse at a gallop. Chunks of grass lifted from the beast's hooves and flew into the air.

Demetrius laughed, encouraged his horse again, and galloped alongside Roshan. As his horse gained speed, Demetrius pushed his body up and let the animal move powerfully beneath him.

Looking ahead, he saw the rocks in more detail. They seemed to break through the plain like a rising Atlantis, and their angle suggested they descended much further into the earth. Wispy grass swayed back and forth beside them, and moss grew at their tops.

Demetrius felt winded. Back at home, he could gallop for as long as the horse would tolerate, but after days of traveling, he was feeling the strain. He slowed and watched Roshan increase the distance between them. In seconds, Roshan stopped his horse and turned back.

"Maybe next time, your highness," he said, laughing.

"Without a doubt," said Demetrius, patting his horse's neck.

They led their horses slowly across the remaining distance to the rocks. Demetrius turned and watched the rest of the unit slowly catch up. He felt sorry for them, for they carried the baggage. As the son of the king, Demetrius had never held that responsibility, nor would it be appropriate for him to assume it.

As Demetrius crested the hill from which the rocks protruded, something caught his eye. He froze. Demetrius called for the others to halt before summoning Peers. When the guide reached him, Demetrius pointed ahead.

Horsemen congregated in the distance. There were about fifteen figures, equidistant from one another, and they were positioned around a large mound of dirt.

"Ah, we've reached them," said Peers, speaking as if he had run into friends in the market.

"Who are they?" said Demetrius.

"Don't worry," said Peers, as he scanned the horsemen. "They are harmless to you." He paused before adding, "At least in this life."

"What do you mean?" Demetrius did not lift his gaze from the motionless riders. He drew his sword.

"You will see soon enough," said Peers. "Just continue moving."

Demetrius and the others rode on in silence. As they approached the mound, nothing moved except the fabric streaming from the bodies of the riders and horses. And then Demetrius saw it. The horses, their fur and skin. It was twisted and pulled close to the bone. The animals looked emaciated. Inspecting the riders, their rigidness suddenly made sense. Long wooden stakes rose from the ground, through each horse and along the back of each rider. Ropes held the figures in place. Their hands were nothing but bones. A rancid smell permeated Demetrius's nostrils, and he pulled his scarf to his nose.

"What is this?" he said, turning to Peers.

"A burial," said Peers. "You see that mound in the middle there?" He pointed at the tall mound of dried and cracked dirt. "It contains a former Scythian chief." He waved at the skeletal horsemen around the hill. "These men are his companions. His protectors. They shared their lord's fate."

"What do you mean?" said Demetrius, as his companions arrived beside him. "What did they do to deserve this punishment?"

"Punishment? No!" said Peers. "To them, this is an honor. These men spent their lives in splendor, as did their lord. In swearing their allegiance to him, their fates interwove with his. His wealth was theirs. And when it was his time to pass to the other realm, it was their fate to pass with him."

Demetrius thought of Alexander's famed Companions. Instead of following him into death, they'd killed each other for his empire.

"And they accepted this fate willingly?" said Ashok, now beside Demetrius.

"Of course," said Peers. "These men had good lives. They lived like kings."

"As long as their lord lived as such," said Demetrius.

"Exactly," said Peers. "Now you understand."

He pointed at the mound and riders. "These men are honored here."

Demetrius studied the decomposing bodies and imagined his own among them. He shuddered.

"Fascinating, isn't it?" said Peers.

"Let's keep moving." Demetrius guided his horse forward.

"But wait," said Peers, drawing Demetrius's gaze. "You still wish to continue after seeing this? Do you really think you can make peace with such people?"

"My mission remains unchanged," said Demetrius. "So yes, we will continue."

"Then I will leave you here," said Peers. "This is as far as I will go. I know enough about the Scythians to know I don't want to become their prisoner. And I advise that you return with me."

"Your help has been appreciated," said Demetrius. "And please let Laodice know to prepare her army for news of our success."

"Very well," said Peers, as he turned his horse away from the caravan. "But when the Scythians are torturing you, don't expect soldiers from home to arrive before death offers mercy."

As Peers rode away, Demetrius looked to his companions. From the looks on their faces, he assumed they had heard Peers's warning.

"Let's keep moving," Demetrius said, guiding his horse into action.

Before passing beyond the next hill, Demetrius glanced at the rigid horsemen one more time. The breeze weaved between their bones and fluttered the fabric.

CHAPTER TWENTY-FOUR

Beleen

Beleen made her way to the horse pasture. She found Kasen eating dried grass, and soon after, twelve warriors joined her, each with a horse and some with donkeys to carry supplies. Most of the warriors were young—this being only their first or second time leaving the settlement in arms. Beleen had protested with Kulka about including the young ones, but he pushed aside her concerns, saying that she'd been young when he first welcomed her on his attacks. She had a tough time arguing with that.

"Are you ready?" she said, impatient to get going.

"Ready for battle!" one of the younger ones yelled.

Beleen turned away, both amused and horrified by the response. She had seen enough battle to know it was nothing to treasure, no matter how much the community celebrated it at their fires and festivals.

Beleen mounted her horse and led it through the pasture gate, followed by the others. Mist hung above the dull-green grass. She drew in the chilly humidity with each breath, and watched steam escape her mouth. While her fingers and face were cold, the sun warmed the back of her neck.

"Wait!"

Beleen turned and saw a horseman approaching from the settlement.

He galloped toward her, his distinctive Scythian headgear flapping against the sides of his head. Despite his familiar appearance, Beleen felt something was off about him. The man lifted his tattooed right arm as he closed the distance.

"Wait," he called again. "I am to join you."

"And you are?" said Beleen.

"One of Alora's bodyguards. She asked that I accompany you."

"Very well," said Beleen, knowing she had no choice in the matter. "But follow my commands. This is my party."

When the man nodded, Beleen guided her horse forward.

Over the hours of riding, Beleen's companions discussed many things, from Alora to the temperaments of their horses. Some even complained about their parents' marriage ambitions. As they spoke, they trotted across the hilly, treeless terrain, and the air grew hot.

"We're getting close to the burial lands," Beleen called to the others, as they entered an area where tall rocks and pink poppies rose from the grassy hills. "Keep an eye out for enemy scouts. They've been known to come this far."

Despite the warning, Beleen had not expected to see Greeks for at least another day of riding, so when she saw figures in the distance an hour later, her heart thumped against her chest. She held her breath as she studied them.

There were maybe ten horsemen. Some wore plates of armor like their Parthian neighbors. Others wore tunics and carried bows. Beleen watched the strangers point to her and talk among themselves. They spread out, forming a broad front. Many pulled arrows from their quivers and drew swords from their sheaths.

"Are they Greeks?" asked Alora's bodyguard. He stopped beside her, an arrow latched to his bow.

"They must be," said Beleen. "Look at the helmet on that one."

Beleen pointed to a man, whose head was covered in a bronze helmet with a black-and-red crest.

Three of the figures, the crested man included, led their horses in front of the others.

"They approach us as if they want to talk," said Beleen.

"Don't trust them," said Alora's man. "And either way, Kulka was clear. We are to attack."

Beleen glanced at the other warriors who rode with her, and whose lives she was responsible for. They looked to her for direction.

"Spread out," she said.

The three riders stopped halfway between Beleen and the Greeks. She studied them, waiting for someone to make a move. Though she was on a mission to attack, she couldn't help but feel that the Greeks hoped to speak with her. But, remembering the report of Scythian traders hanging from the walls of Maracanda, she tightened her grip on her bow and aligned an arrow against the string. The breeze picked up, cooling her fingers and nose. She breathed slowly.

As Beleen exhaled, she heard a twang and then saw an arrow slam into the neck of a man who wore a bronze helmet with wing-shaped cheek guards. The man swayed, then fell to the ground. Beleen looked to her right and saw Alora's companion lowering his bow.

Seconds after the man fell, the Greeks unsheathed their swords, loosed their arrows, and charged. They stayed in close formation as they approached the Scythian line, but the effect was muted as Beleen commanded her companions to create an opening through which the enemy could pass. The Greeks took the bait, and in moments, they moved behind Beleen. She turned to face them, drawing back and releasing an arrow. More arrows took to the air and pierced Greek bodies. Despite the enemy's armor, the projectiles hit points of weakness. Necks, armpits, horses. Men and animals collapsed.

Some of the Greeks turned and charged again, swinging their swords as they came. Beleen pulled the thin, one-handed ax from her belt and charged the enemy. She ducked as one man swung a sword at her face, and then she slammed her ax into the back of the man's neck. Letting go of the ax, Beleen pulled an arrow from her quiver, latched it to the bow, and searched for a target amid the milieu.

In the chaos, she saw a Greek blade catch Alora's man in the throat. His head fell to the ground, and his horse rode off. Beleen found her target in a soldier who swung his sword aimlessly from atop his horse. She loosened her grip, and the arrow slammed through the right eyehole of the man's helmet.

It didn't take long for the remaining Greeks to panic. They broke rank and rode off as individuals. After such disintegration, there would be no recovery. Only fleeing, chasing, and death.

CHAPTER TWENTY-FIVE

Demetrius

Demetrius woke with his face to the ground. Grass tickled his lips and his tongue was dry. He tried to pull himself up, but couldn't. His hands were bound behind his back. And then he remembered. The Scythians. The attack. The slaughter.

Demetrius rolled onto his back. The sky was blue and blinding. He squinted as he managed to sit up and then looked around.

Men surrounded him. Scythians. They talked and laughed as they tended to their horses and cleaned their weapons of his comrades' blood. Demetrius looked past them at a distant pile of bodies. The Scythians had stripped them, and there was a separate pile of armor and weapons.

"You shouldn't have invaded our land, Greek."

Demetrius turned and saw a woman. She was tall and strong, and wore a tan leather jacket covered in plates of bronze metal. Her pants were made of brown wool. Tattoos and gold bracelets covered her arms, and her hair was long, wavy, and black. Demetrius's mind flashed with images of the goddess Athena. Or was this Scythian woman one of the Amazons of legend?

"We were not invading," said Demetrius. "We came to talk."

"Well, whatever you came for," said the Scythian, speaking Greek, "it was ill-advised, and your friends paid the price." She pointed at the bodies.

"Am I the only one who survived?"

"No, there are others," said the woman. "I'll take you to them soon enough."

"We seek an audience with your chieftain," he said, pushing through the pain in his chest.

"Who are you to presume an audience with our chief?" said the woman. The breeze swept her hair across her face.

"We bring information that may interest him."

The Scythian pointed an arrow at Demetrius's face. "You're from Bactria, aren't you?"

Demetrius didn't speak. He just looked straight into the woman's dark-brown eyes.

"You're here to kill, aren't you?" said the woman. She jabbed the arrow for emphasis.

"No, not to kill," said Demetrius. "To talk."

"I disagree," said the Scythian.

"I am Demetrius, prince of Bactria, son of King Euthydemus," he said with force, "and I no longer ask, but demand, an audience with your chief."

The Scythian stared at him, her gaze roaming across his body.

"Okay, Demetrius, prince of Bactria, I will bring you to him. But he may not be as merciful as I am."

"Where is your chief?" said Demetrius, ignoring the threat.

"North of here," said the Scythian. "A quarter day's ride."

Demetrius nodded.

"How do you speak our language?" he then said, surprised at this display of culture from the sort of person he had only known as a barbarian.

"We speak many languages," said the woman, "Greek being one of the easiest. How many do you speak?"

"Just the one," said Demetrius.

The woman stared at him and let the wind push her hair back and forth across her face.

"Come with me." She turned and walked away.

Demetrius struggled to his feet and followed close behind. He passed horses, standing together, their harnesses attached to small shrubs. Some of the Scythians ran combs through the animals' fur.

Demetrius looked again at his dead comrades. For many, this had been their first mission beyond the confines of Bactria. And he had failed them. By the size of the pile, he doubted many others survived, and even if they were still alive, they might only have hours left to live. He'd heard terrible stories of torture and cannibalism on the steppe. But he'd also heard that Scythians were incapable of speaking Greek, and here was a woman who knew many more languages than he.

When the Scythian halted, Demetrius nearly crashed into her.

"There they are," she said, raising her arm.

Demetrius's gaze followed where she was pointing. Three men were lying under the shade of a tall boulder. He ran to them, his arms still bound.

One man had a gash across his face. He looked at Demetrius through bloodshot eyes and crusted blood. "It is wonderful to see you alive, your highness."

As Demetrius studied the wounded man, he felt as if someone had punched him in the gut. The man was Ashok.

"Ashok, what happened?" he said, ashamed he had not recognized his friend at once.

"Not a lot," said Ashok. "I was hit in the face and fell from my horse early in the fight."

Demetrius nodded and looked to the next man.

"Roshan," he exclaimed.

Roshan looked unhurt, though blood was splattered across his face.

"Your highness," said a voice, pulling Demetrius's attention to the last man.

"You're alive," said Demetrius, eyeing Phlotas. "I saw you fall. I thought you were dead."

"Almost," said Phlotas. He twisted to show Demetrius a ghastly cut across his ribs. Demetrius cringed.

As the men waited, unsure of their fate, they recounted what had happened.

The sun was hovering just above the horizon by the time the Scythians mounted their horses. They provided Demetrius and the others with steeds, although not the ones they had arrived on.

"I guess they'll kill us later," said Roshan, struggling to mount the horse with his hands bound. Demetrius couldn't tell if he was joking.

The Scythians piled the dead on the backs of donkeys. As the caravan began to move, more and more birds came to circle overhead. Periodically, they dove toward the donkeys. For hours, Demetrius watched the birds in disgust and shouted to disperse them.

He hardly noticed the streams and hills they passed. His mind was too deep in the past, on the mistakes he must have made to get his companions killed. He wondered what he would tell their families—if he even survived that long.

"Look," said Roshan, after hours of riding.

Demetrius glanced at him in a daze. "What is it?" he said. His head hurt.

"A settlement."

Demetrius squinted. Brown-and-tan tents covered the next hill, surrounded by a perimeter of wooden stakes. Outside of the settlement, there were two fenced enclosures. One contained cattle, the other horses.

"This is the capital of Scythia?" Demetrius said to the woman he had met earlier.

"A regional capital," she said. "The Royal Scyths live further west, on the other side of the Great Sea."

They passed through the gate on foot. A large tent at the end of a wide alley caught Demetrius's gaze. He moved toward it.

"Not that way," said the woman. Demetrius looked to her. "You don't get to meet the chief just yet," she added. "And that's if you meet him at all. I wouldn't count on being alive too much longer."

"Where are you taking us?" Demetrius asked.

The woman pointed to a small wooden cage on his right.

"Very well," he said, stepping into the enclosure. Ashok, Roshan, and Phlotas followed close behind. He did not tell them what she had said.

"Now we wait," said Roshan, settling onto the damp ground.

"Wait to die, it would seem," said Ashok.

"We'll get out of here," said Demetrius. "I promise."

While he had no control over their fates, Demetrius had a feeling the end would not come here. There was still too much to achieve. Unless Menon had predicted everything wrong.

CHAPTER TWENTY-SIX

Menon

Menon sat on his horse. The green pastures of the Indian countryside extended as far as the eye could see. Mist hovered above the grass, swaying like white fire, and within it, bent men and women tended the crops. Their colorful clothing made them look like flowering trees.

"What do you think?" said Arjun beside him.

"The land is certainly fertile," said Menon, looking past the soldiers in front of him.

"That it is," said Arjun. "I grew up on a farm like this."

"I didn't know your family owned a farm," said Menon, surprised at just how little he knew of Arjun's past.

"Owned?" Arjun laughed. "They didn't own anything. They simply worked the land."

"Were they happy that you chose the life of a soldier?" asked Menon.

"Never got a chance to comment," said Arjun. "They were killed in Taxila's war against the Mauryan Empire to the east."

"I'm sorry," said Menon.

"It's fine," said Arjun. "Everyone loses someone."

Menon's jaw clenched as he pushed the memories of his son, Erastus, from his mind.

"We must be approaching Taxila," said Menon, changing the subject. "What do you think? Do you recognize anything?"

"I haven't been here in years," said Arjun. "But the scout said it should be just over these hills."

The scout was right. An hour later, upon ascending a gentle incline, Menon saw the walls of Taxila rising from the ground like mountains. With each step closer, the city revealed its details. Mud compounds and irrigated farms surrounded the settlement. Next to the gate, colorful tents evidenced the passing of a large merchant community.

Two chariots passed along the base of the walls, each covered with a large umbrella. Behind the chariot drivers, men stood like statues as they looked beyond the horses' decorated crests.

While smooth stones formed the walls of Zariaspa, tan mud covered those of Taxila. Where the dirt had chipped away, Menon could see the gray stones that provided the walls' foundations. Large square flags whipped in the breeze atop towers, between which soldiers stood guard.

Menon and Arjun entered the crowd approaching the city's main gate. Shepherd boys led herds of goats, farmers pushed carts covered in freshly picked fruit, and soldiers returned from their patrols. Beside the gate, a man struggled to control a group of cow-like gaur. Short brown fur covered their bodies, but their legs were as white as teeth. Their horns were long, curving toward the sky, changing from white at the base to black at the tip.

On the other side of the gate, soldiers, merchants, children, and beggars hustled on the wide street that led to the city center.

"The palace is at the end of this road," said Arjun. "I hope you still have the king's seal. They won't let us in without it."

"I have it," said Menon, feeling the bronze ring resting against his chest.

As they moved toward the palace, Menon and Arjun passed the famous University of Taxila, where students from all across India studied Buddhism and the sciences. The university was built around a large square of tended grass, enclosed by red-brick walls punctured every few feet by gateways. The scene was beautiful, and to Menon, it seemed wholly out of place in the crowded city.

Menon decided to take a detour for curiosity's sake. He followed Arjun onto the university campus, walking beneath the trees and exploring the square's adjacent courtyards. Benches surrounded trees with large canopies, and Arjun explained that classes took place beneath them, as in the forest academies of the gurus.

"Demetrius would love to see this," Menon said.

One courtyard featured a smooth pillar, perhaps two stories high. A script crept delicately up its surface, and at its top, there was a statue of four lions, each head facing a different direction. It was another one of Ashoka's pillars and looked almost identical to the one Menon had seen in Kabul.

"Beautiful, isn't it?" he said.

"Magnificent," said Arjun.

As the sun fell below the horizon and shadows blanketed the city, they decided to enter the palace. As predicted, the soldiers denied them entry until Menon showed Euthydemus's royal seal.

Leaving their guards at the gate, Menon and Arjun followed a servant to the raja's audience chamber, where they found Raja Manish sitting behind a short table covered in fruit and fried snacks. Manish had long, wavy black hair that flowed down his shoulders and back. His eyes were dark and deep-set, his nose sharp, and his mouth was covered in a long and well-maintained mustache. He wore a loose-fitting white tunic, and gold ornaments covered his neck, arms, and ears.

Menon and Arjun sat on a long, flat pillow across from the raja.

"I must apologize for all of the security," said the raja. "I can never be too careful these days."

"We understand, your highness," said Menon. "These are dangerous times indeed."

After introductions, Menon explained their request for soldiers, going so far as to cite the relationship of Taxila and Bactria dating back to the time of Alexander the Great. But it was to no avail.

"I'm sorry to say no," said Manish, after a time, "but I cannot send one of my units to your king. Not this time."

"We would pay double the normal price," said Menon. He leaned forward and pulled another slice of mango from the table.

"I'm sure you would," said Manish. "I've heard of the size of Antiochus's army. But it's just not possible. We are facing an insurrection in the north, and Sophagasenus is planning something, I just know it."

Menon looked away and into the garden below. Langur monkeys chased one another through the trees, their long, thin tails whipping behind them. Their faces, ears, and hands were black, but light-gray fur covered their bodies. After studying them, Menon turned back to Manish and inhaled the raja's sandalwood perfume.

"What if we can facilitate peace between you and Sophagasenus?" said Menon. "At least for a year."

"He wouldn't stick to it."

"I'm starting to think you want war," said Menon, placing the mango peel on the table.

"Well," said Manish, "it's about time we settle our disputes over the mountain pass that connects us, don't you think?"

"But we can prevent it," said Menon. "We can secure peace between your kingdoms."

"How about I facilitate peace between your king and Antiochus?"

"Now you're mocking us," said Menon.

"No," said Manish. "But you must realize that my responsibility will always be to my people's safety. And only after that is secured can my attention turn to yours. You have been speaking to me as if Taxila is not equal to Zariaspa."

"You're right," said Menon, before looking down and breathing in slowly. "I offer our apologies."

"But we are friends," continued Manish. "So how about this?" He waved toward the wide window through which wafted the smell of spices and the sound of haggling. "Many people come in and out of the city looking for work. They're filling the streets and bothering my more sensitive subjects. I will allow you to recruit freely from them and at no cost."

"From the streets?" said Arjun, visibly shocked. "From the *streets*?"

"It is all I can offer," said Manish. "And besides, there are plenty of strong men out there who can hold one of those long spears and fill the ranks."

"I must say," said Arjun, "this is much less than what we've requested. It's almost insulting."

"Not at all," said the raja. "I am only giving you what I can."

"Then we shall take our leave," said Arjun, standing.

Menon stood, too, contemplating whether to push the issue. But, deciding against it, he followed Arjun out of the room.

An attendant led them from the palace into the large market beyond the palace gate. This market was more extensive than Zariaspa's. Just like at home, though, vendors called and joked. The only significant difference Menon noticed was the lack of Greek. Here, people conversed in a variety of local languages that he did not understand.

With the soldiers surrounding Menon and Arjun, they stuck out among the crowd. Many people gave them a wide berth, but others called to them, clearly understanding that Arjun and Menon could afford many, if not all, of the items on sale.

Upon entering the royal guesthouse, Menon sat with Arjun in the courtyard. The architecture reminded him of the palace of Zariaspa.

"What do you think we should do?" said Menon as he studied the stars.

"Well," said Arjun, "it'd be a shame to come all this way for nothing."

"You really want to recruit from the streets? I can't help but think that Raja Manish wants us to purchase his bandit problem."

Arjun smirked.

"You know I came from the streets, right? I had to go somewhere when my parents died."

Menon blushed and looked away. "I'm sorry, Arjun. I meant nothing by it."

"No need to apologize," he said. "But yes, I'm willing to try. It's that or go home with no one."

"Well," said Menon, "we could always purchase more elephants."

"We can certainly try," said Arjun. "But if Manish is really mobilizing for war, he may have placed a ban on selling elephants."

Menon rubbed his face with the palms of his hands. His fingers were yellow from the food they had eaten at the palace.

"Alright, let's get some rest," said Menon. "We'll start recruiting in the morning."

He went to bed haunted by his failed attempts to secure an alliance with Sophagasenus and to acquire soldiers from Manish. He hadn't imagined both could fall through. Now, he could only hope the prince had reached Maracanda safely and that Laodice had provided the requested soldiers. If not, the future looked grim.

CHAPTER TWENTY-SEVEN

Demetrius

"Demetrius, wake up."

Demetrius opened his eyes to Roshan's silhouette against the rising sun.

"They're asking for you."

Demetrius looked through the wooden bars at a Scythian man.

"Come," said the man, as he opened the door.

Demetrius looked from Ashok to Roshan to Phlotas. He passed through the door and followed the Scythian to the corridor that bisected the settlement. Reaching it, he eyed the large tent.

"Are you taking me to your chief?" said Demetrius.

The man was silent.

Demetrius saw the woman from the steppe standing beside the door.

"Beleen," said the man, nodding at the woman.

So that's her name, thought Demetrius, as the woman opened the door and strode in. Demetrius followed her into a crowded room. He had never seen so much gold. The Scythians' extensive use of it had been one of his biggest surprises since leaving home. He had always imagined them as covered in the skins of their enemies.

Soldiers lined the walls, some swaying back and forth, causing the gold they wore to sparkle in the firelight.

The chief sat on a wooden throne decorated with gold foil. He was a large man, and his grin widened his already broad face. As he moved his head, his beard swayed beneath his chin.

When Demetrius came to a stop before the throne, an attendant stepped forward and spoke.

"Traveler," he said in Greek. "Identify yourself and your business in the lands of Kulka."

"I am Prince Demetrius, son of Euthydemus, king of Bactria, and I seek an audience with your majesty," said Demetrius, drawing closer to the throne.

Kulka leaned forward. "And what is it that you want, Prince Demetrius?"

"I want peace between my people and yours."

"Peace is a strange offering coming from a people who attack us relentlessly," said Kulka. "We've heard what happened to the traders who reached Maracanda."

"That was a mistake," said Demetrius. "And one that will be rectified. Believe me. I want peace between us."

"And what would we get?"

Demetrius was surprised by how quickly the conversation had moved to details. "Exception from our trade customs for ten years," he said, hoping it was a reasonable offer.

The chief scoffed, then whispered with a brightly dressed woman beside him.

"Not enough," he said, to Demetrius.

"We guard the gateways to India and its vast markets," said Demetrius. "We can open that for you."

"And what if we want more than trade?" said Kulka. "What if we want land?"

"There is plenty of land on the steppe," said Demetrius.

"Is there?" said Kulka, looking at the ceiling. He breathed slowly, then brought his gaze back to Demetrius. "There is war north of us," he said. "And this war has pushed the northern people south and onto our land. If we could fight them all, we would. But we cannot."

Demetrius stood silently, waiting. He knew where Kulka intended to push the conversation.

"My people have nowhere to go but south," Kulka finally said. "And as far as we can see, there is plenty of room in the south. There is better land for grazing. More people and animals can survive there. We want a piece of that land. That is my price for peace."

Demetrius looked at the floor. He thought about Antiochus's invasion and the possibility of war with the Scythians. Sacrifices were required if the kingdom was to survive. Even large sacrifices.

"We can provide land. But on one condition." Demetrius knew his next words could undermine a conversion that had thus far gone surprisingly well. But with Kulka appearing open to discussion and with Bactria at risk of annexation by the Seleucids, he thought the risk of appearing weak was worth it. "The condition is that you and your people join Bactria in war against a common foe."

Kulka smirked. "You're not as strong as we thought, it would seem."

"We're more than strong enough for you," said Demetrius, firmly.

Again, Kulka whispered with the woman beside him.

"And this foe being?" he said, at last.

"Antiochus III, the Seleucid emperor."

"I see," said Kulka. "And to what end?"

"To protect both of our lands from domination by a foreign power."

"You are a foreign power," Kulka quipped.

"I am no more foreign than you. I was born in Bactria just as you were born on the steppe."

Kulka didn't respond.

"If your people want a safe home south of here," continued Demetrius, "near the mountains or beyond them, you will face this foe, as well as their new ally, Parthia."

A murmur rippled through the crowd.

"You say that Parthia is their ally?"

"Yes," said Demetrius. "And they may soon ride through your land. Presumably to get to us. But who knows? They just might stay."

"And you think we can hold them back?"

"I know you can," said Demetrius. "After all, your people have beaten all invaders from the south."

"Including your Alexander," said the chief.

"Including Alexander," said Demetrius.

Kulka breathed deeply and slowly, and the woman beside him whispered in his ear.

"We'll have to work out the details," said Kulka, exhaling. "But you have a deal."

Whispers permeated the room, and Demetrius's heart pounded. He had been surprised to gain peace so quickly, let alone this.

Kulka waved to an attendant and spoke to him in a Scythian language. The man nodded and left the tent.

"We have a tradition to solidify alliances," said Kulka, by way of explanation. "We are to unite ourselves with blood."

Demetrius's heart beat faster.

"Nothing too ominous," Kulka added with a laugh.

The man returned, holding a small golden bowl full of milk. The servant placed the bowl in front of Kulka's decorated shoes.

"It is important that you and I keep our promises," said Kulka, stepping down from the throne. "The fates of our peoples depend upon it."

He pulled a knife from his belt. The blade was shined iron, and the handle was gem-spotted gold. He placed the weapon against his palm and dragged it toward him. A line of blood followed. Kulka lifted his hand and let a few drops of blood fall into the milk. Each drop added a crimson splash to the white.

"Your turn," said Kulka, extending his arm, blade in hand.

Demetrius took the blood-covered knife. Though in no mood to slice open his hand, Demetrius placed the blade against his palm and pulled it back in one smooth motion. Blood flowed freely from his skin and into the milk, which turned pink.

"Now we drink," said Kulka.

Demetrius had been afraid of that. But without hesitation, he picked up the bowl and drank the blood-infused milk. He tried to ignore the taste, and he kept his eyes locked on Kulka's.

He handed the bowl to the chief with some of the pink liquid remaining. Kulka lifted the bowl, nodded, and drank the rest.

"It is done, then," said Kulka, handing the empty bowl to a servant. "Our peoples are as one."

Demetrius nodded, still in shock at how quickly he had secured a deal.

"Tonight we celebrate," said Kulka. "We shall drink in honor of our upcoming victory against Antiochus and his Parthian allies."

"You must do one other thing," said Demetrius, stepping forward.

"We'll see," said Kulka, sitting back on his throne.

"You must let me bury my men."

Kulka nodded. "I will have their bodies brought to you."

"Thank you," said Demetrius.

Beleen led him from the tent and to the cage, where the others were released.

"How did it go?" said Roshan.

"There's a lot to tell you," said Demetrius. He placed one hand on Roshan's shoulder, and the other on Ashok's. "But first things first." He smiled and looked from them to Phlotas. "We're free."

CHAPTER TWENTY-EIGHT

Beleen

After leaving the Greek prince with his comrades, Beleen returned to Kulka's tent. She found the chief alone on his throne.

"Alora left?" she said.

"Yes," Kulka said. "And I'm not sure if that indicates her feelings about the alliance, but what is done is done."

"Are you sure that war with the Seleucids is a good idea?" Beleen removed her hat. "I can't help but feel we've only added to the pressures we face."

"I'm afraid we don't have much of a choice," said Kulka. "We need to move south. And besides, we have much to gain from studying the Greek way of war. I have my doubts about how long our peace with them will last."

"Yes, my chief," said Beleen, impressed by Kulka's forethought and fearful about what those thoughts suggested for the future.

"You know, Beleen," said Kulka, "your efforts over the past weeks have not gone unnoticed. Alora was impressed with the new settlement that you and Tul organized."

"Thank you, my chief."

"And because of that," continued Kulka, "I ask that you lead our forces south and into war against the western invader."

Beleen lowered her gaze, using the moment to catch her breath. "It's an honor," she said, looking up. She had waited years to be given such an opportunity.

"But I should note," said Kulka, "that though the Parthians are our enemies, you cannot let your animosity toward them cloud your judgment on the battlefield."

Beleen thought of her brother's dead body on the steppe. By the time she had reached it, vultures had torn out his eyes.

"Understood, my chief," she said.

"Good," said Kulka. "Now, if you'll excuse me, I must prepare for the feast."

Beleen bowed and as she stepped outside, she wiped tears from her cheeks and stood straight. Her past was past. Her future awaited.

CHAPTER TWENTY-NINE

Demetrius

"Just so I'm clear," said Phlotas, sitting across from Demetrius in the tent that had been provided for them, "how did you get the Scythians to not only agree to peace, but also to join us against Antiochus?"

Everyone was watching Demetrius, and he knew his answer would be poorly received. But he had made his decision. He said, "I promised them land in the south."

Phlotas threw his hands up and looked to the others. "You gave them our land?" he spat. "To secure an alliance? That hardly seems worth it."

"An alliance with them is no small thing," said Demetrius. "You know how they fight. Either way, the warriors are a bonus. We came here to secure peace so we can concentrate our forces on the more immediate threat from Antiochus."

"But you gave them our land," said Phlotas, standing. "We told those in Maracanda that we'd stop the attacks, not that we'd bring the attackers closer."

"I'm afraid those two things go hand in hand," said Demetrius, standing as well. "The Scythians need land. They're being pushed from the north. If giving them land brings peace to their realm and to ours, then so be it."

"Mark my words," said Phlotas, his face red. "If the north pushes now, it will push again. And soon enough, these Scythians will be our enemies, and they will attack our home."

"Perhaps," said Demetrius. "But for now, we must ensure that we have a home to fight for."

Phlotas threw his arms up again and sighed.

"Enough of this," said Demetrius, turning toward the door. "Let's join the feast. We've been in this tent long enough."

Demetrius lifted the tent's fabric flap. Dropping it, he turned back. "And Phlotas," he said. "We may be far from home, and your family may hold influence with my father, but you will never speak to me like that again."

After a pause, Phlotas lowered his head. "Yes, your majesty," he said.

"Good. Now let's go."

Demetrius stepped into the chilly evening. The feast was only a moment's walk away.

In front of Kulka's tent, long wooden tables stood covered in food. Scythians swooped around them, pulling items into their bowls like birds clawing at a carcass. There were piles of fresh fruit, their source a complete mystery to Demetrius, a row of different species of fowl, and an entire cow roasting over a fire.

Demetrius watched his men hover beside the table. They took turns approaching it and pulling back. Only after Roshan grabbed from the food did Ashok and Phlotas do the same.

"I believe we have enough variety for you to find something to your liking," said Kulka, coming up to Demetrius.

"I have no doubt," said Demetrius, a little in awe of the display. "How long until your warriors are ready to move south?" he asked. He didn't want the festivities to distract him from his duty.

"I've already sent messengers to the other tribes," said Kulka. "But it will take a few days for our warriors to arrive. It is important that we wait for every tribe. Each one must show their loyalty to my call."

"Very well," said Demetrius. "But please know that the longer we wait, the more prepared our enemy becomes."

"Certainly," said Kulka.

"One more thing," said Demetrius. "I'd like you to send messengers to Maracanda to report the alliance."

"And how can you promise that my messengers won't hang from the walls of that city?"

"Bring the dispatch to me," said Demetrius, "and I'll stamp it with my seal. Your messengers will be respected."

"Very well," said Kulka. "Now, I'd like to introduce you to someone."

Kulka whispered to his attendant, who moved away, and in a moment, Demetrius saw a tall woman approach—the same woman who had been standing beside Kulka in the tent. Tattoos covered her cheeks and forehead, and gold jewelry fell from a diadem that sat atop her blond hair. As she stopped beside Kulka, Demetrius caught a glance from her grass-green eyes.

"This is Alora," said Kulka, stepping back to make room between Demetrius and the woman. "She is from the west. I thought you'd want to meet her, as she often trades with your Greek cousins on the coast of the Black Sea."

The chieftain turned to Alora. He said something in their language and then switched to Greek. "And this is Demetrius, son of Euthydemus, the Greek king in Bactria."

"It is an honor to meet you," said Alora, bowing.

"Likewise," said Demetrius.

"I must note," said Alora, "that you dress differently from your cousins in the west." She pointed at the gold bracelets on Demetrius's hands and his dangling earrings.

"I can only imagine," said Demetrius. "It's been over a hundred years since my people left their homes in Greece to travel with the great Alexander."

"And much has changed in your home since your departure," said Alora. "My people have watched with great interest as the Greeks have fallen from their impressive heritage. We have also watched the rise of Rome. Philip, the king of Macedonia, is at war with them over his alliance with Carthage."

Demetrius had heard little of the Roman polity. Emissaries and merchants came to Zariaspa with reports of the Roman war with Carthage, but the information was cursory.

"I understand," said Alora, "that you and your people are now enemies of Antiochus. Surely you don't think you can beat him."

"We can beat him, and we will," said Demetrius, irritated by the slight. He nodded to Kulka. "And with the help of our northern allies no less."

"Will you meet him in open battle or wait for a siege?" said Alora.

"Whichever comes first," said Demetrius, feigning confidence. "I believe that even a bloody nose will send Antiochus home. He can ill afford to stay in this region for long. Ptolemy of Egypt will only hold back for so long."

"I hope you're right, Greek. For your sake." She looked to Kulka. "And for his."

She spoke with Kulka in their language before walking away.

"Alora has a way with words," said Demetrius.

"She has no reason to mince them," said the chief. "She comes to us from the master tribe."

"Beleen mentioned something about that," said Demetrius.

"Yes," said Kulka. "Just as Beleen and my warriors swear allegiance to me, my people swear allegiance to hers."

"And have they ever called upon that obligation?"

"Not in a long time," said Kulka. "But their leader is old. It's widely believed that his sons will go to war once he dies. I'm worried such a contest will pull my people into the killing."

"And you will have to go?"

"Of course," said Kulka. "We honor our commitments, even unto death. The same is true of our commitment to your king. And I hope it is true of your commitment to us."

"Yes, of course," said Demetrius, beginning to fear he had promised something his father might not give.

"Very well," said Kulka. "I will leave you to the party."

Kulka bowed his head and walked into the embrace of the crowd.

Scanning the gathering, Demetrius saw a line forming beside a small tent. Smoke billowed from a hole at its top. The tent flap opened and a man stumbled out, extending his arms to the sky. He twisted in place and fell to the ground, laughing.

"What do you think he's doing?" said Ashok, stepping beside Demetrius.

"There must be something in the smoke," said Demetrius.

"There is." Beleen joined them. Her hair was thicker than before and seemed interwoven with red fabric. It was pulled into a knot at the top of her head.

"The smoke is a gateway to our ancestors and gods," she said. "People breathe it in, and guided by the priestesses, they go to a middle ground, a space between this world and the next."

Demetrius thought of the priestesses. From everything he had seen, they were all men, although dressed and adorned as women.

"Have you ever been inside?" Demetrius said, looking from Beleen to the tent, where a woman disappeared into its embrace.

"Long ago. But I didn't like what I saw, and I haven't gone in since." She sighed and turned to Demetrius. "I admire the way you spoke with Kulka. You spoke with much regard for your people."

Demetrius lowered his gaze and then looked up at her.

"Is Kulka a good man?" he asked. "Will he keep his word?"

"He will," said Beleen. "Will your people keep yours?"

"I'm not saying it will be easy," said Demetrius. "But I am confident that they will."

"I hope so. Our people see blood promises as unbreakable."

Demetrius nodded.

"Will you drink with me in celebration?" said Beleen.

As Demetrius thought of the milk-based alcohol that he'd tried earlier, his mind flashed with images of his dead comrades on the steppe. Beleen had been one of their killers. His mind then went to Laodice. Her choice to execute the Scythian traders had caused all of this killing.

"No," he said. "I should rest for the funerals tomorrow."

Without staying to hear her response, Demetrius left the gathering. His chest hurt and his stomach was knotted. The deaths of his men weighed heavily on his conscience.

Yet, he felt some weight lift from his mind as he entered his tent. It was dimly lit and calming. Carpets covered the floors and walls, giving the room a welcoming aura.

After removing his dirty clothes, Demetrius settled into bed and pulled the scratchy fur blanket over his chest. Then the pains and regrets of his men's deaths came back to him. As tears rolled down his face, Demetrius hoped the treaty was worth their sacrifice.

CHAPTER THIRTY

Beleen

Beleen watched sparks fly from the central bonfire. Men and women, drunk with excitement and magic fumes, stumbled around the flames. Some tried to coordinate their movements with the rhythmic music of eagle-bone flutes and ox-horn drums, while others wobbled around aimlessly.

Beleen spotted one of the soldiers who had accompanied the Greek prince—one she had noted earlier for his beauty. Roshan. That was his name.

"You're not a Greek, are you?" she said, drawing up alongside him.

Roshan turned to fully face her, the flames reflected in his green eyes. "What makes you say that?"

His frame was large and imposing, and the bronze cuirass he wore was shaped like the muscles of a god.

"I don't know," she said. "You don't look like the prince." She pointed at his long black beard.

"Someone once said that being Greek is not about blood," said Roshan. "It's about outlook."

"Then perhaps *I'm* a Greek." Beleen smiled. Then she remembered the story of the beheaded Scyles and looked down.

"Perhaps you could become one," said Roshan, adding to Beleen's anxiety. "But is that why you came over here? To discuss being Greek?"

"No, not exactly," said Beleen, wanting to move on from the conversation. In truth, she wasn't sure why she had approached. She only knew that she wanted to speak with him. "I guess I'm wondering what it is like to live among the Greeks," said Beleen, unable to find a quick change of subject. "I imagine there are many things to get used to."

"You're joining the warriors?" said Roshan.

"I'm leading them," said Beleen, both proud and offended.

"Well, there's a difference already," said Roshan. "Women in the south don't perform the same tasks that they perform here."

"That's their loss," said Beleen.

"If all women fight like you," said Roshan, "then it certainly is."

"And the prince," said Beleen. "What is he like?"

"You've seen him speak, haven't you?" said Roshan. "He speaks his mind, and he speaks the truth. At least, that's what I've seen so far."

Beleen nodded, hoping for more.

"Demetrius is different from other people," continued Roshan. "He's idealistic but not naïve. It's hard to describe. But I'm sure you'll learn soon enough."

"I'm sure I will," said Beleen, thinking of the many days she would ride with the Greeks on their way to war.

"I must go and prepare," said Roshan. "We're to bury our comrades tomorrow, but you know that."

Beleen locked eyes with him. "I'm sorry about what happened to your companions," she said. "I am sorry for my part in it."

"Thank you for saying so," he said, tears welling at his eyelids. "One of them was a good friend."

"I've lost people, too," said Beleen, feeling guilty. "Not to Greek arms. But I know the feeling of loss. My brother was killed last year in a skirmish with the Parthians." Beleen paused. "Do your people believe in life after death?" she asked.

"They do," said Roshan. "Although, if I'm being honest, I'm not sure what I believe, exactly."

"Then I guess you and I are similar," said Beleen.

"I guess so," said Roshan.

There was a pause.

"I should get some rest," said Roshan, taking a breath. "Good night, Beleen."

He turned and disappeared into the crowd.

"Good night, Roshan," Beleen whispered.

CHAPTER THIRTY-ONE

Roshan

Waking the next morning, Roshan opened his eyes and shifted his gaze from the fabric ceiling to the center of the tent, where Demetrius was quietly putting a golden diadem on his head.

"I should look presentable for the funerals," said Demetrius, not looking up. "We may be far from home, but we must play our part."

Roshan sat up. "They'll be honored that the prince presides over their funerals," he said.

Roshan thought of Feroze. His funeral would be nothing like the Zoroastrian funerals in Zariaspa. But Roshan would do his best. His friend deserved it.

Roshan pushed against the scratchy feeling in his throat. He hadn't slept well. All night, he had twisted in bed, sometimes too cold and sometimes too hot. He didn't want to admit it, but Beleen had been on his mind before he fell asleep and then again as he awoke.

"Ready?" said Demetrius, looking from one man to the next. When his gaze landed on Roshan, Roshan nodded and stood.

"Let's do this," he said. Phlotas and Ashok nodded, too.

Roshan and the others walked to the wagon at the edge of camp where the bodies of their comrades were collected. The Scythians had wrapped each of them in white cloth.

Roshan cried when he saw Feroze. The Scythians had placed his distinctive helmet on his chest. With its unique, wing-shaped cheek guards, the helmet had been one of Feroze's most prized possessions. But their faith did not allow Feroze to be laid to rest with it, and so Roshan set it aside. He would wear it into battle in honor of his friend.

"Alright," said Roshan, wiping his cheeks. "Let's get moving."

As the men hefted the bodies from the wagon, Roshan scanned the horizon until his gaze settled on a tall rock at the top of a hill. It would have to do.

CHAPTER THIRTY-TWO

Beleen

Later that morning, Beleen sat in Tul's tent, deep in thought.

"I've never seen anything like it," she said. "They just left him there."

"What do you mean, left him there?" asked Tul, glancing up from repairing his bow.

"They took his body to the top of the hill," said Beleen. "They placed it flat on a tall rock, and then they left it there."

"Was there any ceremony?"

"I'm not sure. They seemed to say a few words, but from where I was standing, I couldn't be sure." Beleen pressed her memory, but couldn't recall further details.

"Interesting," said Tul.

"I didn't know what to think," said Beleen. "When they came down the hill, the vultures were already circling."

"And what did they do with the other bodies?"

"They burned them."

"So they burned most of them and then left one on the hill?"

"Exactly." Beleen nodded. "It seemed like a punishment."

"Or maybe an honor," said Tul.

"Perhaps," said Beleen, thinking of their own burial customs.

"I think this will be a good one," said Tul, lifting his bow and pulling the string. "I just need to give it some practice."

"How about we hunt?" said Beleen.

"I wish," said Tul. "But Kulka has me doing work with the council. How about you ask the Greeks to go with you?"

Beleen laughed, though it was an intriguing idea. Her mind settled on Roshan.

"I'll ask them," she said, her heartbeat quickening.

"Really?" said Tul. "I was only joking."

"Yes, really," said Beleen. "It might reduce some of the tension between us."

Before searching for the Bactrians, Beleen collected her horse, Kasen, from a walled pasture set aside for the battle horses. Kasen was light brown and his mane was cut short. Beleen placed a simple green saddlecloth across his back, and secured atop it a saddle of wood, wool, and leather. Last, she attached the bridle of bone to the horse's mouth and head.

She found the four men from Bactria just outside the settlement walls. They were leaning against a fence, watching a flock of hundreds of white-fleeced sheep. On the horizon beyond them, a massive wall of clouds rose into the sky, until its white curves blended with the sun's blinding radiance.

"Demetrius!" Beleen called.

Demetrius turned to her. As she came to a stop, he pointed at the sheep.

"I don't think I've seen so many animals in one place before," he said. "It's impressive."

"I will share your kind words with Kulka," said Beleen. "He's been building this flock for years. I first learned how to use a bow so I could protect them from predators, both animal and human."

Demetrius nodded.

"So," said Beleen. "I am going hunting, and I think you and the others should join."

Demetrius paused. He was torn between becoming too familiar with the Scythians and needing to get to know his new allies.

"What animal shall we hunt?" he finally said.

Beleen didn't know the Greek word for the animal she had in mind, so she placed her hands above her head, palms forward, and pulled up her lip to reveal her front teeth.

Roshan, who still leaned against the fence, laughed.

"What's so funny?" She blushed.

Roshan smiled. "That's an excellent representation."

"What is this animal called?" Beleen asked, quickly.

"It's a hare," said Demetrius. "We have those, too."

"Well," said Beleen. "We are to hunt hare, then."

The man called Phlotas pushed away from the fence. "I'll be in the tent."

"Sure you don't want to hunt?" asked Demetrius.

"I'm sure," said Phlotas, glaring at Beleen.

She returned the look as he walked away.

"Don't worry about him," said Demetrius, turning to Beleen. "He will take time to adjust to our alliance."

Beleen nodded and her expression softened. "You know how to handle a bow?" she said, glancing between them.

"We do," said Demetrius. He grabbed a bow that had been leaning against the wooden fence. Roshan picked up another. The bows were similar to hers, made from a combination of wood and animal sinew. The bow that Ashok retrieved, however, was at least twice the length of hers, and seemed to be made of a single piece of wood.

"Your people are not the only ones to have mastered this art," said Roshan.

He drew an arrow from his quiver, placed it on the string, and pulled back. After failing to find a suitable target, he slowly released the tension on the bow.

"I better not waste an arrow," he said.

"Of course," said Beleen. But she was convinced that his skills were lacking.

Beleen led them away from the settlement and toward the well-watered banks of the Jaxartes River.

"This is the perfect place to find our prey," she said, looking at hills of dry, yellowing grass.

She moved into the damp dirt and foliage and scanned the horizon. Each hill seemed to invite exploration, offering the possibility of something new and exciting beyond.

It took them over an hour to spot a hare, and when they did, Beleen missed. Her chosen arrow, which was painted red and topped with a hooked bronze arrowhead, landed just behind the running animal. To make matters worse, it was Roshan who finally downed it. Demetrius and Ashok, who seemed to find the situation amusing, peeled away and left Beleen alone with Roshan.

"Good aim," she said, jutting her chin at the bow.

"Luck," he said, a faint smile now on his face.

Beleen blushed and looked away.

When she turned back to Roshan, her eyes locked with his. Neither of them blinked. Beleen's heartbeat quickened and her breathing slowed.

"I should join the others." Roshan looked away.

"Of course," she said, glancing at Demetrius and Ashok. They led their horses along the riverbank, the wall of clouds behind them. As Beleen watched Roshan ride away, her cheeks prickled.

Later, as Beleen led the others back to the settlement, they spotted a group of shaggy gray saiga antelope. The animals had tall, pointed horns that twisted like seashells. This time, Beleen's arrow pierced a saiga through the shoulder, and it fell after a single leap.

"That's a big one," said Demetrius. "How are we going to bring it back? We didn't bring rope."

"I'd be happy to place it on my horse," said Roshan, stepping forward. "I could use the walk."

"No," said Beleen, glancing at Roshan. "I don't need help. I can do it on my own."

"No doubt," said Roshan. "But if you want the help, just let me know."

Beleen struggled to pull the animal onto Kasen's back. The horse slapped his front hooves against the ground in annoyance.

"Just stay still," she hissed.

Roshan shifted his gaze to the horizon.

After securing the antelope, Beleen grabbed Kasen's reins and led him toward the settlement. As they approached, she saw a column of riders in the distance.

"The warriors are arriving," she called to Demetrius.

"Excellent," cried Demetrius. "We need to leave soon if we're to stop Antiochus."

Beleen still had doubts about joining Bactria's fight against the Seleucid emperor. If they lost the war, wouldn't her people be punished? She wondered if Antiochus was a forgiving man. She had her doubts.

CHAPTER THIRTY-THREE

Antiochus

Antiochus rearranged his position on his horse. For hours, he had been riding up and down the column along the mountain path. "It is important that soldiers see their monarch," he had told Dropidas when questioned. "Especially when they're being asked to leave home and fight."

He considered the long line of men walking two or three wide. They carried their long spears against their shoulders and their personal items on their backs, while pack animals at the end of the column pulled the materials needed to set up camp. Everyone's armor was covered in dirt, and in some places, blood. The journey through the mountains had been much harder than anticipated. The armies, both Seleucid and Parthian, had lost many men and supplies.

"Your majesty." Dropidas rode toward him at a trot, and when he pulled his horse to a stop, the horse's hooves kicked dust into the air. The earthy smell filled Antiochus's nostrils.

"Your majesty," said Dropidas, "the king of Kabul, Sophagasenus, has sent his messengers. They are resting just ahead."

"Take me to them," said Antiochus. "And never call him a king again. He is not a king. He is nothing more than a wayward vassal in need of guidance."

As Antiochus and Dropidas rode to the front of the column, Antiochus studied the pebble-covered hills around them. Except for a few small shrubs, they were mostly bare of vegetation. At the top of a small hill, Antiochus saw a group of horsemen wearing an array of armor that ranged from leather to wicker to metal. They had bows strapped to their backs, quivers at their thighs, and spears in their hands. They removed their bronze helmets as he approached.

"Your highness," said one rider. "Sophagasenus, the king of Kabul, welcomes you."

The title of king infuriated Antiochus, but this time, he chose to ignore it. Instead, he sent the messengers back with demands that Sophagasenus open the hay stores for the army's pack animals and clear the fields for his soldiers.

Before long, Antiochus and his army moved out of the mountain pass and into a wide valley. Here, humble mud-brick homes covered much of the land. Among them rose more significant buildings, with pillars of smoke identifying many as temples. The city was bustling, and on his way through, Antiochus passed three lively markets, where street performers evidenced their craft.

Antiochus approached the fortress citadel, which was made of yellowish stone and rose to about three stories. Rounded embrasures guarded its walkways, and archers stood watching through gaps between the rocks.

Something caught Antiochus's eye: a giant elephant. It stood in the middle of a moat bridge, a red blanket draped across its rotund body. Two men sat on its back. The driver of the elephant, the mahout, sat on the animal's neck. He wore a white loincloth and held a wooden staff topped with a metal spike. Behind the mahout, a man sat on a shimmering blue pillow. Antiochus supposed the man to be Sophagasenus. There was a wooden railing around him, from which a stake rose to hold an umbrella. Gold ornaments dangled from the umbrella's edge like fruit from a tree.

Stopping before the elephant, Antiochus turned to one of the local attendants and asked that Sophagasenus step down from the animal and join him in conversation.

The attendant rode into the shadow of the elephant, where he spoke with Sophagasenus. After a pause, the animal bent its knees and lowered to the ground. Sophagasenus descended to the dusty bridge. He then mounted a horse and brought it to a stop in front of Antiochus.

Sophagasenus was a tall man with shallow shoulders. A black mustache sat on his angular face, and his hazel eyes radiated within deep sockets. He wore jewelry on his neck, wrists, and fingers, and a gold crown, inlaid with lapis lazuli, sat atop his wavy, shoulder-length hair.

"Welcome to Kabul, your majesty," said Sophagasenus. "It is a pleasure to welcome you to our home."

"An unexpected one, I'm sure," said Antiochus.

"Unexpected, yes," said Sophagasenus, offering a weak smile. "But you are a most welcome guest. While your men settle into the areas we've prepared for them, I hope you and your companions will join me for dinner."

"Excellent," said Antiochus. "We will."

Later that night, after making their way through the citadel's successive rings of defense, Antiochus and his entourage entered an entertainment parlor. Sophagasenus directed them to pillows on the floor. Antiochus sat on a purple cushion, leaned back, and placed his weight on his left arm. He watched a peacock weave between the potted plants in the courtyard beside them. Its turquoise-and-blue tail feathers dragged on the ground behind it, picking up dry leaves as it went.

"If I remember correctly," said Antiochus, "you're a bit of a mix. Your ancestors came from Macedonia, but your grandmother came from India. Is that correct?"

"That is correct, your highness," said Sophagasenus, leaning against a pillow. "It is a heritage that has served me well."

"But it seems to have convinced you that you're something special," said Antiochus. He was not interested in pleasantries. "Something outside of the fold. But let me assure you, you are still very much my subject. Your father and grandfather may have sworn loyalty to the Mauryans, but the Mauryans are not here anymore. And before them, your people owed allegiance to me."

"They did many things in their times. Things that I have done differently in mine."

"So you view autonomy from the empire as a permanent affair?" said Antiochus, waving away a servant who offered him wine. "I must admit, I believed that you did not understand your obligations to me. The obligations of your people. In which case, I am here to remind you of them. You, Sophagasenus, are my vassal. But this relationship should not feel burdensome. You can still run the affairs of your valley as you see fit. However, moving forward, your army will answer my calls for soldiers, and your treasury will contribute to mine."

He turned to Phriapa.

"The Parthians were my enemies only days ago. And now we are friends. Isn't that so, Phriapa?"

"As you say," said Phriapa, clearly with difficulty.

"You must know," said Sophagasenus, eyeing Antiochus, "that my generals and soldiers will find it difficult to leave home to fight in your wars in Egypt. What quarrel do they have with the Egyptians?"

"Perhaps they have no quarrel in Egypt," said Antiochus. "That is understandable. But your people should have an interest in the empire's health."

"Why?" said Sophagasenus.

Antiochus heard a laugh and glared at Phriapa.

"I understand that you have an interest in lands controlled by Taxila," said Antiochus, looking back to Sophagasenus. Even without Phriapa distracting him, Antiochus felt more tested than he'd anticipated. He had a massive army outside, after all.

"This is true," said Sophagasenus. "They control much of the mountain pass that leads to India, and they disrupt our trade at will."

"And you have fought with the soldiers of Taxila, have you not?"

"Only minor skirmishes," said Sophagasenus.

"Once I have taken care of Bactria," said Antiochus, "I will help you secure the lands you desire."

Sophagasenus stroked his beard and looked at the ceiling. Antiochus found him exceptionally hard to read.

"What interest do you have in helping us with this?" said Sophagasenus.

"The empire has every interest in securing its borders and controlling trade. Right now, much trade happens north, above the mountains and among the Scythians. It makes them rich and they use their riches to attack our settlements. We must allow for more trade along our domains. You and your people can be part of it. And I should note that further connection with the empire will make you very rich."

Sophagasenus sat quietly and sipped from his cup. Antiochus clenched his jaw, realizing he had allowed himself to negotiate instead of dictating his terms.

"Your elephants," he said. "I want them."

"Each elephant has taken years to train," said Sophagasenus, setting the cup down. "But if sending them with you gets your army moving from my land, so be it."

"My land," said Antiochus.

"How about you take care of Bactria first?" said Sophagasenus, sitting straight. "And then we can talk about what is and isn't your land. After all, taking Bactria will be much more difficult than burning down an innocent village."

Antiochus thought he heard Phriapa let out another laugh.

"News travels fast," added Sophagasenus.

After collecting his thoughts and composure, Antiochus spoke, "Believe me, my friend. I will be back, and that conversation will be had."

"Till then," said Sophagasenus, "I wish you well. But for now, let us eat."

"Very well," said Antiochus. "Bring the food."

As Antiochus ate with Sophagasenus, they spoke of the grains harvested in the valley and the game that roamed it. It wasn't long before Antiochus felt as if they were two friends conversing, but he knew that feeling was a mirage. His counterpart was certainly analyzing everything he said and did for weakness and opportunity. After all, Antiochus was doing the same thing.

A selection of local and foreign wines followed dessert. Antiochus was particularly interested in a wine imported from Spain, near the Pillars of Hercules.

"It's a wonder you're able to get wine from Spain," said Antiochus. "Not only must it travel across Asia, it must pass through a war."

"From what I've heard," said Sophagasenus, "the Romans sent a talented general to Spain to fight the Carthaginians. Scipio is his name, I believe. Such interesting names among the Romans."

Antiochus thought of Rome's war with Carthage. If either of them destroyed the other, it would only be a matter of time before the victor's gaze turned east.

"Do you fear you will have to face Rome in war?" said Sophagasenus, as if reading Antiochus's mind.

"No," Antiochus lied. "And even if we did, no army can stand up to my phalanx."

As Antiochus spoke, a Seleucid messenger entered the room. He wore a simple purple tunic, clasped at the waist with a leather belt. With both Antiochus's and Sophagasenus's permission, he approached.

"What is it?" Antiochus pushed himself from the pillow and straightened his back.

"We've received news from our spies in Merv."

"And?"

"And," said the messenger, "Euthydemus is there with the army."

"Euthydemus? In Merv?" Antiochus glared at Phriapa. "How did you miss this during your reconnaissance?"

"Don't be ridiculous," said Phriapa. "We couldn't get close enough to tell whether Euthydemus was there."

As Antiochus opened his mouth to protest, Dropidas cut him off.

"Phriapa is right," he said. "Our men missed it, too."

Antiochus looked from Dropidas to Phriapa, not sure against whom he should direct his fury.

"Perhaps he aims to attack our supply depot at Saddarvazeh," said Dropidas. He looked to Phriapa. "Or maybe he intends to force the Parthians from their alliance."

"Or," said Phriapa, glaring at Dropidas, "he could mean to come here, to meet us in the mountains, away from familiar refuge. But that assumes that he knows we're here."

"Let's attack Zariaspa then," said Dropidas, "It will be lightly defended."

"No, we won't go to Zariaspa," said Antiochus. "I want to fight Euthydemus as soon as possible. Sieges take time and money. A single battle in the field can bring this unfortunate episode to a close. And while Euthydemus waits at Merv, we can also link with Arsak's growing forces from Saddarvazeh."

Antiochus felt a smile pull his lips apart.

"Phriapa," he said, turning to the Parthian prince, "I need you to ride to Saddarvazeh and tell your father to mobilize the army he's been assembling. We can draw Euthydemus from Merv and crush him from both sides. And once you've spoken with him, harass the enemy as much as you can. If they move, either here or back to Zariaspa, you need to slow them down while we approach."

"I'd be happy to leave immediately," said Phriapa.

Antiochus found his tone, as always, infuriatingly difficult to read.

"And one more thing," said Antiochus. Phriapa turned. "Dropidas will join you."

Dropidas failed to suppress his surprise and dismay.

"As you wish," Phriapa finally said, turning away.

After Phriapa and Dropidas—both clearly annoyed—left the room, Antiochus faced Sophagasenus. "Now, how about more wine?"

As Antiochus waited for his cup to be filled, he thought of the Bactrians. They would soon be surrounded and alone. There was no one to help them. No one at all.

CHAPTER THIRTY-FOUR

Demetrius

"The Scythians are gathering," said Ashok, who stood within the tent's entrance flap.

Demetrius, lying in bed, looked to him. "I'm sure they're just here to wish well those coming south with us."

Still, he got up and walked over to the tent door to lift the flap fully. The sky was gray, and men, women, and children gathered near Kulka's tent. A few of them wore bronze helmets atop their fabric caps.

Having sweat under heavy fur blankets all night, Demetrius embraced the chilly morning air. After dressing, he led his companions into the crowd, which, person by person, stepped aside at their approach. When they reached the inner edge of the group, Demetrius saw Kulka standing in a clearing, speaking to priestesses and advisors. Beleen stood to Kulka's right, but came to greet the Bactrians.

"What's going on?" asked Demetrius.

"We must make sacrifices," said Beleen.

A priestess stepped into the center of the clearing, holding a hare. She lifted it above her head by its long ears and said a few words that

Beleen chose not to translate. Demetrius's heart pounded as, with a thin silver knife, the priestess slit the hare's throat, and then placed the carcass at Kulka's feet.

A commotion on the far side of the circle drew Demetrius's attention from the motionless animal. The crowd moved aside, opening an aisle through which entered a richly decorated horse. Trinkets swayed below the horse's fitted helmet, and a red-and-purple quilt cascaded toward the ground from either side of the animal's back. The man leading the horse had a somber look on his face.

"He raised that horse," said Beleen. "For him, today is both an honor and a burden."

"Why was his horse chosen?" asked Demetrius, needing no explanation for what was about to happen.

"The priestesses identified it as the one most likely to bring victory."

Demetrius watched as a priestess handed Kulka a one-handed ax and then removed the horse's helmet. Demetrius looked away as Kulka lifted the ax over his head and swung it into the horse's skull.

The crowd was silent as the horse tumbled to the ground. Kulka broke the silence with a yell, and the crowd yelled back. Demetrius didn't understand the words, but he understood the sentiment: Much of the tribe was off to war, and protection was requested from the gods.

As the crowd dispersed, Demetrius followed Beleen to the horse pasture outside the settlement walls. After witnessing the sacrifice, he was grateful to see his horse in good health. It lifted its head from the grass to watch him approach.

"We have gone from enemies to allies," said Beleen, handing Demetrius his horse's reins. "I can only hope that you'll fight like it on the battlefield."

Demetrius nodded, and his mind flooded with images of his dead comrades on the steppe. He pushed the scene from his mind.

As Beleen walked away, Demetrius called to his three surviving comrades. They tied their horses' reins to the fence and joined him.

"We started this journey with many men," said Demetrius, his throat tightening. "And now it's just us. We started this journey to better prepare our kingdom for war, and now we ride south having secured the armies of both Maracanda and Scythia. You should be proud of what you have accomplished. I am certainly proud of you.

"Now, I know that we've had our fair share of disagreements since leaving home. But I ask that, starting today, you set them aside for the benefit of our kingdom. I also ask that you set them aside for the benefit of yourselves. The enemy does not care what languages we speak at home. And nor should you. Our destinies were linked over a hundred years ago, and our fates are linked today. As we ride south to Merv, let us ride not only side by side, but also as one. Our kingdom depends on it."

Demetrius looked to Roshan, to Ashok, and finally, to Phlotas. No one spoke, but they each nodded as he met their gaze. Time would tell, Demetrius knew, if his message had been received with welcome.

CHAPTER THIRTY-FIVE

Roshan

Days later, and within the near-waterless expanse of the Karakum Desert, Roshan passed a large group of Scythian warriors. They stayed close and spoke among themselves. Roshan looked fruitlessly for Beleen. Giving up the search, he led his horse forward and joined Demetrius and Ashok. Phlotas rode just ahead of them.

"I've never spent so much time on a horse in my whole life," said Roshan, rubbing his legs. They had been riding all day, and the sun crept toward the hilly horizon.

"I don't think I'll be able to walk tomorrow," said Ashok.

"It's worth it for the view, though," said Demetrius.

Roshan looked at the waves of sand and rock that surrounded them. "If you say so." Suddenly he felt very thirsty. "Did you hear anything of Maracanda?" Roshan turned from the dunes to Demetrius.

"Yes," said Demetrius. "A messenger arrived this morning with news that Maracanda's army left a few days back."

"And how did Laodice react to the summons?" said Roshan.

"Not well, I imagine," said Demetrius.

Roshan met Demetrius's gaze and they both smiled.

"Hey, Roshan," said Ashok. "There she is." Ashok pointed to their right flank, where Beleen rode alone. Roshan's chest tightened and he blushed.

"What of it?" he said, trying to show as little emotion as possible.

"Fine." Ashok smirked. "Don't talk to her."

Roshan looked to Demetrius. The prince must have read his mind, because he nodded his approval. Roshan grinned and rode toward Beleen.

"Have you been here before?" asked Beleen, as Roshan drew near. Her hair danced in the breeze. A gold chain rested above her ears and along her forehead.

"I haven't," he said, slowing his horse beside hers. "But it's certainly interesting. I didn't know a place could be made entirely of sand."

"Why not?" Beleen pushed her hair from her face. "The far north is only snow."

Roshan laughed.

"What's funny?" said Beleen. "I hope you're not amused by my Greek."

"No, no," said Roshan. "You speak Greek very well."

"Then what is it?"

"The snow," he said, chuckling. "It all makes sense now. Someone told us that your people believe that the north is a land of feathers. I realize now that the 'feathers' are snow."

"I've never heard this story."

"Neither had I," said Roshan. "The man had read it somewhere."

"You know," said Beleen. "You shouldn't believe everything you read."

"I guess not," said Roshan, laughing again.

Roshan and Beleen spoke for much of the afternoon, and when the sun approached the horizon, Roshan was surprised by how quickly time had passed.

When the sun touched the hills, a horseman rode toward them, carrying the flag of a royal messenger.

"I'll rejoin the prince," said Roshan. "But I'll see you later."

"I hope so." Beleen beamed.

"We must be close," said Demetrius, as Roshan returned alongside him.

Moments later, the messenger came to a stop before them.

"Welcome, your majesty," said the man to Demetrius. "Scouts noticed your approach and your father eagerly awaits your arrival. Merv is not far ahead."

"Excellent," said Demetrius. "Ride back and tell him to prepare food and water. We're running low."

"Yes, your majesty," said the messenger as he spurred his horse to action.

Roshan's stomach growled and he only now realized that he had not eaten all day.

Shortly thereafter, they finally left the sand dunes and came to Merv. Its tan walls were rigid against the dark, rolling mountains to the south. As the caravan approached, Roshan noticed thousands of tents outside the fortress. The camp was a forest of fabric, and while most tents were made of white wool, some were made of brown leather and colorful linen. Soldiers piled weapons between the structures and built fires in the clearings. It was the largest gathering of soldiers Roshan had ever seen.

"King Euthydemus brought the army, alright," said Ashok.

"Elephants and all," said Roshan, studying the massive animals lumbering beside a well.

"And there's the standard of Maracanda," said Ashok, pointing to a red flag fluttering above a group of tents.

After wishing Demetrius well for his meeting with the king, Roshan and Ashok continued to the camp.

"I hope there's food," said Ashok.

"If the smoke rising from that long tent is any indication, we've arrived just in time," said Roshan.

Ashok tied his horse's reins to a pole. "A while back, Priya spoke of joining the army caravan if it ever deployed. She didn't trust the army to feed me properly. So, who knows, she might be here."

"If Demetrius's stories of her cooking are true, I hope so," said Roshan.

They approached the long tent, which was open on two sides. Cauldrons and tables filled the space beneath the roof, and men and women wove around one another as they prepared food. Between cauldrons of white rice, there were platters of fried dough and bowls of soupy liquids. They varied in color, from bright yellow to orange-red. Stacked flatbreads formed a tower at the end of one table. Beside them, a man flattened dough between his hands and placed it against the inner wall of a large clay oven.

"Ashok!" someone yelled.

Roshan turned in time to see a woman running toward them. The long fabric of her orange saree flew in the wind behind her.

"Priya!" cried Ashok, opening his arms and embracing her.

Roshan stepped back as the woman paced around Ashok, speaking wildly as she pointed to the cuts and bruises across his arms and face.

"My friend," said Ashok, turning to Roshan, "this is my wife, Priya."

"It's wonderful to meet you," said Roshan. "Ashok talked about you a lot during our journey."

After speaking with Priya in a language Roshan did not understand, Ashok turned to him and spoke Greek.

"I've told her that I have many stories from our journey."

"I don't envy you," said Roshan, darkly. "I wouldn't know where to start."

It was then Roshan saw two figures approaching through the crowd.

"Your excellency," said Ashok to one of them. Roshan knew him to be Arjun, commander of the Indian forces. "You're back."

"Yes," said Arjun, looking from Ashok to Roshan. A layer of dust covered Arjun's bronze chest plate, and mud stained his red tunic. "Menon and I only just arrived with soldiers from India," he said, indicating Menon beside him.

Roshan thought Menon looked tired. He wore a gray tunic and a dirty white shawl. His beard was ragged, its hair pointing in conflicting directions, and his eyes looked more sunken than usual.

"I understand you've returned with the prince," said Menon, facing Roshan. "I trust he's unharmed."

"His majesty is healthy, your excellency," said Roshan. "But we lost many men in the north."

"Is it true that you secured an alliance with the Scythians?"

"Yes, your excellency," said Roshan. "The prince ensured our success."

"And I'm sure you did your part," said Menon, placing his hand on Roshan's shoulder.

"I only did my duty," said Roshan.

"Thank you," said Menon. He turned to Arjun. "We must find the king."

"Certainly," said Arjun.

As Menon and Arjun walked away, a smile crossed Roshan cheeks. For the first time in a long time, he felt proud.

CHAPTER THIRTY-SIX

⧖

Menon

Menon followed Arjun into the king's tent.

"Arjun. Menon," said Euthydemus, embracing them. "I am glad to see you safely returned. From what I've heard, you had quite the journey."

The king wore a pale-blue tunic and leather sandals. The jewelry that typically adorned his body was missing, as was the diadem that often graced his head.

Lander hovered near the tent's rear and wore a bronze chest plate, a leather-protected skirt, and greaves.

"Menon!"

Menon turned to see Demetrius approaching with his arms extended.

"Your majesty," said Menon, embracing him. "It is wonderful to see you well."

"Likewise," said Demetrius.

Menon stepped back. "I've been told of the deal you made with the Scythians."

"Yes," said Demetrius. "They are now our allies."

"Remarkable," said Menon. "I certainly didn't expect that when you went north."

"Remarkable, yes," said a woman, who glided forward. Menon felt his fists tighten as he recognized Laodice. She smirked and continued, "But I'd be remiss if I didn't say that the young prince gave too much to secure their friendship. Letting them freely populate the land just north of the Bactrian plain is risky. What's to stop them from pushing further next year?"

"With a place to stay," said Demetrius, turning to Laodice, "they won't have to. And they were coming anyway. There are movements over the horizon that we cannot control. The world is much bigger than we realize."

As Menon listened to Demetrius, he felt like he was meeting a new man.

"I let them settle so they can be our allies," Demetrius went on. "Perhaps together we can hold back the bigger waves to come. But we will not be able to hold anything back—Seleucid or otherwise—if the Scythians remain our enemies. Regardless, you made peace with them a requirement to deploying the army of Maracanda."

"I think you must have misunderstood our conversation, young prince," said Laodice, her face flushed. "But regardless, we're here now. And so are the Scythians."

"And we're grateful for you both," said Euthydemus, nodding to Laodice and then to Demetrius. He turned to Menon. "Now, Menon, you have news?"

"Yes, your majesty," said Menon, stepping forward. "Antiochus and his soldiers are camped in the Kabul Valley. They appear to have joined forces with King Sophagasenus."

"And what do you make of it?" said Euthydemus.

"It doesn't surprise me," said Menon. "Sophagasenus was not keen to join us. Although I doubt he is particularly willing to join the Seleucids. But with Antiochus's forces there, he may not have a choice."

"And what of the army? What can you tell me of its numbers and health?"

"During our journey," said Arjun, wiping beads of sweat from his forehead, "we heard Antiochus faced many attacks from locals. But according to our reconnaissance of Kabul, his forces are still considerable. Maybe thirty thousand men, not including the baggage train. About half are Macedonian and Greek phalangites. I also saw peltasts, slingers, Thracian swordsmen, and Persian spearmen."

"And the cavalry?" said Euthydemus.

"This is where their strength lies," said Menon. "We saw a few thousand Parthian horsemen alongside the Macedonian Companion cavalry. The Parthians seem to have contributed a fair number of cataphracts and many horse archers."

"And the elephants?" said Euthydemus. "Have they been mobilized?"

"It appears so, your majesty," said Menon.

"I see," said Euthydemus, backing into a wooden chair. "Unfortunately, that parallels what I've heard of Saddarvazeh. Arsak is also assembling an army." The king settled onto his cushion. "Lander, how are the defenses in Zariaspa coming along?"

"Your majesty," said Lander, bowing his head. "We need more time."

"Give me specifics," said Euthydemus.

"We've finished building supports on the weak sections of the walls and collected provisions, although many foodstuffs are still on their way from other cities. We have yet to clear the land outside the walls. There are still places the enemy could fortify and plenty of forage for their animals. And the farmers need more time to finish harvesting the fields. It's that or we burn them, so they don't harvest for the enemy."

"Then we should meet Antiochus in the mountains," said Demetrius, moving to the center of the room. "We need to slow him down, if not beat him outright."

Lander cleared his throat.

"Yes?" Euthydemus asked.

"I wonder, your majesty, if it would be better to wait here for Antiochus. His men will be tired by the time they arrive and our men will be rested. Further, we know this land, and we know very little of that in the south."

"True," said Euthydemus. "But we can't afford to let Antiochus combine his forces with Arsak's. I agree with Demetrius. We should strike Antiochus while he's on the move. He'll be stuck in the mountains. His troops will be spread thin. It's the advantage we need. Then we can turn and face Arsak."

"But our men will also stretch within the mountains," said Lander. "We'll be drawn too thin. The enemy could catch us at a vulnerable moment."

"I hear you," said Euthydemus. "But my decision is made. We will confront him in the mountains."

Demetrius glanced at Menon, who was nodding his approval.

"Lander," said Euthydemus, "order a large part of the remaining army in Zariaspa to head south, as well. I understand we need soldiers at Zariaspa to finish preparations, but they'll be put to better use with us. I will not have Antiochus's soldiers set foot in Bactria."

"Yes, your majesty," said Lander.

"Now, Demetrius," said Euthydemus.

"Yes, Father?" said Demetrius.

"You will lead the cavalry. It is a position of honor, but also a responsibility. As Lander said, the enemy can catch us at a moment of disadvantage if we are unprepared. I need you and your men to scout thoroughly. We need plenty of warning of the enemy's movements."

"It would be an honor," said Demetrius, displaying none of his usual uncertainty.

"Good," said Euthydemus. "Lead them well."

"Yes, Father. But I have one request."

"Name it."

"That I pick my men, whether they be native Bactrians or Greeks."

Laodice scoffed. "Now this is too far," she said. "Much too far. The vanguard has always been reserved for our own."

Menon looked from Demetrius to Laodice, and then to the king. Euthydemus's gaze was focused on the prince.

"Pick your men as you please," he said.

"Thank you, Father," said Demetrius, bowing his head. He then turned and left.

Menon met the king's gaze. They both smiled.

CHAPTER THIRTY-SEVEN

Demetrius

The next morning, as the sun climbed above the hazy horizon, Demetrius stood on the walls of Merv with his father and Menon. They watched the army assemble in the clearing between the spiked moat and the fields beyond. It had been many years since Demetrius last saw so many soldiers in one place, and it was a sight to behold. Beside the canal that watered the grain fields, thousands of horses were gathered, each with a fabric bundle strapped to its back. These packages contained the armor that would be placed across the horses' bodies before battle. Because the metal heated so quickly, riders tried their best to keep it off the animals whenever possible. Beside the gathered horses, there were hundreds of tents, around which soldiers from across Bactria assembled. The forces were a potent mix of east and west. Riders from Maracanda mingled with infantry from the eastern town of Aornos. Many soldiers had come with an attendant or two, who helped their masters ready for battle.

"We have enough food for the men and horses?" Euthydemus asked Menon.

"We have enough to reach the Kabul Valley," said Menon. "But we'll need to forage in that territory before returning. It's already hard enough pulling the baggage train as it is."

Demetrius looked at the army of donkeys and wagons assembled just below the walls. Dust hovered around them like a low-hanging cloud.

"Our elephant core should be able to break through Antiochus's phalanx, don't you think?" said Euthydemus.

Demetrius studied a shady grove of trees to his right. Squinting, he discerned movement among the leaves.

"I hope so, your majesty," said Menon. "But I'd advise that we use the elephants only after we break their ranks, and not to achieve it. Antiochus's soldiers are highly disciplined and very skilled. The phalanx will not move for our elephants until their cohesion is already broken. If given the opportunity, I think we should attack first with our horse archers and then with the cataphracts. We should avoid using our infantry at all costs. We simply don't have the discipline and numbers to match the enemy phalanx, and our transition to sarissas has not been completed. Our spears are too short and the sarissas we have are poor quality. As best we can, we should draw Antiochus into a cavalry battle. We have more horsemen than he does."

"Thank you for your counsel," said Euthydemus. "But you know as well as I do that few things go according to plan."

Recent weeks had taught Demetrius exactly that.

"You should get going, son," said Euthydemus.

"Yes, Father," said Demetrius.

His heart rate increased as he moved toward the stairs.

"Follow your instincts, your majesty," said Menon, pulling Demetrius's gaze. "They have proved remarkably good."

As Demetrius descended the stairs, he couldn't help but smile.

Demetrius mounted his horse at the gate and led it outside the walls of Merv, where the vanguard was gathering within a field of tall grass. A group of Scythian riders waited beside them. As Demetrius approached, Eucratides galloped toward him from among the vanguard.

"Your majesty!" cried Eucratides, stopping in front of Demetrius, "I hear you're permitting Bactrians to ride among the vanguard."

"That is correct," said Demetrius, realizing his friend was not there to ask about his journey north.

"But the vanguard is a place of honor."

"Exactly," said Demetrius, guiding his horse around Eucratides.

"And the Scythians," called Eucratides, to Demetrius's back. "Are they really going to ride with the army?"

"Yes."

"But they are our enemies!"

Demetrius turned his horse so that he faced Eucratides.

"Perhaps they were," said Demetrius. "But they're our allies now, so set aside your aggression."

"They constantly invade my family's lands," said Eucratides, throwing his arms into the air.

"Those lands belong to my father," Demetrius snapped. "Your family only lives on them with permission from the king."

Eucratides scoffed. "I never thought you'd speak like that about a noble family."

"And I never thought we'd be fighting a war for our survival."

Demetrius led his horse on, and behind him, he heard Eucratides release a long sigh. As he reached the soldiers, they quieted and turned to him. Moments later, the Scythians led their horses near.

"Comrades!" Demetrius cried. "It is our honor to ride south against Antiochus. And it is my honor to ride with you. As I look across this gathering, I see men I grew up with, as well as men I've only recently met." He looked to Eucratides and then to Roshan, who was wearing Feroze's prized bronze helmet. "Moreover, it is my honor to ride with both the soldiers of Bactria and the men and women of Scythia." He nodded to Beleen.

Demetrius heard whispers from within the crowd. "It is no secret that there has been tension between Bactria and Scythia," said

Demetrius, speaking loud enough to quell them. "And though it is rarely publicly acknowledged, it is no secret that there has been tension between Bactrians whose ancestors come from Greece and Bactrians whose ancestors do not. But for better or worse, Antiochus has brought us together. So together we will destroy him. And together we will remain."

Though pockets of soldiers remained quiet, the group erupted in cheers.

"Now let's get moving!" yelled Demetrius.

When the cheering dissipated, the vanguard moved toward the front of the infantry and the Scythians moved to the baggage train, where they were to guard against attack. Demetrius studied the infantry, which lumbered in a long column toward the mountains. With their spears pointed to the sky, it appeared as if a forest had suddenly risen from the desert sands.

CHAPTER THIRTY-EIGHT

Roshan

By the time the army stopped to set up camp for the night, the soldiers had made their way from the desert of Merv to the valleys of the southern mountains. Roshan was exhausted and ready to be off his horse and on his feet.

The king had picked a long, thin valley for the camp. Bare tan hills rose steeply on either side, and the curving terrain made it impossible to see the entire army at once. As men pulled equipment from the baggage wagons, others went to the top of each ridge to survey the land. But with the scenery divided by ridges, it would be nearly impossible to prevent surprise attacks.

Roshan wondered where Beleen was and if she was safe. He knew she and the other Scythians were protecting the baggage train, and with enemy scouts circling, it was a dangerous place to be. Still keeping an eye out for Beleen, Roshan roamed the camp in search of Ashok.

Roshan found him beside one of the weapon tents. "These spears are such poor quality," he said, picking one up and lifting it toward Ashok. "And they have so many splinters."

"They just need a few days to smooth out," said Ashok, taking the weapon from him and running his fingers against it.

"Where's Priya?"

Ashok returned the spear to the rack. "She's helping at the cooking tent. It seems duty has found us all. But she hopes to steal away later. We will try to organize a little dinner. You should join."

A group of horsemen rode by, the hooves of the animals kicking dust into the air. Roshan coughed, and then, as soon as his lungs allowed, he yelled at the riders, "How about you watch where you're going?"

One rider slowed, turned back, and stopped. Three others did the same. They rode together toward Roshan, their chest plates bouncing. The horsemen stopped beside Roshan, and the one in front reached up and removed his helmet. After running his hand through his short black hair, he glared at Roshan.

Roshan felt himself heat.

"Eucratides," he said. "No surprise there. Riding too close to others. I almost wonder if you were trying to trip me."

"I don't need to trip you," said Eucratides. "We both know you like doing that to yourself."

"Spoken like a true cheater," said Roshan.

It was a foolish thing to say, but the heat had gotten to him. Roshan looked at Ashok and then back to Eucratides just in time to see him, now dismounted, swing his fist at Roshan's face.

Roshan leaned back and avoided the blow, then bobbed below the swing of Eucratides's free hand. He stepped away from the weapon tent. Eucratides followed, chest heaving.

"You better take that back!" yelled Eucratides. "I won't have anyone lying about me."

"Then you have no quarrel with me," said Roshan, knowing the situation would only be resolved with a fight, "because I spoke the truth."

Eucratides swung his arm. Again, Roshan leaned back, but this time Eucratides's fist caught him on the jaw. Roshan heard the bone click out of socket. As he straightened, he caught another punch, this time to the stomach. He bent over, struggling to breathe, and heard laughter.

Roshan stood and raised his fists in front of his face. Eucratides shuffled to the left and then to the right, jabbing his fists toward Roshan. Roshan tilted his head away and then swung hard with his right arm. His fist smashed into Eucratides's face. As Eucratides dropped to the ground, Roshan's hand throbbed. Blood flowed from his knuckles.

Two of the Greeks ran forward and helped Eucratides up. His eyes were bloodshot, and his face was red. Blood dripped from his lip and nose.

"You're dead," said Eucratides. He grabbed a spear from the rack and pointed it at Roshan.

Roshan looked at the weapons, but Eucratides blocked his route to them.

Just as Eucratides stepped forward with his spear pointed, a large brown mass moved in front of him and pushed Roshan back. It was Phlotas, atop an armored horse.

"Back away from each other," Phlotas yelled, shifting his furious gaze between Roshan and Eucratides.

"You can't be serious," spat Eucratides. "Stop fooling around, Phlotas, and help me teach this Bactrian a lesson."

"I, too, am a Bactrian," said Phlotas. "As are you and Roshan. We should not be fighting one another. Our real enemy could be upon us at any moment."

"Is this some sort of joke?" said Eucratides, looking from Roshan to Phlotas.

"Get on your horse and get moving." Phlotas maneuvered his horse to keep it between the two men.

Roshan's chest heaved as he watched Eucratides, who looked from Phlotas to Roshan and then back to Phlotas. Then Eucratides mounted his horse and galloped away.

Roshan wiped the sweat and dust from his face and scanned his surroundings. A small crowd whispered and stared.

"That wasn't good," said Ashok, approaching. "He could have killed you."

"Well, if he wants to, I'm here," said Roshan. "He still can."

Roshan reached down and picked up the spear that Eucratides had tossed aside. With his hand throbbing, he no longer felt the splinters beneath his grip. After placing the spear on the rack, he looked back to Phlotas, who was riding slowly away.

"Hey!"

Phlotas turned his horse.

"I didn't need your help," said Roshan.

"I know," said Phlotas.

"Then why did you get involved?"

"Let's just say that I want to make amends. And I would like to think that people can change."

Roshan studied Phlotas, who was clearly hoping for a response.

"It's a start."

"Thank you," said Phlotas. He then lowered his head, turned, and rode away.

"You're quick to forgive," said Ashok.

"I wasn't in the past," said Roshan. He lifted Feroze's helmet from the ground and brushed dust from the metal. "But who knows," he continued, running his fingers along the bird-feather mold of the helmet's cheek guards, "perhaps people really can change."

Hours later, with the camp prepared, some men organized a game of kabaddi. The rules were simple enough: Two teams stood on either side of a line drawn in the dirt. Then, one member of the offensive team would cross the line and touch as many people as he could—but the whole time, he had to repeat the word "kabaddi" without breathing. After touching as many people as he wanted, he dashed back to the line. If he made it back, the people he touched were out. If, however, the defending team grabbed him and held him in place until he ran out of air, *he* was out. The game continued in this way, with the teams taking turns as offense and defense, until only one side remained.

Those not playing kabaddi settled around pathetic fires made from Zariaspan wood. The army had entered an area of pebbles and dirt, where the tallest plants failed to reach anyone's knees. Roshan had once heard that the Scythians used animal bones as wood for their fires, but as he sat next to the crackling flame, he couldn't remember what had fueled the fire during the celebrations of the Scythian alliance.

Roshan decided against joining the other members of the vanguard. Eucratides was among them, and in his current mood it was best if Roshan stayed away. He sat within shouting distance of the others and stretched his legs before him.

"You don't want to join them?"

Roshan turned and saw Beleen. Firelight flickered across her face.

"I wanted to avoid people for a bit," said Roshan.

"I see," said Beleen, turning away.

"I don't mean you," said Roshan. He offered a smile and shifted over to make room.

When Beleen sat beside him, Roshan's palms started to sweat.

"I, too, left my companions because I wanted to be alone," said Beleen, turning to Roshan. "But I enjoy speaking with you." She bit her bottom lip. "So here I am."

Roshan's heart pounded, and he forgot about the pain across his face.

"Ashok invited me to dinner with his wife," said Beleen after a breathless pause. "Want to join?"

Roshan watched the light weave across her face. The gold beads in her hair looked like balls of fire.

"I should sleep," said Roshan, feeling physically exhausted and emotionally confused. "But say hello for me."

Beleen looked away and back to Roshan. She offered a gentle smile. "Good night, Roshan," she said, standing.

"Good night, Beleen," said Roshan to her retreating figure.

After Beleen disappeared into the darkness, Roshan closed his eyes and lay flat against the dirt. With battle on the horizon, perhaps new bonds were best avoided.

CHAPTER THIRTY-NINE

>>———➤

Phriapa

Phriapa rode among a body of lightly armored cavalry. The moon lit the path before him, though he knew to look out for footfalls and other obstacles. He could not afford a wounded horse at this point in his journey.

Phriapa looked to his right, where Dropidas wiped dust from his forehead.

"We should be closing on them, don't you think?" said Dropidas.

"I'd say so," said Phriapa. "We've been traveling for days." Steam escaped his mouth as he spoke.

"It's too dark and cold to continue now," said Dropidas. "Let's stop for the night."

"No," said Phriapa. "The Bactrians can't be much farther."

"Fine," said Dropidas. "But don't blame me when you can't feel your fingers."

Phriapa encouraged his horse to move faster until he rode just shy of a gallop.

With the moon rising higher above the horizon, Phriapa and his companions followed the low point of a valley, letting it lead them through a maze of rocky hills.

"You see that glow on the horizon?" said Phriapa, pointing at the orange line between dark rock and the purple sky. "That must be their fires."

Dropidas smiled. "Not bad, Parthian," he said. "Not bad."

Leaving a group of men to guard the horses, Phriapa and Dropidas continued on foot. They removed most of their armor to keep noise to a minimum. Phriapa tucked a long bronze dagger in his belt, and slung a leather case of arrows over his shoulder. He kept his bow in hand.

After a short and silent walk, Phriapa ascended a gentle ridge. As he moved, he listened to the rattle of voices and the clanking of blacksmiths. When he reached the top, he ducked behind a tall rock and considered the twisting valley below. He held his breath.

"There they are," said Dropidas.

"Yes." Phriapa's heart beat rapidly. "There they are."

The valley was full of enemy fighters. Thousands of them. They weaved between tents and around fires, cooked food, cleaned armor, and sharpened weapons. In the distance, soldiers worked beside servants and pack animals to bring the large baggage train within the confines of a rudimentary wall. The line of wagons, oxen, and donkeys disappeared behind an adjacent hill. Just below the ridge, horses stood within a basic enclosure. From the decorations the horses wore, Phriapa knew them to be Scythian.

CHAPTER FORTY

Beleen

Beleen approached Kasen. The horse pawed the ground as she reached the makeshift stable. Clearly, he had been waiting for her return. She had been sharing dinner with Ashok and his wife for the last hour, at least.

"You miss home, don't you?" Beleen ran her fingers through his mane.

As Kasen kicked at the dirt, Beleen thought of their grassy homeland. She missed the chilly mornings when the crisp breeze met her skin, and the evenings when the sunset painted the hills gold.

The grinding of dirt alerted Beleen to Tul's approach.

"Beleen," said Tul. "I've been looking for you. We're setting up a fire. And we have koumiss. Join us."

"Thanks, but I think I'll stay with Kasen," said Beleen. "He's been restless lately. He's not used to the mountains."

"Then, if it's alright with you," said Tul, "we'll set up the fire here. That way, Kasen can join us."

Beleen laughed. "Very well," she said.

Before long, Beleen, Tul, and a small group of Scythians sat beside the horses and shared a jug of koumiss and stories from home. For a few rare moments, Beleen even forgot she was deep in the mountains and on her way to war. But the sound of sticks snapping in the darkness ruined the illusion.

As the wind carried the crack of twigs and the scrape of stone from beyond the nearest hill, Beleen realized she was also hearing voices.

"Be quiet!" she hissed to the others, then closed her eyes and tried to listen through the whistle of the wind. Her breathing stopped when she recognized the language.

"Get your weapons," she whispered, before running to Kasen.

She pulled her bow from its leather casing.

"What did you hear?" said Tul, hurrying to her side.

"Greek," said Beleen. "I heard Greek."

"It's probably just the sentries," said Tul.

"I don't think so," said Beleen. "I haven't seen sentries all night."

Without waiting for the others, Beleen ran into the darkness. The cool breeze whipped her cheeks, stung her nose, and watered her eyes as she worked her way up the hill. Sounds seemed to carry farther and louder in the darkness, and Beleen was more aware than usual of her footsteps.

Beleen stopped at the top of the bare, moonlit hill. She saw nothing but darkness.

"Do you see anything?" she asked, as Tul and the others caught up.

"No," a few of them murmured.

"Maybe you're just nervous," said Tul.

"I'm not nervous," said Beleen, offended by the insinuation.

A twig snapped.

"Did you hear that?" Beleen stepped further into the darkness.

"Yes," Tul whispered, "but it's probably just an animal."

He placed his hand on her shoulder.

"Just wait with me," said Beleen, shaking his hand off. "And be ready to fight."

Tul sighed as he pulled a one-handed ax from his belt.

With the breeze picking up, Beleen struggled to distinguish sounds, but she was confident about what she'd heard. For this reason, she sat in silence on the hill for longer than her peers thought reasonable, and well past their return to the camp. When Beleen finally returned to camp, too, the sun was rising above the horizon. Only hours later, and despite her exhaustion, Beleen took up a guard position among the baggage wagons as the army commenced its march. As the wagons rumbled beside her, she fought to stay awake and keep track of the time and soldiers passing by.

"Horsemen!" someone called, sending a shock through Beleen's body.

She looked where the man was pointing, and on the shrub-covered ridge, she saw a group of eight to ten riders, sitting motionless.

"Parthians," Beleen said under her breath, as she nocked an arrow to her bow.

She pulled back the string and aimed at the riders, thinking of her brother.

"They're too far," said Tul, coming to a stop beside her.

"Let's go get them," said Beleen.

"No," said Tul. "We're to protect the baggage, remember? We shouldn't be pulled away unless needed. Let's wait for them to make a mistake."

Beleen tightened her grip on her bow.

"You're right," she said, loosening her fingers.

Throughout the afternoon, and much to Beleen's dismay, the horsemen followed the caravan at a distance. Each time they approached, she nocked another arrow, but then they pulled back. The waiting came to an end, however, when a Greek horseman galloped to Beleen.

"The Parthians!" he yelled. "They're attacking the infantry."

He pointed ahead.

Upon seeing that the enemy no longer stalked the baggage train, Beleen rushed to the fight. As her horse galloped beneath her, she opened and closed her fingers against her bow and looked to the quiver at her waist, which held red-and-black-painted arrows.

"Come on!" she called to Kasen. She squeezed her thighs, telling the horse to move faster. He obliged, and her hair flew wildly behind her.

After ascending a sandy hill, Beleen saw a battle, marked by swirling dust and frenzied combatants. Horsemen rode toward the column, released their arrows on the men hiding behind their shields, and retreated before the terrified soldiers had a chance to even swing their spears uselessly through the air.

Beleen looked at her comrades to get a sense of numbers. She was among ten to fifteen riders. The enemy appeared to have a similar number. Beleen and Kasen galloped directly toward the Parthians. She placed an arrow on her bow and directed her horse into a sharp left turn. She released the arrow. It flew and just missed one rider. Beleen turned and galloped toward the next closest Parthian—who pulled a long knife from his waist. Beleen pulled the ax from her belt. She and the Parthian swung simultaneously, but her ax was longer than the Parthian's knife, and the man fell.

As Kasen ran back into the killing zone, Beleen pulled an arrow from her quiver, placed it on the bow, and let it fly. A Parthian horseman took the arrow in the neck but continued to ride.

Beleen launched another arrow at a less armored man. The arrow found its mark on the man's face and sent him tumbling off the back of his horse. As Beleen reached for a third arrow, an enemy projectile slammed into her waist. An arrow projected from her thick belt. Beleen pulled it from the leather, nocked it to her bow, and sent it flying at her assailant. It ricocheted off the man's helmet, and snapped under a horse's hoof.

With another arrow latched to her bow, Beleen aimed at the rider, but he rode quickly past, their eyes meeting for a moment. Before she could turn, pain exploded in her back. She was hit, and slid from her horse uncontrollably. A moment later, she was rolling in the dust.

When she finally stopped rolling, Beleen pulled the now-broken arrow from her shoulder blade. She stood and turned in place. Horses, both with riders and without, wove around one another and in front of the infantry. Arrows flew through the air, while yelling and screaming reverberated through the dust. She eyed her red hands and wiped the blood against her thighs. Looking up, she saw the Parthians in retreat.

CHAPTER FORTY-ONE

»»——➤

Phriapa

Seeing that the enemy failed to pursue his retreat, Phriapa slowed his horse to a trot.

"Let's head back to Antiochus," Phriapa called to Dropidas.

"You don't want to attack again?" said Dropidas.

"No," said Phriapa. "We've got them on edge. That's enough for now."

"Alright." Dropidas wiped his forehead. "We'll head south then."

Phriapa nodded and nudged his horse back into action.

It took Phriapa and the others two days to reach the Seleucid army. They found it lumbering through the thin valleys of Ariana, where the mountains rose to the sky like walls on either side of the column. The men looked exhausted, and their discipline seemed weak. Men dragged their spears in the dirt and stuffed their armor onto wagons. Phriapa found the scene discouraging. After watering their horses at a small stream, he and Dropidas found Antiochus in the middle of the column, where he was cleaning a wound on his shoulder.

"We were attacked by the locals again," said Antiochus, looking up from his wound, as if Phriapa and Dropidas had been gone for only a moment. "Tell me you bring good news."

"We engaged the enemy," said Phriapa.

Antiochus dropped the bloody rag.

"And? What of it?" he said.

"Your majesty," Dropidas said, "Euthydemus is on his way here."

Antiochus nodded, his expression emotionless.

Dropidas looked to Phriapa and then continued, "And the scouts we sent to Zariaspa report that an army is on the move from there, as well. They're trying to pincer us."

Antiochus poked at the gash on his shoulder with his dirty fingernails. Phriapa wondered why Antiochus was acting this way. Perhaps he was exhausted.

"What's the road like ahead?" he asked, his voice flat. He pulled his fingers from the blood. "Anything of note? Anything to worry about?"

"There's a river," said Dropidas. "The Arius, I believe. The crossing may slow us down and leave us vulnerable to attack."

"Then we must cross it before Euthydemus reaches it." Antiochus pulled his cloak over the red gash. "Tonight is a full moon. We'll march through the night."

"Yes, your majesty," said Dropidas, lowering his head.

After leaving Antiochus and Dropidas, Phriapa found Heron with the other Parthians.

"You look worn out," Phriapa said to him.

"You look no better yourself," said Heron.

"We've been riding for days. And we engaged the enemy northwest of here."

"I'm sorry to have missed it," said Heron. "We've been busy, too. The columns are attacked at least once a day, sometimes twice. We've lost thirteen of our men, and the Seleucids have lost countless more."

"We will honor our fallen when the time is right," said Phriapa. "But for now, the Bactrian army is approaching and our fight has barely begun."

CHAPTER FORTY-TWO

Demetrius

Two days later, Demetrius rode through a narrow gorge at the head of his father's army. The winding mountain path made it impossible to see the entire army at once. Still, he had a limited view of the heavy cavalrymen, their armor carried by their horses or on donkeys beside them.

"Quite the scenery," said Demetrius, turning to Eucratides, who rode beside him.

The path ahead twisted to the left ahead and a rocky hill rose like a wall. Bushes were upended and had turned a stale brown—evidence of a recent rockslide.

"Yes, your majesty," said Eucratides. "It's really something."

Despite the tension and formality, Demetrius was content that Eucratides was following orders without complaint. Battle was no time for personal squabbles.

Demetrius looked up as two scouts galloped toward him.

"Your majesty," said one. "We've spotted dust ahead. And vultures. It must be them."

"Where?" said Demetrius, leaning forward. His legs were sore from the previous days' riding.

"Southeast of here. We saw it from a ridge about twenty stades away."

"Very good," said Demetrius. "I understand that a river runs nearby. Did you see it?"

"Yes, your majesty," said the second rider. "The Arius." His face was covered in sweat. He had removed his helmet and leather cuirass and tied them to the blanket he rode on.

"The river is not far," the first rider added. "Maybe ten stades. It's wide but mostly slow-moving."

"Will it slow down the enemy?" said Demetrius. He was eager to keep Antiochus in place until the rest of the army could catch up.

"If defended," said the man.

"Good. Now go to the king and tell him the soldiers must move up quickly."

As the first horseman rode off, Demetrius looked at the horizon where dust rose above its jagged lines.

"We can't slow them for too long," said Eucratides. "Arsak approaches from the northwest. If we stay too long, we risk being encircled."

"I know," said Demetrius. "But the Parthians from Saddarvazeh are still a few days off, and our forces from Zariaspa should arrive late tomorrow."

"That'll be close," said Eucratides.

"I know," said Demetrius, before letting out a long sigh.

He turned to the remaining scout.

"Head back out and get a better sense of the enemy's speed and destination."

"Yes, your majesty," said the man, turning his horse away.

"It won't be long before we're in battle," said Eucratides.

"Are you ready for it?" asked Demetrius.

"I've sought battle since I could walk," said Eucratides.

Demetrius had never had such a drive, but over the past few weeks, he'd learned that drive had nothing to do with fighting. War was thrust upon you.

"Can you go check on the men?" said Demetrius, looking to Eucratides. "Make sure they're prepared to fight at a moment's notice."

"Of course, your majesty," said Eucratides, in the flat tone Demetrius had come to expect.

Just as Eucratides disappeared from view, Beleen rode up. Her hair was pulled back into a low ponytail, and her neck and ears were covered in gold.

"I hear the enemy is close," she said.

"Yes, they're just over those hills." Demetrius pointed at the ridgeline.

Beleen scanned the hills with her dark brown eyes.

"I'm not sure how we can fight like this," she said, turning back to him. "In this region, you can't see the enemy until it's too late."

"It's different from the steppe, that's for sure," said Demetrius, recalling his battle with the Scythians in the grassy plains.

Beleen looked away and then down at the dirt.

"There's a river ahead," Demetrius continued. "We can stop them there. To cross, they must accept many losses."

Beleen nodded and they rode in silence.

"Have you seen—" said Beleen, pausing.

Demetrius turned to her, a smile crossing his face.

"Have I seen Roshan?" he said.

Beleen blushed and looked down.

"I haven't," said Demetrius. "But when you find him, please give him my regards."

Beleen smiled and her cheeks went from pink to red.

"I will," she said, riding away.

It did not take long for the king and his entourage to reach Demetrius's position. His father was panting as his horse came to a stop. Lander and Arjun were close behind.

"Look." Demetrius pointed at the dust and birds that filled the sky.

"They're close," said his father, who turned and faced the column of infantry behind them. The men looked tired and weighed down by the weapons and armor they carried over their shoulders. "Lander, have the men change into battle gear. And make sure the baggage is moved to the back."

"Yes, your majesty." Lander galloped away.

"Arjun," said the king.

"Yes, your majesty," said Arjun, stepping forward. His bronze chest plate and gold earrings shone in the sunlight.

"Take some men and find a suitable place to camp. If we don't fight today, we should be in well-defended positions for tomorrow."

"As you command," said Arjun, bowing and turning away.

Demetrius locked eyes with his father.

"Demetrius. Take the Royal Guards and some Scythians and scout out the enemy's position and strength. I need to know if they are vulnerable to attack before the sun goes down."

"I sent scouts ahead to determine that," said Demetrius. "They should be returning soon."

"I want to hear it from you," said Euthydemus. "Now is no time for mistakes."

"Yes, Father."

After pulling together a handful of riders—including Beleen, who he found watering her horse at a stream—Demetrius moved ahead and down the winding path.

"Did you find Roshan?" Demetrius asked, glancing at her.

"No," said Beleen, her voice flat.

"We'll find him. I'm sure he's just doing his part. We all have our duties."

CHAPTER FORTY-THREE

>>———→

Phriapa

The Seleucid army had traveled fast to close the space between the armies. Antiochus had only allowed such breaks as were deemed necessary for the horses' survival. But the quick march worked, and it was only a few days before the enemy was reported in the area.

Now, with the coming battle on his mind, Phriapa led his horse to the top of a ridge where Antiochus and Dropidas waited.

"We've been searching for the enemy for days," said Antiochus. "And when we finally find them, there is a river between us. The gods are playing games with me."

Phriapa looked across the wide, flat valley. Jagged tan hills bordered the expanse, from which shadows blanketed the small, olive-green shrubs that peppered the ground. The horizon looked like a serrated blade. The center of the valley was flat and dusty. Its most conspicuous feature, however, was the turquoise river that cut across it like a line of gems on a bronze crown. The afternoon sunlight flickered against the small ripples in the water. The river moved slowly, but a few sections looked deep enough to swamp a horse and rider.

"How long will it take to form up lines?" asked Antiochus, turning to Dropidas.

"We can deploy the skirmishers in short order," said Dropidas, his voice betraying his exhaustion. "But it will take time for the heavy infantry and elephants to catch up. That last section of passes proved difficult for them."

"Bring everyone now," said Antiochus. "I don't care if they're tired. Look at the horizon."

He pointed at the far ridge, above which a cloud of dust rose into the sky.

"Euthydemus is close at hand, and I want our soldiers here to meet him. Neither Arsak nor the soldiers from Zariaspa are here yet, so it's just me and Euthydemus. Whoever crosses the river first controls the day, and we need to finish this before Euthydemus's reinforcements arrive. We must be quick. The phalanx cannot hold together if it must cross under the shadow of the enemy."

"Yes, your majesty," said Dropidas. He disappeared below the ridge, leaving Phriapa alone with the Seleucid monarch.

"Phriapa," said Antiochus, still staring at the river, "it is time to see your famed cavalry in action. Take your men and move ahead. Keep the enemy delayed while I bring up the rest of the army."

Phriapa nodded. He agreed with Antiochus's logic and, after days of planning and skirmishing, was eager for the fight.

It took Phriapa some time to find his countrymen among the long column that was Antiochus's army. The column twisted along the path it had followed from Kabul. Mountains and hills, almost entirely devoid of vegetation, bordered the path on either side. Thracian mercenaries—who specialized in such environments—moved along the ridges to protect against ambush.

Phriapa passed the Seleucid Silver Shields, who held their sarissas against their shoulders, and the Median archers, who nodded to him as he rode by. He found his comrades watering their horses at a small stream, and approached Heron, whose armor was covered in a film of dust.

"Antiochus has instructed us to ride ahead—"

Heron lifted his hand to cut him off. "Ordered us?" he said with disgust.

"Just leave it," said Phriapa. "You know this bothers me just as much as it does you. But the enemy is close and our lives depend on a Seleucid victory." Heron didn't respond, and Phriapa continued, "We are to secure the river ahead, delay the enemy, and prevent them from forming lines. At least until the Seleucid columns deploy."

"Makes sense." Heron patted his horse on the back. "Time to suit up, brother."

In short order, Phriapa, Heron, and the other cataphract riders had covered themselves in layers of metal. With the sun high, it was painful for Phriapa to gaze straight at all of his men, but he knew that they looked beautiful and terrifying.

He instructed his horse to kneel, which the animal did without protest.

"Good," he said, patting the horse's armor plates.

"Let's go," he called to Heron, as his horse stood up, lifting him into the air. He could feel the weight of the metal encompassing him. It was both uncomfortable and reassuring.

Phriapa led the cataphracts in a trot beside the infantry. The lightly armored horse archers followed close behind. As he passed Antiochus, who watched from the final ridge before the river, he nodded, and Antiochus lowered his head in recognition.

Phriapa led his horse into the plain between the hills and the river, his mind clearing. From the small eyeholes in his helmet, it was difficult to get a good view, but as he bounced atop his horse, he could glimpse the turquoise waves. He rode toward them, letting the breeze push through the gaps in his armor. It was little relief, but still, it was something.

Phriapa's horse kicked up water as it trotted into the river's shallows. While bright blue, the surrounding water was also muddy, and Phriapa couldn't see the bottom. His horse stepped forward and back awkwardly.

"It's okay. It's okay," Phriapa said, patting the metal plates, which clanked under his hand.

Splashing filled Phriapa's ears as his companions joined him in the river.

"That was easy," said Heron, stopping beside Phriapa.

Phriapa examined the hills ahead, but they seemed identical to those behind. As he scanned the landscape, he heard a zip and a gurgle. Phriapa turned back to Heron, but Heron was gone.

Phriapa's gaze moved down to the water. There was Heron, lying motionless under the waves, an arrow protruding from his face.

There was a knock against Phriapa's chest, and an arrow dropped into the water.

"They're here!" he shouted, tightening his grip on his lance. He looked at the far hills and kicked his horse into motion and out of the water.

On the far bank, riders galloped parallel to the water, letting loose arrows from their bows. The projectiles tapped against the ground and splashed in the water. There was a zip beside Phriapa's face, and he ducked.

"Pull back!" he yelled. Anyone who fell into the water in cataphract armor would soon drown.

He led his horse farther from the water, followed by the other cataphracts. The Parthian horse archers, however, moved toward the enemy. They rode to the river's edge, turned, and loosed their arrows. Looking back, Phriapa saw horses and men crumple to the ground.

On the other side of the river, enemy riders galloped among the dead and dying. At a quick glance, Phriapa identified the cataphract and horse archers of Bactria, but a second look showed Scythian horse archers riding with them. The Scythians wore leather armor covered in gold, which reflected light with an intensity he had never seen before.

In the following minutes, the forces on both sides of the river— likely realizing their limited impact—pulled back. But as the enemy riders moved up the bluff, a heavily armored man led his horse to the river and rode into the water alone.

CHAPTER FORTY-FOUR

Demetrius

Demetrius didn't know why he led his horse into the river and toward the enemy. He just felt drawn to do it. After so much talking, the invasion was here, and only feet away. As the water lapped at his feet, Demetrius pulled his lance to his shoulder. It clanked against the metal plates of his armor.

The enemy was now too far away to hit him with arrows, and their horses kicked at the dirt. Parthians, Demetrius realized, as he studied them. He had spent so much time thinking of the Seleucids that he had given little thought to facing the famed Parthians on the battlefield.

One of the Parthians separated from the others and galloped toward him, carrying a lance. The rider was tall and built. His helmet was a shiny iron dome from which small, layered plates of metal fell across his face, obscuring it entirely. At the water's edge, he lifted his helmet, revealing his face, a short black beard, and a low ponytail of long black hair. The man stared at Demetrius, no expression discernible.

Demetrius grabbed the top of his own helmet and lifted it from his head, feeling instant relief from the accumulated sweat.

There was a long pause as Demetrius and the Parthian stared at one another.

"It's a hot one," the Parthian called to him in Greek. He lifted his hand toward the sun, and the light flickered off his armor.

"Certainly," said Demetrius, feeling foolish for talking about the weather.

"Who are you?" the Parthian called to him.

Demetrius paused, unsure what to say. After a brief moment of silence, he straightened and called out, "I am Demetrius, son of Euthydemus, king of Bactria, Sogdiana, and Margiana."

The Parthian smiled. "Sogdiana and Margiana?" he said, wiping sweat from his forehead. "I see your imagination expands beyond your borders."

While his father had lost control of those regions years ago, it was the kingdom's official position that they remained part of their domains. But now was no time for technicalities.

"And who are you?" said Demetrius, sitting even straighter.

"I am Phriapa, prince of Parthia, son of Arsak, king of the Parthians." The man lifted his lance as he spoke.

Demetrius had known from the man's clothing that he was someone of importance, but he was surprised to have met the prince.

"I advise you and your people to turn around and go home," said Demetrius. He looked at the other horsemen, many of whom pulled arrows against bowstrings. "Our fight is with Antiochus and his invaders. It is not with you."

"Your fight has always been with us," said Phriapa. "If Antiochus had beaten us and offered your father our lands, I'm certain he would have taken them."

"If?" said Demetrius. "*If* he had beaten you? My understanding is that you *were* beaten. Or are you here by your own will?"

A look of disgust crossed the Parthian's face. He lifted his helmet and placed it back on his head. After the metal plates settled into place, he turned and rode from the river to the other Parthians, who guided their horses back and forth in front of the hills.

Arrows landed in the water around Demetrius. With the fight begun once again, Demetrius fell back to his comrades. Horse archers took turns riding toward the water, loosing their arrows, and retreating out of range. Neither side wanted to be the first to ford the river and risk annihilation by arrows or water if caught in an unexpected section of depth or current.

Demetrius called to Beleen. "Move west and see if you can find a crossing. I'll do the same to the east."

Beleen nodded and led the Scythians in search. On the opposite side of the river, a group of Parthians mirrored her journey. Crossing was tricky business. Timing and position were everything. For Alexander's fight against Porus on the banks of the Hydaspes in India, it had been the difference between death and glory. Today, it was no different.

Demetrius led the Bactrian contingent east. Another Parthian group did the same. Riders from both sides of the river periodically risked death by riding to the shore and loosing arrows at the enemy. As he rode, Demetrius studied the water, but it was too cloudy for him to discern a suitable spot to cross.

Once he lost sight of the Scythians, Demetrius turned back and traversed the same ground, this time leading his horse into the water to test the depth—until arrows forced him back. When archers on his side pushed the enemy away, he led his horse into the river again. It was a deadly dance.

When Demetrius returned to the spot of their initial encounter, he found Bactrian skirmishers filing into the pebble-covered flats. They wore tunics and small bronze or leather chest plates. A lucky few wore helmets. The javelin throwers carried bundles of javelins in one hand and wicker shields in the other. The archers carried only their bows, and arrows protruded from leather cases at their waists. Commanders directed them into the water, where they could attack the enemy and push them from the far bank. The enemy horse archers responded by galloping back and forth toward the water, loosing arrows with each pass. There was a strange rhythm of splashes and screams as arrows cascaded from the sky. The skirmishers wore nothing close to the armor of the enemy cavalry, and with time, bodies piled up and turned the river red.

CHAPTER FORTY-FIVE

Roshan

Standing horseless in the water, Roshan pulled the bowstring against his cheek. Figuring he could better engage the enemy on foot, he had left his horse in safety on the bluff. He searched for his target. A group of slingers stood on the opposite side of the river; the rocks they had been throwing had already killed two of his comrades and struck Roshan painfully in the hip, leaving him to navigate the battlefield with a limp.

A slinger ran toward the river, twisting his sling as he moved. For a moment, it seemed as though the man stared directly at Roshan. Roshan let the bowstring loose and watched the arrow fly across the river and into the man's chest. The man stumbled forward and fell into the shallows, where water swept around the body as if it were a rock.

Roshan drew another arrow and launched it at a javelin thrower who was fording the river. This man fell too, and his javelins spread out and floated down the river.

Now, the far bank was full of enemy soldiers. There were slingers, archers—both on the ground and atop horses—javelin peltasts, and armored cavalry. The warriors moved between one another like fish in the river. Some worked silently while others yelled and screamed along the river's edge. Others cried out when wounded or thrashed when the water became too deep. All around, there was evidence of death. The same scene played out on Roshan's side of the river where Bactrian, Indian, and Scythian soldiers killed the enemy or died by the enemy's hand.

Roshan saw Ashok launch the last arrow from his wicker basket. Roshan's gaze followed the arrow's trajectory from Ashok's bow to the face of an enemy rider. The man toppled from his horse and into the water.

Roshan picked up his spear and ran to Ashok.

"Take some of my arrows," he said, pointing at Ashok's empty basket. "You have better aim."

"Not today I don't," said Ashok, taking three arrows. "Not with all the armor they wear."

"I'm better with a spear anyway," said Roshan, tightening his grip around that weapon. "If only we could cross the river," he added, looking at the current. "We have double their numbers."

As he scanned the riverbank, Roshan saw a group of Scythian riders. Beleen was graceful and deadly on her horse, twisting and releasing arrows as if it were as easy as breathing. Roshan wanted to go to her, but now was not the time. He had his duties.

He looked to the opposite riverbank, over which enemy skirmishers continued to spread. He dropped his spear, pulled an arrow against his bow, and released.

CHAPTER FORTY-SIX

Antiochus

"Move the archers up faster!" yelled Antiochus. He stood on a bluff, watching the river, where the enemy was securing a foothold. Horse archers, cataphracts, and the river's unpredictability offered the only resistance to an enemy crossing. Not that they'd be foolish enough to cross without the heavy infantry needed to hold the position.

"Push them back," he cried, as Median archers ran past him toward the water.

Antiochus rocked atop his horse. He had been riding all day, and his body ached.

"This is ridiculous," he grumbled to himself.

Antiochus turned as Dropidas crested the hill.

"Where is the phalanx?" said Antiochus. "The enemy seems disorganized. If we can deploy faster than they can, we can take the day."

"Our soldiers are still moving up," said Dropidas. "The passes are narrow and slow us down."

Antiochus closed his eyes and breathed deeply.

"Fine," he said. "But as soon as possible, have the phalanx deploy for battle. Form up the center line with the Gold and Bronze Shield units. I want the Silver Shields divided and placed on the flanks. Is that clear?"

"Yes, your majesty," said Dropidas.

"Parthian cavalry on the left flank and Companions on the right," continued Antiochus. "The phalanx is to move over the hill only when in lines. The cavalry can join the flanks when the infantry is fully formed on the riverbank. How long until this is done?"

"Maybe an hour to prepare," said Dropidas. "But some are ready now."

"That's too long," snapped Antiochus. "Get them moving faster. I don't know how long the skirmishers and cavalry can prevent a crossing, and we need the enemy to stay on the other side until we're ready."

"I'll see what I can do."

Dropidas rode toward the columns of infantry that snaked through the mountain passes beyond.

Antiochus looked at the opposite ridge across the river. He knew that beyond it, Euthydemus's army approached, and on the beach, enemy skirmishers blocked any easy crossing.

CHAPTER FORTY-SEVEN

Beleen

Beleen's horse took her to the edge of the river, where she loosed an arrow, which ricocheted off an enemy helmet.

Tul pulled his horse next to hers. He smiled at her as he pulled an arrow from the quiver beside his leg. He brought the feathers of the arrow to his cheek, breathed out, and released.

"How long are we supposed to stay here?" he called to Beleen. "This is hardly good land."

"We're to hold the enemy back for as long as we can. The infantry is moving up."

"We can try our best," said Tul, walking his horse in a small circle. "But if the enemy crosses now, we won't be able to stop them."

"Just do what you can," said Beleen.

"Is that new?" Tul pointed to Beleen's back, which was covered in blood.

"It's from the baggage train attack," she said. "Must have reopened. But that's no matter."

Beleen rode from the river and scanned the commotion along the bank. Roshan stood knee-deep in the water, struggling to pull a body from the current. Beleen rode to him and dismounted, then ran into the water.

"Help me with him," said Roshan.

The man was face down, and Beleen grabbed him by the armpits and helped to drag him from the water. When they reached the sand, they pushed the man over. Beleen gasped. His right cheekbone and eye had been crushed.

"Must have been a sling stone," said Roshan, straightening.

Beleen caught Roshan's gaze. Her heart pounded even more than when she'd been fighting.

"I was looking for you," she said.

"Here I am," said Roshan.

An arrow flew between them. They ducked and ran from the riverbank.

As they slowed, Beleen turned back to see Tul riding parallel to the river. He pulled his bowstring back, bringing an arrow to his cheek. Suddenly, his arms jolted and he launched the arrow nearly straight up. Beleen saw an enemy arrow sticking from his face. Tul's body splashed into the water.

"No!" screamed Beleen.

She grabbed Kasen's loose reins, threw them into Roshan's hands, and ran to the river. But she couldn't see Tul's body. There were plenty of corpses in the water, but none of them wore Tul's bright-red cloak.

When a javelin landed beside Beleen, she realized she was exposed. She grabbed Tul's horse, mounted it, and rode from the water.

Beleen reached Roshan and pulled Kasen's reins from his hold.

"I must keep fighting," she said, trying to keep her voice calm.

"I'm with you," said Roshan.

Beleen mounted her own horse and Roshan took Tul's. With arrows latched to bows, they galloped back into the fray.

CHAPTER FORTY-EIGHT

Antiochus

Dropidas's prediction proved correct, and an hour passed before the army stood in lines behind the ridge. Frustrated at the wasted time, Antiochus rode behind the front lines of the phalanx, which was at least fifteen men deep already, and yelled at the men to close ranks. Dropidas rode beside him.

"Why aren't the elephants up yet?" Antiochus demanded. With the infantry in place, Antiochus was now concerned for the secondary units.

"They're still at the stream, your majesty," said Dropidas. "Their handlers say the elephants are dehydrated. Apparently they'll start fainting if we don't let them drink and rest."

"Drink and rest?" said Antiochus. "Now? Why is this only an issue now?"

"It was brought up earlier, your majesty, but you were—" Dropidas shut his mouth as Antiochus glared.

"Just get them up here," said Antiochus. "And move the phalanx over the ridge. We've waited long enough."

"Yes, your majesty."

It did not take long for Antiochus's orders to pass from Dropidas to the lesser officers, and from them to the men. The phalanx—a glimmering mass of armor and blades—ambled up the ridge that shielded them from the river.

CHAPTER FORTY-NINE

Demetrius

The deep buzz of horns sounded from the opposite ridge. Demetrius stared hard at its large boulders and small bushes, and as he watched, a blanket of flickering light covered the line between earth and sky. Sparkling blades lifted into the air atop long, thin poles. Demetrius's knees grew weak, and for a moment, he couldn't breathe.

In seconds, the ridge filled with the famed Seleucid phalanx—its shields polished to perfection, its pikes forming a forest in the sky. Its soldiers moved together like an animal covered in bronze scales and colorful clumps of hair. Demetrius watched in shock as the Seleucid phalanx passed over the ridge and approached the river's edge. They had formed lines much quicker than anticipated, and their presence closed the opportunity for Demetrius and the others to ford the river relatively unopposed.

He turned and led his horse away from the bank. When he reached the top of his own side's ridge, he halted and took a deep breath. Ahead of him, in a wide valley hidden from the enemy's view, the Bactrian infantry waited in lines. Demetrius's father rode at the front of the bronze-clad hoplites, who, under the barked orders of their commanders, took their place in the phalanx. Shields and pikes clattered as the men drew themselves into tighter and tighter ranks. While some carried sarissas, many used the same small spears as had been used by Greek phalanxes for centuries.

Indian mercenary spearmen and native Bactrian swordsmen extended the main line to the right and left. The Bactrian cataphract cavalry was on the far right. The far left flank was left empty. The plan was to have the Scythian cavalry fill that flank, but they were currently skirmishing on the riverbank.

Demetrius rode toward his father and Arjun. Arjun wore a green tunic, which matched the blanket that covered his horse. His wrists, neck, and ears glittering with gold and bronze jewelry. He wore no helmet but had a plate of bronze across his chest and greaves on his legs.

"My son," Euthydemus said, as Demetrius slowed his horse to a stop beside him. Euthydemus wore bronze armor and a blue cloak. Without a helmet, his gray hair waved in the wind. Dust clouded his beard and mustache.

"Where have you been?" said Euthydemus. "We're getting the men together. I hear the enemy has already formed ranks on the beach."

"I know. I was just down there," said Demetrius.

"And?" said Euthydemus. "How do they look? What of their size? Is it as we've been told?"

"Unfortunately, yes," said Demetrius. "Their phalanx is much larger than ours."

He thought back on the bronze and spiked wall that had formed across the river. A bead of sweat dripped down his nose.

"Did you see any elephants?" asked Arjun.

"No," said Demetrius.

"Good," said Euthydemus, nodding. "Good."

He turned to Arjun. "Bring the elephants up and make sure the best archers are in their castles. We need to break that phalanx."

"Yes, your majesty," said Arjun.

"And did your men find a place to camp?" continued Euthydemus.

"Yes," said Arjun. "There's a valley twenty stade back. I've assigned people to clear the land around it and start setting up camp."

"Is that the closest spot available?"

"As far as our scouts could find, yes," said Arjun.

"That's not ideal," said Euthydemus, "but it will have to do. Now carry on. I want those elephants here as soon as possible."

As Arjun rode away, Demetrius asked Euthydemus, "How are you doing, Father?"

"I am fine, my son," said Euthydemus. "We'll be victorious before sundown."

Demetrius read doubt in his father's sunken brown eyes. He didn't push the matter, but instead shifted his attention to the mass of hoplites climbing the ridge on their way to the river and the enemy.

CHAPTER FIFTY

Antiochus

Antiochus felt confident as he watched his army fill the riverbank. Officers straightened the lines and encouraged the men. They were all doing the best they could given the challenging ground. All the phalanx needed to do was remain cohesive until the enemy mass broke.

When Antiochus saw the far ridge, however, his confidence wavered. The Bactrian army covered its curves. The phalanx stood in the middle, missile troops waited on the edges, and cavalry rested at the far flanks. The old king had done it, Antiochus thought. He had brought a real army.

With the main battle lines forming, the skirmishers on both sides of the river pulled back. A few of the more adventurous still ran toward the river and released a missile at the enemy. Some found their mark and the glory they sought. Others were struck and died in front of thousands.

At first, the two armies were silent, save for the clanking of armor, weapons, and shields as they moved into position. But then, as the lines came to a halt, men hurled insults across the river and banged their weapons against their shields. They were impatient to fight—or perhaps scared to do so.

Antiochus stopped behind the center of his line and beside Dropidas.

"Have you found a crossing?" Antiochus asked.

"Not yet," said Dropidas. "Although there are a few places that seem promising. They're narrow, maybe twenty men across. We don't know the depth yet. The enemy skirmishers are defending the area."

Phriapa rode toward them from the river. "Your majesty," he said, bringing his horse to a stop beside them. "I don't see my cavalry being much use until the enemy crosses the river. I suggest that I pull them back."

"Fine," said Antiochus. "But take men and scout another crossing. Somewhere close by, but out of sight of the enemy."

Phriapa nodded.

"And take some Thracian mercenaries," said Antiochus. "They'll keep up."

"Very well," said Phriapa. He galloped away, leaving dust in his wake, and the Thracians joined him at the bottom of the hill. Their masks glistened in the sun, the bronze beards molded onto them appearing to flutter in the wind.

Antiochus turned back to Dropidas. "Send part of the phalanx across the shallows you mentioned. We're running out of time to disrupt the enemy as they form lines."

"Are you sure, your majesty? We don't know the depth—"

"Just do it," snapped Antiochus.

Moments later, Antiochus watched Dropidas ride through a gap in the phalanx. Once he reached the front, he spoke with a large man with a red-and-white plume on his helmet, its length running from ear to ear. The man nodded and barked orders at the phalanx. Groups of men took turns stepping forward, and soon a square of men had separated from the main line. The square followed the large man to the river's edge, turned right, and walked parallel to it.

Further to the right, Dropidas led a group of heavy cavalry into the river. As they reached the middle, they moved slowly, the water reaching the horses' chests. Fortunately, it rose no higher.

On the other side of the river, enemy riders and skirmishers coalesced around the crossing point like flies on a carcass. They launched a barrage of arrows, rocks, and javelins at the heavy cavalry. One man fell from his horse and disappeared into the water. While the river was shallow, his heavy armor would almost certainly hold him under. Then a horse collapsed, a javelin sticking from its neck. The rider thrashed in the waves as the beast pulled him under, too. Finally, the cataphracts, with Dropidas still in the lead, reached the opposite bank and smashed into the enemy. Wearing little in the way of armor, the enemy skirmishers began falling in droves, their bodies pierced by lances and slashed with swords.

With the heavy cavalry across, the chosen square of infantry followed. The process was slow, and the men struggled to stay together. Some stumbled, either falling to their death in the water or requiring others to lift them back to safety.

"Push!" shouted Antiochus, though no one in the river could hear him. "Push ahead!"

The men stepped onto the far bank and formed a line three deep. The line was small, but it was a start.

Despite harassment from Dropidas's cavalry, which had lost much of its formation, enemy skirmishers relentlessly launched missiles at the shield wall. Every few seconds, a rock, javelin, or arrow found its mark, and a man fell. This continued for a minute or so, until Dropidas led a group of horsemen into the skirmishing line, sending the enemy away in chaos.

CHAPTER FIFTY-ONE

Beleen

At the far right of the Bactrian line, Beleen brandished an ax. She looked down the river to her left, her view framed by two thick lines of bronze. Since leaving the steppe, she had seen many new things, but nothing compared to this. She had seen men in the thousands at home, during the large festivals or when populations moved between camps, but she had never seen men in the tens of thousands, and certainly not placed together in uniform lines as they were today. The river meandered between the two armies, turquoise-blue like a necklace traded on the steppe. Dead bodies crowded either side like gems.

Scanning further, Beleen noticed that a group of enemy infantry had forded the river and formed a small wall. Enemy cavalry hacked at the skirmishers that attempted to dislodge them.

As Beleen watched the milieu, someone yelled, "Charge!"

The horses around her pushed toward the river. She nudged her horse and followed, tightening her sweaty fingers around her ax. The mass of horses ran parallel to the Bactrian phalanx and across the beach. Beleen blinked as the sun reflected against armor and into her eyes, and she coughed as dust enveloped her.

She wiped her eyes and looked ahead. Through the bobbing, helmet-covered heads in front of her, she could make out the enemy infantry. Their lines were not tight, and by the time they realized a cavalry charge was underway, they could do nothing to prepare for it.

The soldiers tried to escape. If only they had held their ground, they might have had a chance, but instead, they scattered, opening gaps for the horses to push through. Beleen swung her ax at a man's head, and pain radiated through her hand as the blade slid against his metal helmet. The man was saved for the moment, but the force of the blow sent him tumbling to the ground. Beleen lost sight of him as her horse continued through the line and into the river. Kasen slowed as he entered deeper water, and Beleen's feet dipped under the waves.

"Let's go, Kasen," Beleen urged, pulling his reins.

Kasen struggled through the water. Arrows flew past Beleen's head, and soldiers charged her from the left. Just as they reached her, a second Scythian charge attacked them from behind and knocked many of them over. One man was slammed against Beleen's leg. Sharp pain pierced her knee as the man fell and disappeared in the agitated water.

As Beleen guided her horse toward the shore, she considered what was left of the enemy infantry who had crossed the river. Many lay dead on the beach. Others thrashed in the water. Some dropped their weapons as they followed the retreating Seleucid cataphracts. Others pushed their comrades out of their way, sending them under the blood-soaked waves.

Just as Beleen turned her gaze from the chaos, Kasen lifted her with his hind legs. He had done it before, but when he started tilting to the side, Beleen knew something was wrong. She fell. Beleen had never been underwater before, and she thrashed in panic. She slapped her hands against the surface as she struggled to find her footing. Finally, she grabbed something and lifted her head from the water. As she stood, she realized that she had pulled herself up using Kasen's body. Water dripped down her face and hair.

Kasen lay on his side, struggling to keep his head above water. An arrow stuck from his neck. Seeing the panic in his eyes, Beleen tried to pull his head higher above the surface, but each swell of bloody water blanketed his mouth and nose.

"Come on," she yelled, pulling at his head.

Kasen thrashed. He sneezed as red water passed across him.

"Come on!"

Kasen's right eye widened as one side of his head inched above the water. But only for a moment. The next red wave submerged him.

Beleen looked to the sky and clenched her jaw. With Kasen still shaking, she let go of him with one hand and searched the water for her ax. She found it on the riverbed and tightened her fingers around it. Tears streamed down her face as she pulled the weapon into the air.

"I'm sorry, Kasen," she cried, before slamming the ax into the horse's head.

Kasen's eyes rolled back, and he stopped moving. Beleen sobbed as she lowered his head below the waves.

In horror and confusion, she backed away toward the beach. Shouting surrounded her. Bodies floated in the water, while others were under the surface.

The far riverbank was covered in bronze. The army of Antiochus. Beleen turned to see a similar shining wall. The phalanx of Bactria. The scene was both beautiful and terrible. Standing at the river's edge between the two armies, she was mesmerized into immobility.

A javelin pierced the water beside her, jolting her to action. She ran from the river and followed the skirmishers through the Bactrian line, which was at least ten men deep. As she moved farther up the ridge and away from the killing zone, she realized there were bloody scrapes on both of her arms, and her shirt was torn, its left sleeve only held to her shoulder by her bronze cuirass.

She looked to the top of the ridge, where Demetrius sat on his horse among a group of heavy cavalry. Beside him sat his father, the king of Bactria.

CHAPTER FIFTY-TWO

Demetrius

The river below had changed dramatically since Demetrius's first approach. Where before it had been calm and pristine, now it was chaotic and stained. The once turquoise water was now a reddish-tan, and the banks were crimson with blood. Skirmishers darted between bodies, launching missiles across the water. As if to frame the onslaught, both bronze-plated phalanxes stood still, their spears facing forward. Demetrius had seen battle, but he had never seen anything like this.

"Your majesty." A horseman rode up the ridge toward his father. "The skirmishers have been unable to find a suitable crossing. The enemy tried to cross along the middle, but it was too narrow, and we killed many."

Euthydemus nodded silently. "This cannot work," he said after a time.

Below him, the spears of the phalanx swayed back and forth, and the men who gripped them shouted insults across the water.

"What do you mean?" Demetrius asked his father.

"The timing can't work." Euthydemus did not turn to face his son. "We needed to cross the river to properly engage them. We needed to fight them in pieces to deal with their strength. Head on like this—" he waved his hand at the armies, "—and with the river causing so many obstacles, I'm not sure we can win."

"So you want us to retreat?" said Demetrius.

"Perhaps," said Euthydemus. "For now, let's wait. Antiochus may grow impatient and make a mistake."

Demetrius gazed at the far riverbank. Skirmishers shuffled between the river and the Seleucid phalanx. On the ridge beyond, countless soldiers stood and waited. And Antiochus—the cause of all of this death—waited among them.

CHAPTER FIFTY-THREE

Antiochus

Antiochus's attention was drawn from the river to a horseman riding up the hill. After a moment's pause, Antiochus realized the rider was Dropidas, dripping with water and blood.

"It was a massacre, your majesty," said Dropidas, panting. His face was smeared with dirt. "We can't do it. We must find another way across."

As Antiochus watched Dropidas struggle for air, a messenger slowed his horse beside him.

"Your majesty," he said. "The elephants are ready to deploy."

"No," said Antiochus.

"Your majesty?" said Dropidas, finally able to catch his breath. "You've been waiting for them. That might be what we need to get across."

"It's too late now," said Antiochus. "The sun is falling, and the enemy is ready. It will be impossible to cross the river like this. The elephants will only get in the way."

Antiochus stared at the far ridge, where a group of enemy horsemen stood motionless. He wondered if one of them was Euthydemus.

As Antiochus squinted, Phriapa halted beside him.

"Antiochus," said Phriapa, neither using "your majesty," nor appearing to care. "We found a crossing." He was breathing heavily and his horse scratched the dirt with its front hooves. "And we found the enemy camp. It's many stades back from the river, in a valley beside a small town."

"So they will need to pull back considerably to reach their camp?" said Antiochus.

"Yes. Absolutely," said Phriapa. "Unless they mean to keep most of their soldiers here, they will have to give up the beach to keep their army together and guarded within the camp."

Antiochus felt himself begin to smile. This was just the break he needed.

"Excellent," he said, looking from Phriapa to Dropidas, and on to the far ridge. "Now, let's make them feel safe."

Antiochus prodded his horse and let it carry him slowly down the ridge. Phriapa and Dropidas followed. As he rode, Antiochus looked to the small group of cavalry on the far ridge.

"Come and beg for mercy," he muttered under his breath.

CHAPTER FIFTY-FOUR

Demetrius

Demetrius watched the far riverbank in shock. The enemy phalanx created a gap through which several horsemen rode, approaching the river. The skirmishers from both sides pulled back.

"That's him," said his father. "That's Antiochus. He wants to talk. See, even he knows this day cannot be won. Let's go."

Demetrius followed his father down the ridge and toward the back of the phalanx. Officers forced the men apart—a concept anathema to the center of a phalanx—and slowly a gap opened in the line like a gate in a rock wall. Demetrius rode through it and to the river's edge, his horse stepping carefully around the fallen bodies.

Demetrius lifted his chin and straightened his back as his steed came to a stop in the shallows. He knew the eyes of both friend and foe were on him and his father. Both armies were quiet.

It didn't take long for Demetrius to discern which of the horsemen was Antiochus. He was the most ornately dressed and bore no sign of combat or exertion. He wore a shined bronze cuirass, with animals battling across the chest, and a thin gold diadem. A red cloak fell from his shoulders.

He was flanked by Phriapa, the Parthian prince Demetrius had met earlier, and a solidly built cavalryman. Only Antiochus smiled. He rode deep into the middle of the river, leaving the others to follow.

Demetrius and his father did not hesitate to lead their horses forward. When they were within speaking distance, Demetrius's feet slipped below the surface.

"An interesting place to meet," said Antiochus, drawing up a horse's length away.

"And both of us so far from home," Euthydemus replied.

"Very true." Antiochus smiled again. "But when duty calls, an emperor must answer."

"As must a king," said Euthydemus. "But tell me, Antiochus, what brings you down from your perch and into conversation? If it is for terms of peace, I will gladly accept and wish you and your men well on your journey home."

"I'm afraid we'll be staying here a bit longer," said Antiochus, the smile disappearing from his face. "In fact, I don't plan to go home until I've visited your famous city of Zariaspa."

"If you intend to visit as an invader," said Euthydemus, "I can promise that you won't even reach the gate."

"Enough of this," snapped Antiochus. "I came down here to offer you and your men a chance at peace. Today, if you swear fealty to me and accept the title of vassal king, my men and I will leave. But if you continue this intransigence, I promise I will adorn the great hall of Zariaspa with your head."

"I am no more your vassal than you are the rightful heir to Alexander," said Euthydemus. "Emperor, king, vassal. These are all words if you cannot back them up with force."

Antiochus pointed at the sarissas swaying behind him. "I have no problem proving my claim with force."

"Nor do I," said Euthydemus, stretching his arms wide.

Demetrius looked from his father to Antiochus, and then to Phriapa. He and the prince were only bystanders now, witnesses to the wordplay of more powerful men.

"So," said Antiochus, reclaiming Demetrius's attention. "You hope to conclude a battle tonight? It is getting dark, and I'm sure your men are tired."

"It sounds like you're scared," said Euthydemus. "We, however, will fight in the moonlight if we have to."

"I hope your army is better than your bluffing," said Antiochus. There was a pause. "Now, it is true that my men need rest, and I'm sure yours do, too. So, while my men would gladly kill the amateurs you brought any time of day, I'm sure everyone would be content to fight in the morning. What do you say to retiring for the night?"

With much of their army still in the rear and the army of Zariaspa still approaching, Demetrius hoped his father would agree. The horses breathed and kicked at the water, the sounds filling the tense silence.

"We will see you at sunrise, then," said Euthydemus.

"Looking forward to it," said Antiochus.

Before Demetrius turned his horse away and followed his father, he looked over to Phriapa. The Parthian was staring at him and, as their eyes met, the man bowed slightly. Demetrius did the same and then nudged his horse into a trot. In seconds, he was back on the bank, the soldiers in front of him murmuring with news of the delay.

"What a fool," said Euthydemus. "By tomorrow morning, we will have twice the number of men."

Demetrius was glad for the delay but confused as to why Antiochus had offered it so willingly. Perhaps there were problems within his army. Maybe the Parthians were proving a challenging ally. Deep in thought, he followed his father up the ridge.

CHAPTER FIFTY-FIVE

Antiochus

"That man has proven himself an unworthy king," said Antiochus, as his horse carried him from the river and toward the phalanx, which had already started filing up the ridge. "He is a fool."

"Yes, your majesty," said Dropidas, riding beside him. "But why let him get away? Half his army is not even here yet. Even if we had lost many, we would have beaten them."

"Perhaps," said Antiochus. "But I'd rather avoid such bloodshed. And you heard Phriapa. He found a nearby crossing, as well as their camp. We shall cross late tonight and attack their camp before sunrise." Antiochus watched his army snake between the hills and smirked. "We will have them beaten before they emerge from their tents."

CHAPTER FIFTY-SIX

Demetrius

Demetrius's father ordered men to make fires so it looked like the army camped near the river. It was imperative that the enemy did not know the true camp was farther back.

"I want the light cavalry going up and down the river throughout the night," Euthydemus called to an officer. "The enemy may try to find a different way to cross."

"Yes, your majesty," the man yelled, riding away.

Before passing over the ridge, Demetrius turned back to look at the gently moving river. Bodies framed it on either side, and the sand was reddish-brown. Taking a deep breath, he turned and started on the short journey through the mountain passes and toward the camp.

As he rode, soldiers approached to ask why they had retreated, while others lay on the ground and cried out for help—or for death. Demetrius tried his best to assign soldiers to help the wounded, but the scale was overwhelming. By the time he reached the camp, he felt sick and exhausted. His throat scratched, but he kept swallowing until it dissipated. When he felt fully composed, he went to his father's tent. There was still much to do.

CHAPTER FIFTY-SEVEN

Beleen

Beleen walked between the camp tents holding a blood-soaked rag against her left forearm. The sun had now fully retreated and stars had taken its place in the sky. Despite the long day, Beleen wasn't tired. Instead, she was missing home. With soldiers and mountains surrounding her, her view of the sky felt exceedingly constrained.

Beleen squeezed her shoulder to test the pain. The gentle pressure elicited a burning sensation, which traveled down her arm. She winced, partly from pain, and partly from recognizing that she had nearly died. Her mind went back to the riverbank, where friends had died, as had thousands of strangers. She remembered a man struggling to pull himself above the water, and there'd been no one to help.

Beleen pulled her mind from the killing and turned in place. A group of Scythians had tied their horses to a log that leaned against a house. Beleen felt her throat tighten as she thought of Kasen, dead in the river, his skull punctured by her ax. As tears crested her eyelids, she led her new horse to a log and secured it among the others.

Ahead of her, a young man tended to a four-wheeled cart beside a large tent. Food covered the platform from end to end. Sliced and whole mangoes lined one half. Bronze cups and a clay jug lined the other. The man stirred the contents of a metal bowl that rattled over a fire. As Beleen passed, he lifted an empty cup and looked at her inquisitively. She shook her head, and he set the cup back among the others. Beyond the cart, a pebble-covered path meandered up a rocky ridge and ended at the center of a small village.

Beleen climbed the ridge to her left. Reaching the top, she studied Euthydemus's army and its hundreds, perhaps thousands, of small fires. With the flicker of flames below and the sparkle of stars above, Beleen could imagine she was flying. She wondered if spirits felt this way.

A cool breeze passed through her clothes. She rubbed her arms and glanced at the nearest campfire, and when she descended to it, she found Roshan among the group, watching the flames.

"Good evening," Roshan said at her approach.

"To you, too." Beleen studied him. Dirt and dried blood covered his arms and face.

Her gaze moved from Roshan to the others. Ashok and Priya were among them. Most of the group had paint on their foreheads. They had been speaking in their language but stopped when she sat down. Ashok welcomed her in Greek.

"How was today for you?" he said.

"I'm still alive," said Beleen, suddenly feeling tired.

"Have you ever seen that much death?"

"Never," said Beleen. "And I hope never to see it again."

She fell into a reflective silence. Demetrius approached.

"Your majesty," said Ashok, standing. "It is wonderful to see you. And without a scratch."

"No need for formalities, Ashok," said Demetrius. "For now, I just need a friend."

Ashok nodded quietly.

"I'm sorry," said Demetrius, taking the seat opposite Beleen. "I interrupted your conversation. What were you talking about?"

"Kurukshetra, the battlefield of our ancestors. As we had not seen battle before today, the war of the Pandavas and the Kauravas was our only reference. And we were sad that today was nothing like the stories. There was none of the individual combat and the honor and the glory that we had expected. Only death and agony."

"No chariots either," said Demetrius.

"I see you remember the stories I told you," said Ashok.

"Some of them," said Demetrius. "It's hard to forget the scene you painted in my mind of Bhima, Drona, Arjun, and the others fighting one another for days on end."

"Yes," said Ashok. "But we have only seen fighting for one day, and I am ready to be rid of it."

"Did I ever tell you the story of the Greeks and the Trojans?" asked Demetrius. "Their war lasted years, and if there was ever a Greek war like the one in your *Mahābhārata*, that would be it. It also had great men on chariots, and great women and gods. Your story has Arjun, Karna, and Draupadi. Ours has Achilles, Menelaus, and Helen. I've come to realize there are not many differences between our ideas and yours. At least, not at a deeper level. Your sages and gurus, and the teacher, Buddha, encourage their followers to seek truth over ignorance, Atma over Maya. Our men of learning, Socrates and Aristotle, for example, teach much the same thing."

"Even Homer's journey of Odysseus is not unlike the story of Rama in search of his Sita," said Beleen, eager to contribute the knowledge she had gained over the years. "Both face trials on their way to their loved ones."

Demetrius turned to her, a quizzical look on his face.

"We Scythians trade in more than gold and trinkets," she said, satisfied by his surprise. "We have learned many of your stories over years of trading and war."

"Well, you're certainly full of surprises," said Demetrius.

They continued speaking through the night about the philosophies of east and west. For moments here and there, Beleen forgot the enemy was near. She forgot that she was waiting for the hours to pass before she was to fight them again. But each time, the reality came crashing back. Eventually, the group fell silent, and as Beleen watched the flames weave across the logs and spray sparks into the air, she wondered if the enemy was doing much the same thing.

CHAPTER FIFTY-EIGHT

⟫——→

Phriapa

Phriapa walked through the forest of campfires that the Seleucid army had created on the ridge. It lit up the entire valley, which was bordered on each side by barren hills. Past the hill to his left and within the valley, water crept through the sand and washed the blood away. Across the river, campfires lit the far ridge, though Phriapa knew them to be diversionary and not a true reflection of Euthydemus's actual camp.

He joined Antiochus and Dropidas at the fire in front of the emperor's tent. Dropidas moved to make room for him, dirt scraping beneath his sandals.

"We were just talking about tomorrow's fight," said Dropidas. "We're eager for this to be done."

"I see," said Phriapa, settling into place on the cold, dusty ground. He looked to Antiochus. "Your majesty, what will you do with Euthydemus and the others once we beat them?"

Antiochus was quiet at first. When he finally spoke, it was in a soft voice, as if he had deeply considered each word. "I gave Euthydemus the choice of friendship today, and he denied it. I will not offer it again."

Phriapa nodded and watched Antiochus through the fire. The monarch's face was hidden in shadow.

"Has anyone ever told you," continued Antiochus, "what Alexander did with the Thebans when they rebelled against him?"

"No," said Phriapa, fed up with how much the westerners spoke of Alexander.

"Well," said Antiochus, leaning forward and letting the light invade his face. "The Thebans had sworn fealty to Alexander before he invaded Persia. Not unlike how the predecessors of Euthydemus swore fealty to mine. But as soon as they were afforded the chance, the Thebans rebelled. Alexander was just about to cross the Hellespont into Asia, so they must have assumed he was too far along to turn back."

Antiochus threw a twig into the fire. "They were wrong, because as any good monarch would, Alexander returned to Greece to reclaim the loyalty that he was due. He reached the land of the Thebans, much as I have reached the land claimed by Euthydemus. When he arrived, he gave the Thebans a chance to reform their ways and take their place once again within the fold."

Antiochus used his sword to flick a wayward piece of burning wood back into the fire. The shadow on his face had returned. "But the Thebans refused the offer and took refuge in their city. From this, Alexander realized that only force would work. More importantly, he realized that an example needed to be made, so that no rebellion would ever hold him from his plans again. So, when he finally defeated the city, he had every single man executed, and the women and children were sold into slavery. The city he leveled to dust."

Like Phriapa, the other men sat in silence. The fire crackled.

"Do you think such a fate is befitting of Euthydemus and his kin?" Antiochus asked, finally filling the void.

"It is not my place to comment on the demands of fate," said Phriapa.

For a long moment, Antiochus was silent.

"Very well," he said, standing. "Let's get moving then. The moon has risen, and the fates await."

Firelight sparkled against his armor and lit his face. His eyes were sunken and dark, and his mouth quivered between a smirk and a grimace.

Phriapa followed Antiochus along the low point of the next valley, letting it lead him to the river's edge. Reaching a ridge that overlooked the water, Phriapa considered the area, first looking for the enemy, and then looking for the crossing he had identified during his battlefield reconnaissance. While he did not see any enemy soldiers, his view was full of movement.

The river sparkled as it passed by the steep, sand-colored cliff and rushed on as it squeezed through a series of rocks that sat in the river.

"Phriapa," Antiochus said, pulling Phriapa's gaze from the water. "Is this the spot?"

"Yes, this is the spot."

"Because I don't want any accidents. If people or horses make a big commotion, it may draw the enemy sentries."

"This is the spot," Phriapa repeated, more firmly.

"Then lead the way."

Phriapa led his horse by the reins down the ridge and toward the glimmering river. The Parthians followed, and behind them, the Seleucid infantry took their place at the top of the hill. As per Antiochus's orders, no one wore armor. Instead, they carried their armor wrapped in blankets taken from the baggage train. Any amount of noise could alert the enemy, and if the army was caught during the river crossing, disaster would follow. Urging his horse deeper into the river, Phriapa looked back to see Antiochus watching his progress.

CHAPTER FIFTY-NINE

Antiochus

Antiochus looked down at the moonlight glistening on the river and took a deep breath of crisp air. The breeze passed over him and sent a refreshing shiver down his back. He felt alive and eager for the fight.

His horse's warm breath spread through the air like blood in water, billowing and twisting. With the others quietly mounting their horses and the stars providing the only light, Antiochus felt more nervous than he had since hunting alone for the first time as a child. There was something eerie about the air. It felt fragile, the quiet ready to break.

Ahead, Phriapa waded waist-deep in water, and Antiochus wondered if it was cold. He pushed the thought from his mind and scolded himself for thinking such a foolish thing. He would walk through ice if it meant defeating his enemies and taking his place in the histories beside Alexander. For too many years, the Seleucid Empire had been nothing but a collection of spoiled rebels. Now, with Rome on the rise and Egypt eyeing his lands, it was time he brought the house to order.

Dropidas rode up behind him, the sound seeming unnecessarily loud in the darkness.

"Everyone is on the move, your majesty," Dropidas said. "The army should cross within two hours."

"Excellent," said Antiochus. "And you told the mahouts to keep their elephants silent?"

"Yes. They'll do what they can."

Antiochus turned back to the river. Phriapa had reached the other side and was leading his men into the hills beyond. It was time for Antiochus to cross. He didn't want a Parthian in the lead for too long.

When Antiochus reached the river and his feet dipped just below the surface, he stopped and considered the sparkle of light around him. He closed his eyes and spoke the words of Hesiod, a long-dead poet: "Never wade through the pretty ripples of perpetually flowing rivers, until you have looked at their lovely waters, and prayed to them, and washed your hands in the pale enchanting water."

Antiochus opened his eyes and leaned down to the river, letting the cold water slip through his fingers. He wrung his hands together and let the water drip from his fingertips. Calmness and anticipation buzzed, contradictorily, within him as he stepped further into the river's cold embrace.

But as Antiochus looked up to see Phriapa disappear over the far ridge, worry passed through him. The surprise of the attack was everything. If Euthydemus knew what was going on, he could attack the Seleucid army at the worst moment. Antiochus's mind found poetry once again: "He does mischief to himself who does mischief to another, and evil planned harms the plotter most."

But Antiochus reassured himself that his actions were not evil. In fact, they were just, and he stepped further into the cold. By the time he reached the other side, the water had risen to his chest, and his body shivered beyond control.

He looked to the pink horizon. The sun would rise above the hills soon enough. They needed to hurry if they were going to catch the enemy at their camp.

As he reached the top of the next ridge, he considered the land ahead. There were hills as far as he could see, appearing like the sand dunes of Mesopotamia. Though he had only seen that desert a few times in his life, it was more familiar to him than this barren land, and the thought made him miss home.

He looked back at the river, where the peltasts struggled to cross. They held their javelins above their heads and stumbled into one another in the darkness. With no fires, everything was covered in a blue haze. Behind them, a group of Seleucid heavy cavalry waited their turn. A smile curled across Antiochus's numb face. Everything was going to plan.

CHAPTER SIXTY

Demetrius

Demetrius woke. He opened his eyes and saw his father standing above him in full armor, the light from the campfires flickering against the metal plates.

"Get your armor on," said Euthydemus.

"What's going on?" said Demetrius, getting to his feet. He looked past his father and into the forest of tents, which were painted pink by the coming dawn. Men were hurrying into their armor and throwing leather and metal onto their horses. They handed lances to one another. Breath steamed from both man and beast.

"One of our scouts saw Antiochus's army crossing the Arius a few stades to the west of where we engaged them yesterday."

Demetrius rubbed his arms and looked up into the clear, star-filled sky. Bats zipped in the air above him, and the wind that filled their wings passed across his lightly covered body. He shivered. The mountains, though warm in the day, grew considerably colder at night.

"We will attack them before they form up lines," continued Euthydemus. "Now get your armor on and join the others. There's no time for the infantry. We're going with the cavalry alone."

"Yes, Father," said Demetrius, feeling more and more awake with each breath. He pulled on a leather coat that would both warm him and keep the metal armor from scraping against his skin.

As he secured his armor, he looked past the other Greek cataphracts to the Scythians. They consisted of a mix of heavily armored spearmen and lightly armored archers. He wondered how effective the archers would be against the Parthian cataphracts. Then again, he had seen the Scythians do many things he'd once thought impossible.

"Did you sleep at all?" he called to Beleen, who was speaking to a group of Scythians. She straightened and looked at him.

"Not a moment," she said. "But we can sleep when this is over."

She held her bow in one hand. Her ax, its blade browned with dried blood, rested in her broad leather belt, and gold jewelry covered her arms. On the battlefield, below the moon, she would be quite a sight.

To Demetrius's right, Ashok placed arrows in a thin wicker basket that he would sling over his shoulder. His tall bow, the string pulled taut, leaned against a boulder behind him.

"Ready to follow our dharma, brother?" said Demetrius, referring to a Hindu concept of duty.

"Ready to become the next Achilles?" Ashok replied.

Demetrius smiled and patted Ashok on the shoulder. He nodded to Roshan, who sharpened the blade of his spear with a whetstone. A bow was strapped to his back.

Before mounting his horse, Demetrius accepted a cup of water from a local boy who he had earlier seen wandering the camp. After returning the cup to the boy, Demetrius accepted the help of a servant in getting onto his horse. With most of his body covered in metal, his range of motion was limited. Once mounted, he took his lance from the servant and patted his horse's neck, letting his armor clatter against the metal on the horse's mane.

When the rest of the cavalry were mounted, he led his horse away from the tents, through the thin gate of the makeshift camp's defenses, and out into the cold, starry night.

CHAPTER SIXTY-ONE

Antiochus

Sitting on his horse beside the river, Antiochus lamented the loss of time. A horse's hooves clattered against the ground, and he spotted one of the light horsemen he had sent to watch the enemy camp. The man, who wore a simple black tunic covered in a crude bronze chest plate, stopped his horse in a cloud of moonlit dust.

"Your majesty," the man said. "The Bactrians. They're on the move. I saw hundreds of horsemen gathering in battle attire."

"Damn it!" yelled Antiochus, squeezing his horse's reins. "Did you see where they were going?"

"I saw their scouts follow a path that could bring them here."

Antiochus looked back at the river, where a group of elephants was making its way across. The animals were pulling water into their trunks and spraying it over their heads and backs.

Behind them, men were tying items onto the baggage train wagons. Donkeys and carts extended up the ridge as far as he could see, blocking the main path to the water. Hardly any of his army had made it across the river. And the enemy would soon arrive.

"How many men did you see gathering?"

"I'm not sure," said the messenger. "It was dark, and the hills blocked much of my view, but perhaps ten thousand."

Antiochus realized his expression must have shaken the messenger, because the man quickly revised the number down to five thousand. But Antiochus knew the revision to be untrue. Euthydemus would not pass on the opportunity to bring his full cavalry against him. This was his chance to save his home from invasion.

Antiochus called to Dropidas, who came running.

"Yes, your majesty?" said Dropidas.

"How many men have crossed the river?"

"About two thousand horsemen," he said. "And maybe three thousand peltasts, archers, and phalangites."

Antiochus's neck tightened. That wasn't enough. But there was no time.

"Have your men mount," he said. "Quickly. The enemy is upon us. Ten thousand strong."

Dropidas's eyes widened. "Yes, your majesty." He dashed back to his horse, calling orders to the other men.

When the men were mounted, Antiochus ordered the peltasts and archers to follow at a jog and to be ready to offer support if needed. He explained to the cavalry officers that they were to draw the enemy riders back toward the river and the skirmishers. If the battle remained only horsemen against horsemen, Antiochus would not live to see the sunrise.

CHAPTER SIXTY-TWO

Demetrius

Demetrius joined his father in a wide valley that ran perpendicular to the camp. King Euthydemus wore layers of leather and metal armor, and with his horse covered the same way, he had the look of a centaur. As he stared back at Demetrius, his lip twitched, and he blinked in quick succession.

"This is it, my son," he said. "This is our chance to be rid of them."

Demetrius tightened his grip on his lance. "Yes, Father."

Demetrius's heart thundered in his chest. Something about the chill of the morning made him distinctly aware of the armor that wrapped around him. His body knew he was off to battle, to kill or be killed.

Across the valley, horsemen wove between one another on their mounts. The glow of the horizon reflected against their shining armor, giving the valley the look of a rippling pool.

Eucratides rode up beside Demetrius. "Are you ready?" he asked.

"I'm ready to be finished with this," said Demetrius. After riding north into Scythia and then riding south in pursuit of Antiochus, his body and mind were tired.

"As am I," said Eucratides. "And soon enough, this will be done. In days, we will be back in Zariaspa, drinking and flirting as we should be."

To Demetrius, their old habits of partying with the noblewomen seemed so far away. So artificial. It had not been until Demetrius rode into Scythia that he felt fully alive. He had the same feeling now.

Demetrius looked at the path they would take to the river. A lightly armored horseman galloped toward their group. News of the enemy, he assumed. The horseman stopped before his father, sending dust into the crisp morning air.

"Your highness," the man gasped. "Horsemen are coming this way. They number about two thousand."

"Where?" said Euthydemus.

"Just a few stades over that ridge." The man pointed at a group of far hills outlined in bright red, which announced the rising sun.

"Let's go," called Euthydemus to the cavalry. "We have them far outnumbered. Let's end this war today."

Demetrius's stomach tightened. He took a deep breath and let it out slowly. Then he nudged his horse, and in seconds the animal was carrying him forward amid the rumbling army.

As they worked their way between the hills and along the path, the sun broke above the horizon and sent bright, fire-colored light smashing into the hillsides. Parts of each hill turned red and orange, but other parts stayed in shadow. The scenery looked like a steppe deer torn to pieces by a lion's claws, blood flowing across its fur.

Demetrius expected to discover the enemy at each bend. With each turn that brought nothing more than red rocks and dark shadows, his heart thumped under his armor.

Finally, as the sun rose above the horizon, Demetrius reached the top of a ridge and saw the enemy cresting the opposite. A wide, flat valley covered in knee-high bushes separated the armies. Compared to Demetrius's horde of horsemen, Antiochus's cavalry looked insignificant. Maybe this would be easy, after all.

As planned, Beleen led the Scythian horse archers on the far left flank. Euthydemus, lit brightly by the rising sun, led the cataphracts on the right.

Demetrius, in the center of the line, rearranged his helmet to better align the eyeholes, and he saw a section of the enemy cavalry form a line. Once the group of roughly two hundred horsemen reached the flat, dusty surface of the valley, they charged at a gallop. They kicked up dust as they went, clouding their comrades behind them, and as they grew closer, Demetrius noticed that these men carried bows, not lances. They were archers.

He opened and closed his fingers around his lance, took a deep breath, and yelled, "Charge!" There was no time to wait for his father's orders: They couldn't just sit there and wait for the arrows. The crash of galloping hooves and clanking metal grew deafening. Demetrius's helmet shook, and the eyeholes jostled with each lunge forward, momentarily blocking his view.

Ahead of him, the enemy horsemen came to a stop. They lifted their bows, and arrows rose into the sky like a dark cloud. In a flash, the arrows disappeared from view, and Demetrius tightened his body and pulled his arms to his chest. He didn't see the arrows land, but he heard men screaming and horses smashing against the earth. The man just ahead of Demetrius fell, and Demetrius's horse jumped over his rolling body.

The enemy horse archers did not stay to engage the survivors. By the time Demetrius got his bearings, they were galloping away, leaving a large gap between the armies. The enemy horde then turned sharply to the left. Demetrius and his companions turned in pursuit, riding into the dust cloud left behind by the enemy.

It was through that dust cloud, and without the slightest warning, that Antiochus's heavy cavalry smashed into the flank of Demetrius's exposed line. Demetrius could hardly see—his eyes closing and blinking beyond his control—as lances, swords, men, and horses passed by him in a terrifying frenzy. And it wasn't just his eyes that were overwhelmed. His ears could no longer discern one sound from another—screaming and trampling and clashing metal all rolled together into one deep hum.

Something dark passed in front of Demetrius. He had no time to decide if the darkness was friend or foe before something else crashed against his left arm. The plate metal spared him a cut, but not the concussion. His arm fell limp and he let go of the horse's reins. With his right arm, he stabbed his lance toward the darkness. Again, something struck him, this time in the right shoulder. The pain burst through his whole body. He stabbed again in desperation until he heard his lance snap. As he pulled the splintered weapon back, he was thrown from his falling horse.

He was on the ground and coughing amid the dust. He couldn't see, couldn't hear, and couldn't stand. The fates had planned his death, he thought, and this was the moment.

His mind veered wildly, offering him a scene of the River Styx, passages from the *Bhagavad Gita*, and a phrase from Buddha. As he faced death, his soul came to the crossroads of his mind. Which path would it take? All of them? One of them? None? And then, as his mind settled on the present, on the dirt below his face, his vision went black.

CHAPTER SIXTY-THREE

⁓

Beleen

Beleen rode on the far left flank of the Bactrian line, where the valley curved into the hill. She searched for a target. In the center of the valley, the cavalry of Bactria and Seleucia fought viciously. Farther back, the Parthian horse archers, who had initiated the attack, took roving shots at any horseman who pulled away from the milieu. She galloped toward the Parthians, the other Scythians close behind her.

A few Parthians sent arrows flying at the approaching Scythians. Beleen pressed her body against her horse's neck to dodge an incoming volley. Once it passed, she straightened and pulled an arrow from the quiver at her waist. Beleen led her horse at a diagonal to the enemy, giving her a clear shot into their ranks. She loosed an arrow into the neck of a Parthian rider, who toppled from his white horse into the dust.

Beleen led her horse back in the direction from which she had come. Enemy arrows landed all around her as she placed one of her own against her bowstring. Twisting around, she looked back at the Parthians, some of whom were giving chase. She released the arrow, sending the man in the lead tumbling off the back of his galloping horse. Men and women fell from their steeds around her or crashed to the ground atop their dying animals.

CHAPTER SIXTY-FOUR

Demetrius

Demetrius opened his eyes. He lay on the ground, his face in the dirt. He coughed, and dust flew into his eyes. As he pushed himself up, the bloodied bodies of men and horses filled his view.

"They're retreating," Demetrius heard someone yell through the chaos.

Getting to his feet, Demetrius looked ahead, where the enemy was disappearing over the ridge. Most were on horses, but some went on foot.

"Demetrius, are you wounded?" a rider called to him.

"Eucratides, is that you?"

"Who else?" Eucratides called back.

Demetrius looked down at his arms and torso. He didn't see any blood, but his left arm and his head both throbbed.

"I'm fine," he said, as he grabbed the reins of a riderless horse. "What happened?"

"They're retreating. We've got them beat."

As Eucratides spoke, horsemen in pursuit rode past Demetrius and toward the ridge.

"Come on," called Eucratides, throwing him a lance before drawing his sword. "Let's ride them into the river."

With his head and arm aching and his vision clouded, Demetrius pushed his horse into action and toward the far ridge. As he approached, he saw his father halfway up the hill, helmetless. Dust, sweat, and blood caked his face and beard.

Euthydemus yelled encouragement to the others. "We've got them. No mercy for the invaders!"

"Father," Demetrius said. "You're hurt." He pointed at the blood running freely down Euthydemus's face.

"Not as badly as we've hurt them," his father replied. "Now is the time to finish them. Let's go."

Demetrius followed his father over the ridge, where horsemen funneled in a narrow defile, and joined the procession weaving toward the now invisible enemy. But something felt wrong. He looked around for his father to no avail. The current of cavalry cut through the valley, getting thinner and thinner as it went.

Finally, the path widened into a broad valley, similar to the one in which they had just fought. The enemy horsemen were weaving back and forth in the clearing.

Just as Demetrius got a good look at them, yelling diverted his attention. He twisted in the saddle and looked back at the rocky hills through which they had come. Objects flew from them like water from an elephant's trunk. Demetrius only realized they were javelins when one stuck in the chest of the rider beside him. On the hill, men ran across the rocks, stopping every few feet to throw a javelin. They were aiming for the horses that were still in the narrow path. With bodies piling up, the pass was quickly blocked.

Drums banged, and Demetrius turned back to the clearing. Dust rose like a wave, and in its trough, armor and spears glittered in the now bright morning light as horsemen charged toward them.

He tightened his grip on his lance, encouraged his horse to action, and charged the approaching enemy. He held his breath as the distance closed faster than his mind could process. In a flash, riders were beside him, galloping in the opposite direction. The forces had met, and the already loud battlefield erupted into cacophony. When riders passed in front of Demetrius, he stabbed at them with his lance. He hit something hard, and vibrations traveled through his arm. He pulled back and found the lance had snapped in two. He turned it around and faced the pointed counterweight forward. Though much shorter than before, the lance would still work.

Demetrius urged his horse back into action. It led him across the battlefield, and finally, out of the dust. Horsemen circled the battle, releasing arrows into the fray, but he couldn't tell if they were Parthian or Scythian.

He looked to his right and saw a lone rider, surrounded by swordsmen. The rider's red cloak whipped back and forth as the man stabbed at his assailants. In the frenzy, the gold diadem flew from his head. He fought like a demigod, and Demetrius was mesmerized. The man was Antiochus. He fought off his assailants like Hercules fought the many heads of the Hydra, swinging his sword at one man while dodging the assault of another.

"Let's go!" Demetrius called to his horse, leading it into a gallop. Above the animal's flying mane, Demetrius eyed his target.

Once upon him, Demetrius jabbed the broken lance forward, smashing the counterweight into the monarch's shoulder. The blade did not stick, and instead slid off Antiochus's armor, but Demetrius knew the impact had been powerful.

Looking back as he rode on, Demetrius saw Antiochus fall to the ground.

Demetrius turned his horse and studied his lance. The counterweight had broken off. He threw the now much-shortened pole to the ground and pulled a sword from its sheath. The inlaid gems sparkled. When he looked back up, Demetrius could not see Antiochus. Only a pile of dead bodies remained, and the red-cloaked figure was gone.

CHAPTER SIXTY-FIVE

»——→

Phriapa

Phriapa reached into the pouch of arrows at his waist and found that none remained. He looked to the killing field, around which he had been circling, and into which he had been releasing the deadly projectiles.

Horsemen darted past one another with no sign of organization. Arrows, rocks, and javelins flew above them, while lances and swords stabbed and swung between them. The bodies of horses and men peppered the ground like oddly painted stones.

Despite the near-deafening sounds of death, Phriapa heard the blare of horns in the distance. The signal for retreat. The enemy was retreating. But then he heard another horn, this time from the opposite side of the battlefield.

"No!" he yelled, looking back at the ridgeline that covered the path toward the river. With the enemy retreating, now was the perfect time to push the attack. But instead, Antiochus had also called a retreat. Neither army of Greeks appeared ready to go in for the kill. Yes, an animal was most dangerous when cornered and wounded, but that did not mean one should avoid the strike.

With much of the battle's belligerents on horses, it did not take them long to separate, leaving a collection of the dead and dying in their wake. Reluctantly, Phriapa followed the others toward the valley that would lead them back to the river. To the far right, he saw the enemy struggling to escape the battlefield through the thin pass. They trampled over the dead horses and riders that blocked the way.

The path away from the battlefield looked different in the daylight, the hills less imposing but no less striking. The rising sun left parts of them golden and other parts deep brown. As he reached the river, he saw thousands of men on either side. Between them, a column of infantry was carefully making its way across. Elephants stood in the river beside them, splashing water on their bulbous, gray-brown backs. The colorful paint that had been applied to their faces streamed down their wrinkles and into the river.

Phriapa spotted Antiochus at the edge of the water, his officers beside him. Phriapa squeezed his horse, which carried him down the hill toward the Seleucid emperor.

"Why did you call a retreat?" demanded Phriapa, stopping beside Antiochus. "We had them. They had just called a retreat themselves."

"We did not have them," said Antiochus, not taking his eyes from the soldiers crossing the river. "I was not about to lose my best cavalry in that engagement. No. After they learned of our plan, our only purpose was to stop them from coming here, where most of my army is still crossing the river. At this point, I am perfectly content to let Euthydemus run back to Bactria with a bloody nose. We stopped him from combining his armies. We stopped him from attacking us at the river. I consider this a victory. Even if we can't catch him until he is safely behind the walls of Zariaspa, he doesn't stand a chance against the resources I will bring to bear."

"We could have killed Euthydemus today," said Phriapa. "On the battlefield. And finished it."

"I have spoken," said Antiochus. "And I will speak of it no more."

Phriapa felt himself heating. He took a deep breath, and to prevent himself from saying something he'd regret, he turned his horse and rode away.

CHAPTER SIXTY-SIX

Demetrius

His body was sore. His clothes had left him overheated. His mouth begged for water. Still, when Demetrius saw the walls of Zariaspa in the distance, all discomfort seemed to fade away. With the sun sending its rays toward the city, the walls were bright white, though their natural color was muddier.

In the fields, the grains had been harvested and there were massive piles of dried leaves. Nearer the city, the burned remains of houses covered the ground like skeletons in a desert. Clearly the news of defeat had reached the city, and the scorched earth policy had begun. They were to leave nothing of use for the enemy outside the city walls.

To the left, the Scythian contingent rode alongside the fields. Demetrius tried to imagine how they felt. They had traveled from the steppe to the mountains for his father. Now, they were closer to their beloved home, but their numbers were much reduced.

"I'm sorry we're not coming back as victors," Demetrius said to his father, who rode beside him.

"We gave Antiochus a wound," said Euthydemus. "That counts for something."

Ahead of them, riders came toward them from the gates of the city. Euthydemus and his entourage galloped away from the columns to meet them.

As the columns reached the walls, thousands of people streamed past the trench and into the open. The crowd was mostly full of women and children, who eyed the soldiers' faces, eagerly seeking their loved ones. Many, though, would not be found. In the rush to escape annihilation, the army had left most of the bodies on the battlefield. Euthydemus had sent a messenger to Antiochus asking that the bodies be given the proper ceremonies, but no one could be sure the monarch would respect the request.

By the time the procession reached the upper city, most of the soldiers had peeled away and gone to their homes in the lower city.

Demetrius met his mother and father for a quiet dinner that night. His mother did not ask about the battle, and his father did not offer details. Everyone knew the gravity of the situation. Antiochus's army would reach their valleys in a matter of days, if not sooner.

The next day, Demetrius helped the soldiers deepen and widen the trench. In the distance, others put fire to the remaining buildings outside the walls and used the elephants to rip trees from the ground. They collapsed the wells throughout the countryside and covered them in stone and dirt.

Demetrius thought of the stories he had heard of the Trojan War. He imagined the Trojans preparing their city against the Greeks, who had promised to raze it to the ground. He wondered if Antiochus would really put them under siege like Agamemnon did to Troy. With Ptolemy of Egypt always poised to invade Syria, perhaps Antiochus would be unable to stay. That was what Menon and his father were hoping for.

In the days that followed, Demetrius often looked toward the horizon, hoping to find nothing but the peaceful movements of the clouds, but two days later, he saw more than that. Dust floated into the sky and birds of prey circled. He had seen those signs in the mountains, and he knew what they meant. Antiochus and his army had arrived.

CHAPTER SIXTY-SEVEN

Antiochus

Antiochus stepped from his horse beside a pile of blackened earth. He reached down and picked up a burned stalk of grain.

"Fair enough," he said, throwing the stalk to the ground. He turned to face Arsak, whose forces had joined Antiochus's as the army approached the valleys of Bactria.

"That shouldn't be a problem," said Arsak. "After we take Merv, we'll be able to bring in food shipments regularly. It will be the Greeks behind their walls who will have a problem."

"Yes," said Antiochus, looking at the sun-painted walls of Zariaspa. "I'm not worried. But I'd rather avoid a long siege. My ambitions extend much further than this tiny province. Tomorrow, I will send a messenger to Euthydemus and ask him to speak once again."

"Do you think he will be any more amenable than he was at the Arius?"

"After what my soldiers did to his army, I would think so," said Antiochus.

"I'm concerned about the Scythians," said Arsak. "I heard they were present at the battle. It seems Euthydemus formed an alliance with them."

"What is your concern?" said Antiochus. "They're disorganized barbarians. What threat are they to us?"

"They can harass the supply lines, attack the camp. I learned a long time ago not to underestimate them. In fact, many a statesman has learned this lesson the hard way."

Antiochus tried to ignore the comment. He considered himself superior to those men. He would succeed where they had failed. After all, Alexander—a more apt comparison, he felt—had laid both the Persians and the Scythians low in his time.

"I trust that your men can keep the Scythians busy," said Antiochus.

"They can try," said Arsak.

"Good," said Antiochus, glad to be done with the matter. His attention was on the walls of Zariaspa. They were much more extensive and better built than he had anticipated. And the valleys of Bactria were limited in their provisions of wood. It would take him some time to prepare the siege engines. It would be much better if Euthydemus simply agreed to his terms. Life as a vassal could have its benefits, after all. And the life of a rebel often ended violently.

CHAPTER SIXTY-EIGHT

Demetrius

The sun went down before Demetrius could see the enemy in full, but the fires of their camp confirmed their presence later that night. Demetrius stood beside his father and Menon atop the gate tower and watched the flames twinkling like stars.

"I guess they're not going home," said his father, his voice flat and quiet.

"This gives us a chance to finish what we started," said Demetrius, hoping he sounded strong.

"At least we have the alliance with the Scythians," said Euthydemus. "Perhaps we can call on them to attack Antiochus's supply lines. Unless he plans on farming, he will have a hard time feeding his army out there. We've destroyed the wells and the irrigation ditches. We've salted the fields and burned the storage buildings. They'll have to start from scratch. And we'll harass them the entire time. If the Scythians attack their supplies, they'll quickly starve."

As Euthydemus walked away, Menon approached Demetrius.

"I'm proud of you, your majesty," he said. "In many ways, you saved the kingdom."

"Many people saved it together," said Demetrius.

"Absolutely," said Menon, "but I want you to know that you've grown a lot these past weeks, and when I think of you, I'm confident for the future."

"Thank you, Menon," said Demetrius. "That means a lot. And with you at my side, I'm confident for the future, as well."

Menon bowed and left the tower. Demetrius remained.

The next morning, Demetrius stood atop the palace and looked out at the Seleucid army. He turned when Eucratides entered the observation platform. The cut on his face—a wound gained in battle—had crusted into a scab.

"Antiochus has certainly brought an army," Demetrius said.

"That he has," said Eucratides.

Beyond the walls, covering much of the horizon, the army of Antiochus prepared their camp. No longer obscured by the mountains and the darkness, sun rays bounced from their ranks as the soldiers swung axes and hammers. They did not look like an army preparing to leave. On the contrary, their camp looked ready to house men indefinitely. There was a wooden wall between the soldiers and the clearing, and men were digging a protective ditch in front of it.

"Will you join your father for the negotiations?" asked Eucratides, perhaps trying to repair his rapport with Demetrius.

"He asked me to go with him," said Demetrius. "He says he wants Antiochus to see that the kingdom has a secure future."

"Or perhaps he wants to offer you in marriage." Eucratides grinned and punched Demetrius on the shoulder. "I hear his unmarried daughter is a sight to behold."

The thought of a marriage alliance had not crossed Demetrius's mind. But now he didn't know what to think.

"No," said Demetrius, slowly. "I don't think marriage is on the table. At least not now."

Demetrius's mind moved from the battle at the Arius to the army beyond the walls, and then to the prospect of marrying to save his father's kingdom. Leaving the platform, he felt lightheaded.

The lower city was quieter than he had ever seen it. As he and his father followed the winding street toward the city gate, people watched them from their windows and doors. There was none of the usual cheering that accompanied his father's passage.

Menon rode just behind Demetrius. He, too, was quiet. The moment was a heavy one. They rode to meet Antiochus and his generals—men who had beaten them at the Arius and who now camped an army outside their walls.

As they neared the gate, the street was increasingly filled with people. Demetrius studied the crowds. He noticed the worry in their eyes, but also the determination.

Demetrius spotted Ashok and Priya. They waved to him and smiled. On the other side of the street, Roshan and Beleen stood together. They bowed their heads as Demetrius passed. Just beyond, Phlotas nodded. As Demetrius thought of everything that others had done to get him to this moment, his throat constricted. His emotions swung between gratitude for his companions, fear for their futures, and pride at their accomplishments.

Demetrius and his father stopped their horses at the closed city gate. The doors had been studded with metal reinforcements.

"Are you sure you want to do this?" Demetrius asked, looking at his father.

"Absolutely," said Euthydemus. "As you suggested, we will talk and learn about our enemy. But we will never surrender."

Demetrius nodded.

The gates then opened, and Demetrius led his horse from the city and into the light.

AUTHOR'S NOTE

Coverage of Ancient Afghanistan overwhelmingly focuses on Alexander the Great's invasion of the region, then called Bactria, in 330 BC. By comparison, the periods before and after Alexander's conquest are given scant coverage by ancient scholars, and even less attention by novelists. I wrote this novel because I was particularly interested in the period of cultural fusion in the centuries following Alexander's invasion. During my writing journey, the interplay between fact and fiction (an interplay experienced in all historical fiction) was my constant companion. I encourage you to dive deeper into this fascinating time, and to forgive any historical inaccuracies that have peppered my attempt. I also invite you to write a review for this novel on Amazon. Your thoughts are much appreciated. Thank you!

David Austin Beck

www.davidaustinbeck.com

CPSIA information can be obtained
at www.ICGtesting.com
Printed in the USA
FSHW022337170122
87694FS

9 781736 184004